I0785024

HER FRONTIER SWEETHEARTS
Book 2 in the Frontier Matches Series

Cover Design and Interior Format

HER FRONTIER
SWEETHEARTS

REGINA SCOTT

FIND MORE WARM, WITTY ROMANCE TO LOVE.

Sign up for Regina Scott's free newsletter to hear when the next book is out or on sale, plus get exclusive access to stories from her beloved series. When you sign up, you'll receive two free stories, "Never Capture a Captain," a sequel to her bestselling Fortune's Brides series set in the Regency period, and "A Joy Worth the Wait," set in the world of her critically acclaimed American Wonders series. Don't miss out.

PRAISE FOR REGINA SCOTT'S WORK

"Regina Scott writes some of today's best Historical Romance novels!" Huntress Reviews

"Scott dazzles." *Booklist* on *A Distance Too Grand*, which was given a starred review and named one of the top ten romances of the year

For *The Perfect Mail-Order Bride*, Book 1 in the Frontier Matches series: "5 stars! Readers who enjoy historical romance set in the West will enjoy this lovely story. I can't wait to read more from this series." Among the Reads

*To Victoria Pann, for the name of Ciara's restaurant,
and to the Lord, who knows our names before we do.*

CHAPTER ONE

Seattle, Washington Territory, July 1876

SHE WAS ABOUT to enter a whole new world.

Ciara O'Rourke hugged her carpetbag close, watching as the rough skyline of Seattle disappeared behind a wall of trees. The summer sun speared through the limbs and warmed the shadows of the forest bracketing her. Still, she couldn't help her shiver.

"Everything all right back there?" Harry Yeager called from the bench of the wagon, as if he'd heard the thoughts piling up inside her head like a storm over the Olympics.

Ciara shifted to set the carpetbag among the other belongings crowding the bed of the wagon. "Fine, Harry. Thanks for asking. And thanks again for driving me out to Wallin Landing."

"I was coming for the mail anyway," the logger said. She glanced over her shoulder at him in time to see his broad shoulders move in a shrug of muscle inside his red flannel shirt. "Besides, I can't wait until you're the one doing the cooking."

She drew in a breath. The mixed scent of briny salt water and dusty mill shavings was fading, to be replaced by the moist tang of the forest. Above the tall treetops, clouds scudded across a blue sky. Somewhere in the wood, a bird called.

Her entire life, she'd seldom stepped outside the borders of a city—first the warren of tenements that was Five Points in New York, where she'd been born, then Seattle. Oh, sailing through Patagonia and the Straits of Magellan to reach Washington Territory had been a grand adventure, but that had been ten years ago, when she'd been only eleven. Then, she and her brother, Aiden, had mostly remained aboard ship. Now she was going into the wilderness to start her own business.

The first restaurant in the settlement of Wallin Landing.

Another shiver went through her, and she raised her chin. Already, the breeze was tugging strands of her dark hair out of her coronet braid to flick past her eyes. She should have worn a bonnet or a hat, but she'd been in too much of a hurry, as if Harry would have left her, and the mail, behind.

"Sure you don't want to ride up on the bench?" he asked over the creak of the wagon.

"I'm fine," Ciara repeated. Harry had made no secret of the fact that he was seeking a wife. She didn't plan to give him the least encouragement. She'd heard him enlisting the help of her friend, Ada Rankin, in writing for a mail-order bride. He was handsome enough, with his wavy brown hair and confident swagger, and he'd proved up his claim, so some lady might leap at the chance to marry him.

Not her. If she had been looking to wed, she would have had her pick as one of the few unmarried ladies in a sea of bachelors. Since it had become known she was leaving town, she'd had to refuse six proposals. She hadn't shed a tear over any of them. From what she'd seen, a husband was more hindrance than help, especially when it came to a lady with dreams for her future.

"Looks like trouble up ahead," Harry said, and she felt the wagon slowing as he must have reined in Lance and Percy, the team of sturdy steeldusts pulling it.

She gathered her blue chambray skirts so she could rise to her knees and peer up over the wagon's plank side. A black horse stood at the edge of the rutted dirt track that led out to the settlement, an older man squatting next to it. As Harry drew the team to a stop, Ciara could see a baby sitting among the wildflowers, rubbing fists into eyes red from crying. The pitiful sobs pierced the air.

"Need any help, friend?" Harry asked.

The older man rose. He wore pin-striped black trousers and a jacket that looked far too fine for Seattle, much less the forest, even covered as they were in dust. His long face sagged. There was a hint of desperation in his voice as well.

"How much farther to Wallin Landing?" he asked as if he'd already traveled a great distance.

"At a gentle pace for your horse, about an hour and a half due north," Harry supplied with a nod in that direction. "You're welcome to ride along with us. We're heading to the landing."

The man's face cleared, and he bent and picked up the baby. Closer now, Ciara could see the little girl had eyes as deep a brown as hers, and black wisps of hair stuck out from the edges of the white ruffled cap on her head. Aiden had been between one and two years when he'd reached that size.

The fellow thrust the baby at Harry. "Take her with you. Please."

Ciara started, but Harry recoiled, setting Lance and Percy to fretting in their traces.

"There's room in the wagon for you both," Harry told him. "I have no call to take her."

"I can't keep this up," the man said, turning his tortured gaze now on Ciara. "I'm a manservant, not a nursemaid.

She needs her family, Christopher Weatherly. All you have to do is deliver her."

"Kit?" Harry asked. "Why? Where's the mother?"

The man lifted the baby over the wagon's side and dropped her into Ciara's lap. Ciara's arms came around her to steady her, even as the baby hiccoughed her surprise at the sudden movement. Before Ciara could protest, the man slung a carpetbag and an envelope into the wagon bed as well.

"Everything is explained in the note," he said, backing away from the wagon. "Please. I must go. They'll be following me. If I disappear, Grace has a chance."

"Now, wait a minute," Harry said, but the man flung himself up into the saddle and urged his horse back toward Seattle.

"What'd he mean, grace has a chance?" Harry demanded, as if Ciara could know any more than he did.

She glanced to the baby, who was studying her, one fist lodged in her mouth. At least she'd stopped crying for the moment.

"Grace might be her name," Ciara mused. "Is that right, Grace?"

Grace dropped her hand and beamed, as if Ciara had done something particularly clever.

Harry shifted on the bench to glance back at them. Grace's beam turned into a scowl.

"What are we supposed to do with her?" he asked, and now the desperation in the stranger's voice had infected his as well.

"I suppose we better take her to Mr. Weatherly," Ciara said. "Isn't he a member of Drew's logging crew?"

Harry nodded. "Me, Jesse Willets, and Kit."

She knew Harry, and she'd met the stoic giant that was Jesse. She couldn't recall meeting Kit Weatherly.

"Does his wife live in town?" she asked. She wrinkled her nose at the baby, and Grace's happy smile returned.

She leaned her head against Ciara's shoulder with a sigh. Ciara's arms tightened even as something fluttered inside her. She recognized the sensation: a need to comfort, to protect. She'd felt it for her little brother and the children in the home where they'd lived for a time when their older sister, Maddie, had come West ahead of them ten years ago with the Mercer Expedition.

Harry snorted. "Kit doesn't have a wife. Never had a sweetheart, either, that I can tell. Keeps to himself mostly. That manservant fellow must be touched in the head to send a baby to him."

"Still, we don't have any other choice," Ciara pointed out, rocking Grace gently in her arms. Already the baby's dark lashes were sweeping down over her reddened cheeks. "We'll deliver Grace as requested. Let's go, Harry."

Shaking his head, Harry faced front and clucked to the horses. Lance and Percy picked up their paces as they headed for home.

Ciara gazed down at the baby in her arms. What sort of man abandoned his child? Maddie might have left her and Aiden behind, but neither sibling had been this little. And Maddie had sent for them as soon as she could raise the fare for passage. Kit Weatherly had been only a couple of hours away, less on a fast horse.

Why had he left Grace behind? Had he no feelings? No sense of responsibility?

Either way, she'd have a few choice words for him once she delivered this precious bundle into his care. And then she would get on with building her dream.

Kit Weatherly stretched sore muscles as he lowered his ax onto the porch of the cabin. A good day's work, Drew Wallin, their leader, had said, and more logs ready to be shipped down Salmon Bay to the Sound. A satisfaction he'd been searching for most of his life curled around him like smoke from a campfire. Good work, good friends, good weather. A man couldn't ask for more.

Well, maybe an edible dinner.

He grimaced as he glanced in the window, sighting Jesse staring at the stove in the rear section of the building as if he could cook the food from sheer force of will. He, Jesse, and Harry managed to take care of themselves, but, since Beth Wallin had married and moved into town, her brother Drew had had a difficult time finding a cook for his logging crew. The last few weeks, the three of them had been taking turns at the task. His stomach growled as if protesting another night of it.

But all that was going to change soon. Miss O'Rourke had made a proposal to Drew. She'd cook for the crew, and he'd allow her to turn the bottom floor of the big cabin into a restaurant that would cater to travelers and those around the area who wanted a good meal.

A good meal.

His smile tilted up. Though he'd eaten a treat or two at the Pastry Emporium in town since moving to Seattle two years ago, he'd never crossed paths with the sister of the famous owner. But if she could take over the cooking, he liked her already.

Sutter Murphy came pelting around the cabin, straw-colored hair every which way and untucked cotton shirt flapping about the trousers he perpetually outgrew. "Wagon coming in. Frisco spotted it through the trees. Do you think it's the baker?"

Kit smiled at the energetic ten-year-old, kin to their local minister, Levi Wallin. "Harry went to fetch her today, so it stands to reason."

Sutter vibrated faster than the wings of a hummingbird. "I hope she brought cinnamon rolls with her. Her sister, Mrs. Haggerty, makes the best cinnamon rolls." He heaved a sigh, as if he could see the creamy icing dripping down the sides even now.

"She might not have had time today," Kit warned him as the wagon rolled into the clearing and pulled up next to the barn.

Sutter took off running anyway. His twin brother, Frisco, came out of the woods to join him.

Their own baker and cook. What a blessing! And what a boon to Wallin Landing, which was small as settlements went. The biggest cabin, which housed him, Jesse, and Harry in the loft, sat on a bench overlooking Lake Union. Along the shores next to the lake lay the mercantile, which included the post office. Across the clearing, beyond the massive barn, Drew and his family had a cabin, with his brother Simon up on the hill. Brothers James and John had spreads just beyond, and Levi had a log parsonage next to the church. At the back of the clearing stood the schoolhouse. Other homesteads were beginning to grow along the lake.

Beth's old cabin was through the trees to the north. He'd heard Drew intended to allow Miss O'Rourke to use it.

He could just spot a dark head peeking up above the side of the wagon. She didn't seem to be in a hurry to leave its shelter. Was she already reconsidering her decision to move out so far? His stomach rumbled again. Maybe he should welcome her, assure her they were all eager for her help.

Harry was seeing to the horses, so Kit ambled closer. The wagon was full of crates, boxes, and sacks. Some would be supplies for the settlement. Others, he hoped, would be supplies for the kitchen. She'd already sent ahead one wagon load, and he and Jesse had stood over the boxes studying their contents.

"Why would she need a bowl with holes in it?" Jesse had asked, poking a thick finger at the perforated mass of tin.

"I think it's a colander," Kit had told him. "For straining things. My sister's cook had one."

Jesse had eyed him. People often did that when he mentioned his family, so he mentioned them rarely. It was easier if no one questioned why the brother of one of Tacoma's wealthier matrons was slinging an ax instead of directing the wheels of industry.

Frisco and Sutter had beat him to the wagon bed and were holding out hands to Miss O'Rourke. She managed to stand, and he stopped in his tracks.

Somehow, he'd expected someone older, more seasoned. Mrs. Haggerty was in her thirties. Her sister was quite a few years younger, with hair as warm and rich as hot chocolate and cheeks as rosy as an apple. Combined with a slender figure and her ability to cook, she was guaranteed to draw the attention of every bachelor within miles.

Likely they wouldn't have a cook for long.

"Would you hold her a moment, Frisco?" she was saying, bending toward one of the twins.

Her?

Frisco opened his arms, and Miss O'Rourke surrendered a chubby-faced baby into them.

A baby? Odd. He didn't recall hearing she'd married. Would her husband be moving out with her? Why did that disappoint him?

"That's Kit," Sutter volunteered, pointing at him as if Miss O'Rourke had asked his direction.

She jumped down from the wagon, arranged her blue skirts, took back the baby, and marched up to him. Her eyes were as dark as hot chocolate too, but at the moment they were more fire than warmth.

She held out the baby to him. "Mr. Weatherly. Your daughter."

Kit blinked. "Daughter? I don't have a daughter."

"Told you," Harry said, striding past with a crate in his arms.

Her pretty face set into surprisingly firm lines. "We were told to deliver this sweet child to you. Do you deny your responsibility, sir?"

The baby kicked its feet as if none too pleased to be left dangling between them. Kit reached for her to steady her.

Eyes as dark as his peered into his face. Curls as dark as his escaped her little cap. A smile that reminded him of what he saw in the mirror on a good morning turned up her lips.

Small wonder they thought she was his. She looked just like him!

"She can't be mine," he said aloud. "I've never had a sweetheart."

"Told you," Harry repeated, passing them for the wagon.

Miss O'Rourke's face melted into confusion. "Are you certain, Mr. Weatherly?"

Kit peered closer at the baby, a frown of his own gathering.

The baby met his gaze, opened her mouth…

And shrieked at the top of her lungs.

He nearly dropped her, but he managed to hang on as the sound rent the air. Crows launched themselves off their perches in the cedars. Frisco and Sutter clapped their hands over their ears. Chickens in the coop nearby ran in agitated circles.

"Is she all right?" Miss O'Rourke asked, moving closer.

The baby grinned at them both, showing a few pearly white teeth.

"I think she's rather pleased with herself," Kit marveled.

Miss O'Rourke lay a hand on his arm. "Perhaps we should bring her into the house. The man who gave Grace to us left a note. You should read it."

He should at that. Tucking Grace a little closer, he joined Miss O'Rourke as she retrieved a carpetbag and envelope and headed for the cabin.

They had barely set foot inside before Jesse ducked his massive frame to poke his russet head through the kitchen archway.

"You cooking?" he asked Miss O'Rourke, holding up a wooden spoon as if ready to coronate her with it.

"I wasn't planning to start until tomorrow morning, Mr. Willets," she told him, dropping the carpetbag to the planks. "I have much to do to settle in first."

Kit could feel Jesse's sigh from across the room. The big man shambled back to the stove.

Miss O'Rourke handed Kit the envelope and held out her arms. He gave her Grace, and she began walking the baby around the room, murmuring words no doubt meant to calm. Over her shoulder, Grace watched him.

Kit broke open the envelope to pull out the letter inside. The first words took his breath, and the next few took the heart right out of him. He sank onto the bench at the table near the door and devoured the rest. How? When?

Why?

He lowered the note to find Miss O'Rourke standing in front of him, waiting. As if she saw the blow he'd been given, she perched on the bench beside him, jostling Grace on her knee.

"What's happened?" she asked, dark gaze searching his.

"Grace is my sister's child," he told her, amazed he could still form sentences. "I didn't know she had one. She always wanted children, but none came. We haven't spoken in years, though I write her to let her know where I am and what I'm doing. It seems she and her husband have died, and I'm all Grace has left."

"Take a moment," she murmured. "I'll put the kettle on."

He shook himself as she rose with the baby and turned for the kitchen. "But you're just getting settled," he protested.

"That doesn't mean I can't help," she countered before disappearing into the kitchen with his newfound responsibility.

Help, she'd said. He had a feeling he was going to need it.

CHAPTER TWO

POOR MAN. FAMILY gone, suddenly a father. Ciara kept glancing out of the archway between the little kitchen at one side of the cabin to check on Mr. Weatherly and Grace.

It had taken only a few moments to locate the kettle on the sideboard that took up much of one wall, along with a window over the porcelain sink. Another moment to fill it from the pump and set it on one of the six burners of the big stove. She'd always envied Beth that stove, black iron all decked out with silver trim, with two ovens and a warming drawer. Still, with the stove, the box of wood to feed it, another cupboard with supplies, and Mr. Willets' big frame stuffed into the space, there wasn't much room to move. And she couldn't like the acrid, singed scent of whatever was under the lid of that big copper pot.

"What's that you're cooking?" she asked the logger, who had backed up against the rear wall as if to give her room.

"Dinner," he supplied.

That much she could have guessed.

"Stew?" she tried. "Soup?"

"Little of both."

The kettle began whistling, and she took it off to pour it over the tea she'd found in the caddy Beth used to use.

She returned with a cup for Kit Weatherly and set it

on the table at his elbow, then seated herself beside him again, baby in her arms.

The news seemed to have robbed him of speech. She started jiggling little Grace, watching as the color gradually returned to the logger's face. Another time, she might have considered him handsome, with his black curly hair that fell to his collar and neatly trimmed beard and mustache. Now his eyes looked sunken, his cheeks hollowed, as if that letter had drained the life from him.

It sounded as if his sister had been his only relation. She couldn't imagine such a loss. She might have left her sister, brother-in-law, and brother behind in Seattle, but she knew they were there and that she could go home any time.

Home. This was to be home now. So long as she managed to start her restaurant before she ran out of funds.

She glanced around the main room of the cabin. She'd been out to visit Wallin Landing any number of times, so she knew this cabin had once been the Wallin family home, until they'd outgrown it. Her sister had been good friends with Catherine, who had married Drew, the leader of the clan. Ciara and Beth, the Wallin sister, had only grown closer over the years. Beth had a way of looking at the world, as if it held untold possibilities. Maybe that's why she'd gained such a reputation as a matchmaker.

Now memories crowded closer to Ciara. She knew how cold the wood plank floor could feel on bare toes in the winter, even close to the fireplace built from rounded lake rocks in muted tones of brown, white, and gray. She remembered the comfort of curling up in Mrs. Wallin's bentwood rocker with a good book. She understood the love that had gone into every stitch of the braided rug on the floor and Mrs. Wallin's colorful quilts, which were still draped over chair and bench.

And she could still taste the lighter-than-air biscuits that were famous in the Wallin family, served on the long plank table by the window and baked in that top-of-the-line stove, which would shortly be hers to command.

Mr. Willets lumbered out of the archway and thumped the pot down on the table.

"Dinner," he announced before heading back into the kitchen, presumably for the rest of the meal.

Mr. Weatherly stirred himself. "Allow me to set you a place, Miss O'Rourke."

He was up and moving toward the kitchen sideboard before she could tell him otherwise. Either he was more polite than the other members of the crew, or he was terrified of the baby in her lap.

She would have bet on the latter.

Grace grabbed a hold of Ciara's sleeve and attempted to bring it toward her mouth.

"I bet you're hungry too," Ciara told her, gently removing the chambray from her little fingers.

Grace pouted.

Mr. Willets must have signaled to Harry, for the other logger came in from outside, slamming the door behind him. Grace jumped.

"So, who does she belong to?" he asked, hooking a leg over the chair at one end of the table.

"She's my niece," Mr. Weatherly supplied, bringing back a pile of plates, with tin cups teetering on top. "My sister and her husband passed. I'm all she has left."

"Poor little thing." Harry reached out and patted Grace's head.

Grace shrieked.

Her uncle barely managed to catch the dishes before they toppled out of his grip. Harry shuddered. Mr. Willets dashed into the room, fists up and gaze darting about as if he expected to find a catamount climbing down the chimney.

"Does she have to do that?" Harry asked.

Mr. Willets lowered his fists with a frown.

Grace snuggled closer to Ciara and sighed happily.

"She seems to find it calming," Ciara said with a shake of her head. "She might grow out of it once she feels settled here."

Her uncle sorted plates onto the tables in four places. "I hope so. I'd hate to concern the Wallins."

Harry stuck a finger in his ear and wiggled, as if he was worried he'd popped an eardrum. "I'd hate to concern the folks in Olympia. That's how far that scream would travel."

Mr. Willets went to the head of the table and began ladling something onto the plates. It was brown, watery, and lumpy. Was this their typical fare? No wonder Drew had been so eager for her to come start her restaurant.

Mr. Weatherly went for a pewter pitcher and poured water into the cups. She knew Wallin Landing had several good wells, so she wasn't surprised to find the liquid cold as she took a sip. Grace pursed her lips as if she tasted it too.

He returned once more with forks, then sat on the bench beside her while Mr. Willets took the chair at the head.

"Who's saying grace?" Harry demanded.

The baby perked up. "No, no, no, no, no," she said in a little piping voice.

Harry's brows rose.

Mr. Weatherly smiled. "I'll say the blessing." He bowed his head, and the others followed suit. Ciara lowered her gaze to the baby, who frowned up at her.

"Dear Lord," he said. "We thank You for this food and this company, the beauty of Your creation, and the success of our labor. May we be a blessing to others even as You have blessed us."

"Amen," the other two murmured, voices low and deep.

"Amen," Ciara agreed.

"No, no, no, no, no," Grace said agreeably.

"Yes, yes, yes, yes, yes," Ciara told her with a grin. She attempted to stick her fork into one of the lighter-colored lumps, thinking it might be a potato. The tines bounced off.

She glanced up to find the three loggers digging in. In fact, by the way they ate, the slop was the finest entrée in the swanky Bay View Restaurant in Seattle. Either that or they were starving.

"Would there be any bread?" she asked.

Mr. Willets looked up long enough to shake his head emphatically no.

Grace reached for Ciara's plate.

She nudged it away. It wasn't as if she planned to eat from it, and she certainly wasn't going to feed that to the baby.

"I'm done," her uncle announced, rising. "Let me take her, Miss O'Rourke. I should have thought. Of course you wouldn't be able to eat with her on your lap. Please forgive me. I'm new to this."

He was so embarrassed, pink climbing above his beard, that she couldn't be angry with him. "I understand," she told him as she surrendered the baby into his arms. "But is there truly nothing else to eat in the house? I was told there'd be staples on hand."

"Potatoes," Mr. Willets offered around a mouthful of dinner. "Leeks."

"And all the game and fish you could want," Harry added. He too pushed back from the table. "You wash, Jesse. I'll dry."

"I cooked," Mr. Willets protested before shoveling up the last of his meal.

"And Kit has his hands full," Harry reminded him.

"Besides, Ciara doesn't start work until tomorrow morning. This is your last night in the kitchen."

The giant gave a lopsided grin. "I'll wash."

She didn't scold when Harry piled all the dishes on top of each other, hers included, and trotted them to the kitchen.

"Was it that bad?" Mr. Weatherly murmured, jiggling Grace up and down in his arms as if he'd noticed Ciara doing the same earlier.

"Eat my breakfast tomorrow," she said with a grin. "And you tell me."

He grinned back. "I can hardly wait."

Something fizzed inside her, as if she'd mixed vinegar and saleratus and set them to bubbling. Very likely it was just her stomach informing her she should have eaten while she'd had the chance.

The door opened just then, and Drew and Catherine came in. Like most of the brothers, the eldest had straight, dusky blond hair that hung to the collar of his flannel shirt and deep blue eyes. His shoulders were an impressive width, though she thought Mr. Willets was as tall. Catherine's hair was also blond, but a pale, shimmering shade, and her eyes were a cool blue, particularly in the fine lustring gown she wore. However did she manage to keep her white cuffs and collar so clean?

"Welcome to Wallin Landing," Drew called to Ciara, smile as wide as the arms he spread out.

"And it seems you brought company," Catherine said, sweeping closer and brows up in question.

"This is Grace Virden," Mr. Weatherly told them both. "My niece. My sister and brother-in-law have passed away, and I'm her only family."

Catherine pressed a hand to her mouth, and Drew's smile faded. Worse, Grace's face was turning red, and Ciara feared another shriek was imminent. Instead, the baby started squirming and fussing.

Catherine dropped her hand. "She needs to be changed."

Mr. Weatherly glanced down at her. "I don't even know if she has another dress with her."

"I don't think she means her dress," Ciara told him.

Comprehension must have dawned, because those cheeks were turning pink again. "Perhaps you could…" he started.

Drew took a step back. So did Ciara.

"There's an easier way," Harry said, coming back for another load of dishes. "Just leave off any under things and let her do her business in the grass."

Catherine snatched the baby out of the logger's arms. "Certainly not. Come with me, Kit, and bring whatever belongings were sent with her. I'll show you how to contrive."

Drew hesitated. "Do you need any help?" The question begged for a negative response.

Grace provided it. "No, no, no, no, no," she said as Catherine carried her up the stairs, Mr. Weatherly trailing with the carpetbag.

"Show Ciara around." Catherine's voice drifted down a moment before she disappeared.

"Right." He rubbed his big hands together as if pleased to be given a task more to his liking. "Ready to see your new home?"

For a moment, she hesitated. Why was she feeling a pull up those stairs? Catherine was a nurse; she ran the settlement dispensary. She also had three children of her own. She knew what she was doing. And Ciara had no ties to Kit Weatherly, other than the expectation that she would feed him and the other members of the logging crew. And now a baby.

"Ready," she said, and she went to fetch her carpetbag.

Kit's mind was still reeling as he followed Catherine into the smaller of the two rooms at the top of the stairs. He'd been told it had once been the bedroom of the Wallin parents. Harry had it now, as the most senior member of Drew's logging crew, and only temporarily until he moved into his own cabin nearby. His belongings were strewn about, from the big bed in its iron bedstead to the washstand and carved chest on the opposite wall. Kit and Jesse shared the large loft next door.

"Look in her bag," Catherine instructed, laying the baby down on Harry's quilt. "See if you can find any nappies."

"What's a nappy?" Kit asked, unlatching the bag. Inside was a jumble of clothing, as if someone had shoved in whatever they could grab.

"A muslin or linen cloth, very likely with buttons or ties at the sides," she said, smiling down at Grace. "Then wet a washcloth for me."

Harry wouldn't be too keen on them using his things, but these were desperate times. Kit located several of the cloths she had described in the bag and laid them next to the baby before going to the washstand and wetting a washrag. The water was tepid, but he didn't think it had been used. Harry wasn't the most fastidious of the crew.

He returned in time to see her finish working some ties at either side of Grace's chubby torso.

"Now, watch," Catherine said. "And then you can give it a try."

It was a fairly simple process. Even he might manage it. She did up the nappy, then undid it. And stepped back.

Kit moved in.

Grace wiggled.

He frowned. "I can't have tickled her. I haven't started yet."

"And you'd better hurry," Catherine said, going to wash her hands in the basin, which Kit would have to refill for Harry. "They don't willingly hold still for long."

As if to prove it, Grace started inching closer to the edge of the bed.

"No, you don't," Kit said, picking her up and repositioning her. He sped through the actions he'd seen Catherine take, then stepped back.

Catherine returned to his side and looked down at the baby. "Very good. You're a quick learner."

And that's about all I'm good for, according to my family.

He would not say the words aloud. His family was gone. There would be no more recriminations, no more complaints, no more demands to do better. The letter had said as much.

I regret to inform you that your sister, Hannah Weatherly Virden, has passed away of influenza. Her death follows that of her husband, Rudolph Virden, from the same cause. The staff will be paid to close up the house and then dismissed. The estate will be settled some time in the future. In the meantime, someone must take care of their child, Grace Wilhelmina. I understand you are the closest relation, and, before she passed, your sister advised me to send the child to you. I will bring more details when I am able. Dixon Hitchcock, Attorney.

He couldn't quite make himself believe any of it, that Hannah was gone, that she had had the daughter she'd always prayed for, or that she had wanted Kit to raise that daughter.

Grace didn't seem to have any doubts. Those big brown eyes gazed up at him, trustingly, hopefully.

As if Catherine knew the responsibility he'd been given, she lay a hand on his arm. "What are you going to do?"

"I don't know," Kit said. "I can't log and care for a baby."

"Nora would likely be thrilled to care for her," she said. "She loves babies. Callie's niece, Mica, is already walking, and she was the youngest we had in the family. We can find a cradle and clothes too, if you need them."

"I'd be grateful for anything you can provide," he told her.

Catherine patted his shoulder. "It's a big responsibility and a big adjustment. If there's anything we can do, just ask. I'll take the nappy when I leave. The next time she needs changing, rinse out the soiled nappy and hang it to dry. Wash day is either Monday or Tuesday around here, depending on what else needs doing. Callie, Rina, or I can likely add Grace's things in with ours." She shook her head. "I'm even more glad Drew hired Ciara to cook for you. At least you won't have to worry about that."

Kit stared at her, panic pricking. "But she doesn't start cooking until the morning. What should I feed Grace in the meantime? She only has a tooth or two. Is that enough to chew?"

Catherine eyed the baby. "If I had to guess, I'd say Grace is about a year and a half old. Is that what you were told?"

"The letter didn't say," Kit admitted, gaze going back to the baby, who had managed to roll herself onto her stomach and was wiggling toward the edge of the bed again.

Catherine bent and picked up the little girl, adjusting her long cotton gown to cover her stockinged toes. Grace appeared to be studying her face, as if she would memorize the high cheekbones and vivid eyes.

"Let's start from there," Catherine said. She wiggled a finger against Grace's lips, and his niece obligingly opened her mouth to reveal four teeth, top and bottom.

"Enough to begin chewing," Catherine pronounced, pulling back her finger when Grace showed every indication of being willing to take a bite. "You'll want things like porridge, applesauce, maybe some mashed carrots and beets. Ciara may have ideas. In fact, you may find she's your best ally. She helped in a children's home when she was a girl."

An ally he wasn't even sure liked him, if her initial reaction was any indication. But, then again, that was nothing new.

CHAPTER THREE

SHE DIDN'T REALLY need a tour. Ciara and Beth had wandered all over the settlement when they were younger. But she listened as Drew pointed out the location of the nearest well, waved a hand toward the side of the house, where there was a garden she could use, and then led her down a path to the north, to Beth's old cabin.

Ciara had sent her trunk ahead, so she wasn't surprised to find it already in the little cabin. It was one of two, the other carved wood, on the main floor, which boasted a sitting area and kitchen. The sleeping loft above the kitchen was big enough for a large bed, washstand, and another chest. All the furnishings were of wood, carved by Beth's brothers and father, and the fireplace was also of rounded rock. Her carpetbag looked as if it were hunched in on itself next to the ladder leading up to the loft.

"Jesse laid in a store of firewood," Drew told her, "and Catherine and the ladies stocked the kitchen with everything you might need. It doesn't have a stove; Beth and Nora before her made do with the hearth. But Nora and Callie laid out the bed linens."

Ciara offered him her best smile. "Thank you, Drew. I'm so grateful for this opportunity. I won't let you down."

He snorted. "Your sister raised you. You couldn't let me down."

The smile was hard to keep as she showed him out the door.

Yes, that was her fate. Maddie O'Rourke's little sister. The assumption as to her talents had followed her even from Seattle.

Not that it was a bad fate.

She set about opening her trunk and putting her own things around. Madeleine O'Rourke Haggerty was a legend in Seattle. She'd opened one of the first bakeries and was still the favorite among the millworkers and their families. Her husband, Michael, led the Irish Brigade, which had rescued many from a burning building. They were even now helping establish the first official fire department in Seattle. Her sister and brother-in-law cast long shadows.

Shadows she struggled to step outside.

But this, this was all her own. Her own cabin, her own restaurant. A shame her sister couldn't understand.

"Sure-n but you could start your own restaurant here," Maddie had protested when Ciara had told her her plans. "Much as I love the Wallins, there's no need for you to be moving out into the wilds."

There was every reason. She was as good a cook as her sister. If she had opened a restaurant in Seattle, people would be forever comparing them. If Ciara came out second-best, Maddie would have been mortified. And if Ciara had come out best, she would never have forgiven herself. Here, she had hoped, she could do her best, with no one losing in the process.

Maddie had wanted to know every detail, as if determined to spot some flaw in Ciara's plans.

"And how will you be after buying supplies?" she'd challenged as she'd helped Ciara pack the cooking equipment she'd inherited or purchased over the years. "James Wallin may have fishhooks in that mercantile of his, but I'm doubting he has cinnamon sticks."

"He has sufficient stock to supply Wallin Landing and the nearby homesteads," Ciara assured her, wrapping the heavy glass measuring cup in an apron for protection. "And someone comes into Seattle at least every other day for the mail, so I can send for what I need if necessary."

Maddie added the tin sifter to the crate. "And how are you to be paying for those supplies, until your restaurant starts turning a profit? I had to take a loan from Clay Howard to start my bakery, and then I had to pay it off, with interest."

"I've a little put by," Ciara hedged.

Maddie shoved in the colander. "The money set aside for you to attend university!"

"I've no interest in continuing at the university," Ciara informed her. "That's for teachers and the like. I just want to cook."

Maddie had sighed, eyes brimming. "And I forever cannot see why you cannot be doing that in Seattle."

The pain of the statement was still fresh. The parting with her brother had only made matters worse.

"You're really leaving," Aiden had challenged, standing in the doorway of her bedroom in Maddie's house up on a hill overlooking the city.

"It's only Wallin Landing," she'd reminded him, bundling a cloak into her trunk. "I can come back to Seattle any time I like."

He folded his arms over his chest. At seventeen, he was still a few inches shy of Michael's tall frame. "You won't," Aiden predicted. "You'll go out there and get busy with this restaurant, and we'll never see you again."

"Well, you can come out," she countered, tossing an apron after the cloak. "The road runs both ways."

"For those who have horses," he jibed. His arms fell. "You said we were a pair, Ciara. You said you'd never leave me."

She met his gaze, swallowing her guilt. "I remember.

But we were children then. Mum and Da had died. Maddie was off in a far land. You don't need me like that anymore."

His dark eyes were stormy. "You didn't even ask me to come with you."

"Because you're still in school!" she protested.

"Last time I checked, there's a school in Wallin Landing. But then, what do I know? Maddie still thinks I'm a child, and it's clear you do too."

She wiped at the tears coming down her cheeks now. She hadn't even started her restaurant yet, and she'd paid a price for it. But her brother, and Maddie, would surely come around once they saw her success.

It didn't take long to set the cabin to rights. The handiwork of the ladies of Wallin Landing was readily evident, even if Drew hadn't mentioned it, for there was no dust to be seen, and the wood furniture smelled of beeswax, proving it had been recently polished. It was a fine cabin for one, though she knew Beth's second oldest brother, Simon, had shared it for a time with his wife, Nora, before building her a bigger house on the top of the hill.

She was fairly certain Beth was planning on the cabin holding two again. Beth had had a hand in matching each of her brothers and their friend, Scout Rankin. She was already planning on matching up the logging crew, and Ciara suspected she intended one of them for her.

That, she was determined, would not happen. She knew what her future held. She fully intended to build a legend as great as her sister's. And all that started tomorrow.

Twilight had slipped in while she'd been working. She lit a lamp and stood, listening.

It was so quiet, as if the entire world held its breath.

She listened harder. Before Maddie and Michael had moved them to a house higher on the hill, Ciara had been lulled to sleep by the sounds of the sawmill and men spilling out of establishments on the Skid Row. Even among the more affluent families on the hill, there had been the sounds of wagons trundling past, people calling.

Wallin Landing had other noises. Something swished against the roof. She jumped. Silly. It was probably the bough of a fir tree swaying in the breeze. The floor creaked as she shifted. The cabin was more than ten years old now. What else would she expect? A mournful hoot sounded from the wood. An owl?

And were those footsteps on the porch?

She tensed. The sound came again, furtive, as if the person was trying not to get caught.

It couldn't be one of the Wallins, but there were others in the area, the same bachelors she hoped to attract to her restaurant. Could one have decided to investigate a cabin that had been empty until tonight? Or was a thief sneaking up on her?

She set the lamp on the table, moved to the kitchen, and picked up the largest of the cast-iron frying pans that had been left her. Then she stalked to the door and threw it open, pan swinging.

"Yow!" Harry scuttled back, one hand up over his head in defense. "It was just a song!"

Ciara lowered the frying pan. "Harry? What are you doing here?"

He raised the guitar in his other fist. "I was going to sing to you. They claim its romantic."

Ciara's eyebrows climbed. "Romantic?"

"Never mind. See you in the morning." He tucked the instrument under his arm and strode off into the night.

Ciara shook her head. Well, at least that might deter any thoughts of courting. His mail-order bride would look far more appealing after tonight.

She was about to close the door when another sound rose, tugging at her heart. A baby, crying.

Poor Grace.

Once more she stood, listening in the cool night air. The sobs seemed to go on and on. Did her uncle have no idea how to comfort her? She highly doubted the other two loggers knew much about babies. And the rest of the cabins were likely too far away for their occupants to hear the wailing.

She set the frying pan aside, snatched up her lamp, and hurried down the path for the big cabin.

"Walk her around some more," Jesse urged, watching from the safety of the table as Kit wore a circle in the middle of the braided rug.

"I'm trying," Kit said, jiggling her up and down the way he'd seen Ciara do. "It's not working."

"Is she hungry?" Jesse asked.

"Catherine fed her applesauce before she left."

Jesse's face scrunched up. "Does she need to, uh, you know, again?"

"I changed her ten minutes ago," Kit informed him. He gazed down at the baby. "Aren't you tired, sweetheart?"

"No, no, no, no, no!" Grace shouted, and she punctuated it with a screech that had Jesse heading for the kitchen.

Kit sagged.

The door opened, and Ciara slipped into the room. He could have kissed her. Well, not that. He had no right to do that. But the thought of help made his breath come easier than it had for the last two hours.

"What's wrong?" she asked, setting her lamp on the table and tiptoeing closer.

Grace's head whipped around, and her arms reached out.

Ciara took the baby from him and cuddled her close.

"I don't know," Kit admitted. "She's eaten. She was changed. You'd think she would be tired. *I'm* tired."

"I can imagine." She rubbed one hand against the baby's back. "What's the matter, sweetheart? Are you missing your mama?"

Something twisted inside him. If that was what Grace wanted, he could never give it to her.

Grace's sobs stuttered to a stop as she rested her head on Ciara's shoulder. Ciara went to the rocker by the fire and sank onto it.

"This was Mrs. Wallin's," she told him as he sat on the chair nearby. "I remember her rocking her grandchildren." She set the chair in motion.

Grace started, then snuggled closer, as if she liked the rhythm.

"I imagine she rocked most of her children in that, too," Kit said.

Ciara nodded. "So Beth told me. When they held services in this room, before the church was built, many a mother made use of it. And a few fathers."

The hint was obvious. "Would you like me to take her?"

"It's all right. I find it soothing." She tilted her head until it rested on Grace's, sleek dark hair next to wispy curls.

"By the way," she said as Grace's eyes drifted shut, "did that letter mention anything about who else might be after Grace?"

Kit stiffened. "After Grace?"

She nodded, and Grace's eyes popped open again. "The man who gave Grace to me and Harry mentioned something about being a manservant, I presume for your sister's family. He said someone was coming after him, and if he left right then, Grace stood a chance."

"No," Grace murmured, then she paused to yawn. "No, no, no, no."

"Sorry," Ciara said. "I should be trying to get her to

sleep." She started humming a tune, and Kit settled back in his chair.

But his mind refused to quiet. Who could be coming after Grace? The manservant was likely Bottles, his brother-in-law's butler and valet. The letter had claimed all the staff would be dismissed. Had delivering Grace been his final duty? Then why not complete it?

The letter had been signed by a lawyer who claimed he'd arrive in due time. Perhaps that was who was coming after. Yet what had Bottles meant that Grace stood a chance? A chance of what?

Darkness crept up around them until her lamp was the only light besides the fire. A log shifted in the grate, sending up sparks. Tensions he'd held so long began to slide off his shoulders like a badly fitted jacket.

The humming stopped. So did the rocker.

He glanced over to find two pairs of eyes closed.

His heart turned over.

Slowly, making no sound, he rose and walked on his toes to gather one of the many quilts that clustered around the room. He draped it gently about the two of them.

Ciara sighed. Grace stuck her thumb in her mouth.

He stepped back to fetch more of the quilts and made himself a little nest near the fire. Jesse leaned out of the kitchen, and Kit urged him through with a jerk of his head. He did the same with Harry, when his friend came in a short time later.

"You sure?" Harry mouthed.

Kit nodded.

Harry sat on the bench by the table, removed his boots, then padded in stockinged feet up the stairs.

Kit lay on the floor, watching the two females that had somehow been thrust into his life. He had no intention of leaving Ciara O'Rourke alone to deal with his niece.

He'd be here to take charge of Grace when she woke. It was his duty.

Memories tugged. He'd been only six, his sister Hannah sixteen, when their father had decided to uproot everyone and bring them West on a wagon train. He didn't recall a lot about crossing the country, but he did remember laying under the wagon, snuggled next to his mother and sister, watching their father stand sentry by the fire.

Even then, Hannah had had the care of him, helping him gather kindling for the fire or chips left by the massive buffalo, taking his hand to urge him along as they walked beside the wagon. And when their mother had died before they reached the Rockies, Hannah had stepped into her place.

And never left.

He could not blame her for wanting the best for him. Only for not seeing that what was best for her might not be best for him.

"What do you mean you quit?" she'd railed when he'd confessed he wouldn't be going back to the tiny desk in the windowless office her husband had given him at the company the Virden family had built. "Rudy is counting on you!"

"Rudy has plenty of men ready to rise to the occasion," Kit had told her. "I can't sit and stamp papers the rest of my life, Hannah."

"It's hardly stamping papers," she insisted. "You have important work to do. The Virden company fulfills orders for the railroad. How will travelers be fed or housed without our help?"

"Someone else will know the answer to that question," he said. "The tea fleet's due to sail for Japan in a few days. I plan to go with it."

He hadn't looked back. From the teas and silks of Japan to the brick mansions of Victoria in the British Territories, he'd plied one trade after the other. Able seaman, longshoreman, bootmaker, hop picker, trapper, rail track layer, and others he sometimes forgot. He'd come to this area to work on the Seattle and Walla Walla line, even though it was only as a volunteer as he looked for the next thing of interest. And that's where he'd met Drew Wallin.

"I like your dedication to the job," the logger had said as they'd labored side by side one Saturday. "I could use a man like you on my team."

"Why not?" Kit had said with a grin. "Cutting down trees sounds like more fun than slinging a pickax."

Drew had laughed. "Well, I don't know about fun, but it's steady work, with room and board included, and a chance for land of your own."

The last hadn't interested him then. Wallin Landing was merely another stop on his road to adventure.

A stop that might last longer than he'd thought, now that Grace had been brought into his life. But since he had been unwilling to continue in any of those jobs, what made him think being a father would be any different?

CHAPTER FOUR

SOMETHING WAS PRESSING against her chest, wiggling and whimpering. Ciara opened her eyes to meet those of Grace. The baby's lower lip was starting to tremble. Ciara immediately set the rocker back in motion while she tried to shake herself awake.

The rocker. Grace. What time was it?

She glanced over the long table to the big window. Sunlight was falling into the main clearing in golden beams, anointing the shakes on the roofs, the cows in the pasture. Morning? Had she slept here all night?

Something clanged from the kitchen behind her. Breakfast!

She gathered up the baby and rose, and one of Mrs. Wallin's quilts tumbled down onto the floor. How odd. She didn't remember picking it up last night. Stepping carefully over it, she hurried for the kitchen.

Mr. Weatherly had the stove stoked and the teakettle on. His dark hair stuck out all around his head, as if he hadn't taken the time to comb it this morning, and he appeared to be wearing the same red plaid flannel shirt and dark trousers from the day before, now thoroughly rumpled. And why could she see his stockings? Where were his boots?

Either way, he looked all the more like the baby in her arms, a baby that was starting to fret again.

"Sorry," he said, setting a cast-iron frying pan onto a burner. "I didn't want to wake you."

"You should have," she said. "I have work to do, and so do you." She offered him the baby. "She'll need to be changed. And I have three hungry loggers to feed."

He hurriedly wiped his hands on his trousers and took Grace into his arms. "Thank you."

He disappeared through the archway into the main room.

Ciara pulled the strands of her own hair back into the bun behind her head as she assessed the kitchen. Stove ready? Yes, and plenty of wood in the box should she need more. Dishes washed—Harry and Mr. Willets had taken care of that last night. Time? Too late to start bread or rolls. She'd have to bake later for the rest of the day.

Supplies? Mr. Willets had said something about potatoes and leeks. She located them in crates against the back wall. And there was salted meat hanging nearby, along with an apron Beth must have left behind. At least, she couldn't imagine the cream-colored cotton being big enough to drape Mr. Willets' frame. It would all have to do.

By the time her three loggers and Grace were downstairs and seated at the plank table, she had a credible hash ready. She'd also located jars of canned fruit and set out applesauce as well.

"This looks good enough to eat," Harry said, plopping down into the chair he'd used last night. He at least had combed his hair and wore a clean shirt. "Nice to have a lady who knows her way around the kitchen," he added, grabbing his fork.

He said the blessing, and the three of them tucked in.

"It's good," Mr. Willets said with a lopsided grin around a mouthful of hash.

"Thank you, gentlemen," she said with a bob of a curtsey. She glanced to Mr. Weatherly, but he was trying to get a spoonful of applesauce into Grace's mouth. The baby batted the spoon away, sending a shower of golden drops across the table.

Mr. Willets frowned at him. "You're doing it wrong."

"Well, feel free to show me how to do it right," he shot back. "I was the youngest in the family. I've never had to deal with a baby."

"Try a little of the hash," Ciara suggested, wrapping the apron around the handle of the kettle to pour more tea into Harry's cup.

Harry nodded his thanks, gaze on the baby as well.

Mr. Weatherly sliced off the tiniest of slivers and dangled it in front of Grace's nose. The baby crossed her eyes trying to focus on it.

Ciara set the kettle on the trivet in front of Harry. "Here. Let me."

She settled on the bench and took Grace into her lap. Then she found a choice morsel of hash and swung it toward the baby's lips. "Open up, little bird."

Grace obliged, and Ciara slipped in the food. The baby's eyes widened as the taste must have hit. She wiggled her mouth around, chewing, then opened it for more.

Her uncle shook his head. "You make it look easy."

"It's not that easy," Ciara allowed, tipping in another bite. "I was only a few years older than my brother, Aiden, but I used to help Mrs. McNeilly with the little ones. She was the owner of the children's home where my brother and I stayed until our sister could send for us. Some of the wee ones pine so much for their mothers they aren't interested in food."

His dark eyes looked as hollowed as a cave. "But she has to eat!"

"And it's up to us to find a way to see that she does," Ciara agreed, keeping the hash moving.

The door opened then, and Drew came in, making the big room seem smaller. He glanced around at his men and nodded. "Good to see things returning to normal around here."

Mr. Willets shoveled in the last of his hash and pushed back from his seat.

"Where are we working today, boss?" Harry asked before doing likewise.

"North, close to the bay," Drew said. "I don't expect we'll be back before dinner."

Mr. Willets grabbed his cup and guzzled down the tea.

Mr. Weatherly rose as well, gaze on Ciara. "Would you mind taking care of Grace?"

Did he have any idea how much work she had to do today? She gritted her teeth.

"No, no, no, no, no," Grace said.

"Do you think that's the only word she knows?" Mr. Willets murmured to Harry, who shrugged.

"Grace may only know one word, but I agree completely," Ciara said, rising carefully. "I came here to open a restaurant, Mr. Weatherly. I'd be giving Mr. Wallin a poor return on his investment if I turned into a nanny instead. I'll take her up to Nora, as Mrs. Wallin suggested, just for today. In the future, you'll need to plan on time to do so yourself."

"Of course." He inclined his head as if that was sufficient apology.

"I don't expect any trouble," Drew told Ciara, "but if you need us, use the rifle hanging outside the back door. One shot for trouble, two for dinner."

She'd seen Beth use the notification system more than once. Voices only carried so far in the wilderness. A rifle shot carried farther.

But to fire a gun? She'd never had call to learn and wasn't sure she wanted to try. So she merely smiled as the men headed out for their day of work.

She managed to get a few more spoonfuls of applesauce into Grace, then put the baby in the empty wash tub to hold her long enough that Ciara could bank the stove. There wasn't any food left to put away; they'd devoured every last mouthful. It likely wasn't a testament to her cooking so much as a hint of their appetites. She'd have to make larger portions in the future.

She picked up Grace and started for the door. "Let's get you settled, little lady."

She knew the path up the hill started behind the school, so she crossed the clearing in that direction, a breeze from the lake bringing a brush of moisture. James Wallin, the third brother, waved to her as he came out of the big barn. Grace waved back. Ciara also spotted Catherine, steps brisk and head high, as she started for the dispensary, which was located on the road to Seattle.

The woods seemed deeper as Ciara climbed the series of switchbacks. She might not have spent much time in the woods, but she recognized tall fir, thin aspen, and spiky fern. Their shadows striped the path. Birds darted among them. A squirrel scampered up a fir, paws skittering on the rough bark. Grace's head didn't stop moving as she tried to take it all in.

Ciara felt the same way. Everything seemed so much bigger, wider, the depths of the fir-scented forest impenetrable. That tightness was gathering in her shoulders again, as if even her body knew it didn't belong here. She made herself keep walking.

They had come to the third turning of the path when a wildcat stepped out as if to block their way. It stood a little above her knee, with mottled fur that dipped under its chin into two peaks tufted in black. The golden eyes stared unblinkingly at her, measuring her. She froze.

Grace opened her mouth and shrieked.

Birds rocketed out of the trees. Small things scuttled away through the undergrowth. Tufted ears laid back, the cat dove into the forest and disappeared.

Still Ciara couldn't make herself move. Had it truly

gone? Was it circling back? Would it drop on them as she passed under a big cedar?

The bracken crackled, and she tensed, arms tightening to protect Grace. A plumed tail rose above the ferns a moment before a dog trotted out onto the path. The snowy white of his fur was covered by black on his head and upper body, as if he were wearing a hooded cape. Pointed ears stood at attention as he glanced her way.

She knew that look. Nora's dog, purchased from a trader who had traveled to the far north, was part of the history of Wallin Landing. Ciara sighed in relief, then quickly patted her skirts with her free hand to encourage him closer. "Fleet! Here, boy! Good dog! Oh, but I'm glad to see you."

Grace reached chubby hands toward the dog, who ambled closer.

Fleet came to sit in front of them, pink tongue lolling and almond-shaped dark eyes shining. Grace anchored on one hip, Ciara sank the fingers of her other hand in the soft fur. "Let's go find Nora."

She located Beth's sister-in-law in the fine plank house at the top of the hill. Another member of the Mercer expedition, Nora Wallin had come to the landing in a marriage of convenience and stayed in a marriage of love. As Catherine had predicted, her gray eyes glowed at the sight of the baby in Ciara's arms.

"And who is this?" she asked, cocking her head so that the sun flashed on the threads of silver in her thick black braided hair.

"This is Grace," Ciara said, glancing down at the little girl, who was eyeing Nora thoughtfully as if she wondered at the many colored pieces of thread speckling the seamstress's fanciful gray gown with hearts embroidered on every edge. "She's Mr. Weatherly's niece, and she's come to live with him." She lowered her voice, though she couldn't know whether the baby would understand her next words. "Her parents are gone."

Nora's face fell. "Oh, the poor little thing." She opened her arms, and Grace reached for her.

"We'll see you raised, sweetheart," Nora crooned, hugging her. "You're going to love it here. I did."

"Then you'll be fine with her?" Here she had come to deposit the baby, and all she wanted to do was take her back. "She can be a little fussy."

"No, no, no, no, no," Grace said as if to confirm the fact.

Nora smiled. "Oh, we're at that stage, are we? It's no trouble, Ciara. I'm used to babies—mine, Catherine's, Rina's, even Callie's little niece. Busy mamas and papas need someone to help. Will you be back for her later?"

"Mr. Weatherly will be back for her," Ciara said firmly. "And he'll be the one delivering her in the future. I imagine it will be early."

She shrugged. "We're all up at sunrise. I'll be waiting."

She turned to go, and Ciara felt a sudden panic. "Nora?"

She glanced back. "Yes?"

"There was a big cat on the trail coming up."

Nora's soft face hardened. "Lynx. He's been prowling around the hen house for the last week. Simon's hoping to stop him."

Ciara shivered, but at the fate of the lynx or her own, she wasn't certain. "Can I borrow Fleet?"

Nora's usually happy smile returned. "Of course. Though I can't promise he won't find something else that interests him. We have that sort of arrangement."

She looked to the dog, who had been sniffing about the area while they talked. "Fleet, go with Miss Ciara to the main house."

The dog stopped and eyed her. "Nooooo," he said.

Grace stared at him.

Ciara had heard the native dog give voice before. Some

of the children believed he talked back. She was fairly confident it was just another way of barking.

Nora seemed to think otherwise. "Don't you argue with me," she scolded. "She needs our help. She's new. Now, go."

He ranged ahead of Ciara toward the path. All she could do was thank Nora and hurry to follow.

Kit listened all day for the sound of a rifle in the distance. Surely it would be needed. What if no one could get Grace to eat? What if they couldn't get her to sleep? What if she fell or rolled off the bed? Dozens of scenarios flashed through his mind, each more horrid than the last. Was this what it was like being a father?

"Good day's work," Drew said as the sun settled on the tips of the firs to the west. "And at least an hour ahead of schedule. I don't recall you three ever chopping so fast."

Harry slung his ax up onto his shoulder. "We never had something so good to return to before."

"Dinner," Jesse said with his crooked grin.

Drew barked a laugh. "Ciara O'Rourke is a fine cook. I'm glad you appreciate that. Let's head for home."

He started off, ax in one hand and long cross-cut saw bouncing over one shoulder. Jesse followed, but Harry fell in beside Kit.

"Don't think about courting Ciara," he said. "You may have an advantage with her spending time with that baby, but Jesse and I figure she's marrying one of us."

Jesse glanced back and nodded.

Something inside him protested. Baby or not, he'd seen the pretty cook first. He shook off the thought. "I'm not looking to court anyone," he assured Harry.

"Good," Harry said. "There aren't enough women in these parts, and the mail-order brides are getting pickier all the time. I don't have Scout Rankin's kind of money to attract one. And neither does Jesse."

Few did. A good friend of the Wallin family, Thomas "Scout" Rankin had made his money on the gold fields and come home a wealthy man. Kit had been tempted to follow his path. Panning gold was one job he hadn't tried, and the British Territories to the north were said to be untamed and beautiful. Now he could only be glad he'd decided to stay in Wallin Landing. Bottles and the lawyer Hitchcock might never have found him to deliver Grace. She might have ended up in a children's home, like Miss O'Rourke and her brother. If they even had such things in Washington Territory. Few women meant fewer families.

"I can only wish you the best of luck," Kit said.

Harry snorted. "I'll likely need it. Once she opens that restaurant, every man in five miles will be sniffing at the cabin door. We need to marry that gal, and fast."

He moved ahead to talk to Jesse. Kit did his best not to listen. Marriage? A long-term commitment? No, he wasn't ready, though he understood why some ladies might be willing to become mail-order brides. According to Hannah, marriage brought a wife financial stability, a home of her own, and a family. He wasn't in a position to offer a woman any of that.

Even a woman as little as Grace.

Yet didn't the baby need a mother? He was learning as fast as he could, but the right wife could comfort his niece, help raise her into a lady. For if his sister had had high expectations of him, he could only imagine what she would have expected from her daughter.

CHAPTER FIVE

CIARA HAD HAD a productive day. She'd arranged all the utensils, bowls, cookware, and other tools she'd brought with her to her liking; inventoried the supplies; and planned her meals for the rest of the week. She'd baked bread for today and cinnamon rolls to ice in the morning. A stew was simmering with the dried meat and vegetables she'd had on hand.

Better, she'd mapped out her plan to turn the bottom floor of the old Wallin cabin into a restaurant that would attract diners from all over the area. It wasn't so easy as to open the front door and holler for customers. While she'd built her own book of recipes, she'd mostly served them to family and friends, and she wasn't sure how well they'd work with larger groups. Besides, whoever else she ended up serving, she must honor her promise to Drew to feed his team.

So, first, she had to establish a routine with the three loggers as to breakfast and dinner. Second, it was obvious she'd need a better line of supply for fresh vegetables and meat, so she'd have to talk to Simon and John Wallin, who had the largest farms in the area. She also wanted a closer look at James's mercantile.

Then she'd test her recipes with her loggers, though she was beginning to wonder whether they'd eat anything she set before them. Once she was satisfied she had a rotation of meals that could be relied on, she'd test them on Friday and Saturday nights with the closest population to perfect them. Only then would she feel confident opening the restaurant to serve dinner Mondays through Saturdays, with a picnic hamper available Saturday night for Sundays.

It was a grand plan, an ambitious plan, and she could hardly believe she was making it happen. She just had to count her pennies and spread them as far as they would go.

And she was also rather proud of the fact that she only glanced out the window, checking for the lynx, once or twice.

It helped that she had so many visitors. Catherine brought ointment for chapped hands, as if she thought Ciara might need it with all the dishes she'd be washing. She had barely left when Dottie, John's wife, tapped on the kitchen door.

Ciara opened to the golden-haired blond and her little boy, Peter, whose arms were piled with colored wooden blocks.

"We heard there's a new baby at the Landing," Dottie said with a gentle smile, one hand resting on her calico skirts, which were rounding with another new life to come. "Peter wanted to give her some of his things."

"I'm a big boy now," the four-year-old announced, letting the blocks fall on the floor with a clatter. "I fish with my pa."

"I'd be happy to take any extra fish you might have," Ciara assured him and Dottie.

"Let's bring the blocks onto the rug," Dottie suggested to her son, who scooped them up and suffered himself to be nudged toward the main room of the cabin.

They stayed for tea and were heading for home when Callie, wife of the local minister, Levi Wallin, and sister to the twins who had welcomed Ciara yesterday, popped in the door.

"Still looks more like home than a restaurant," she said, blue-gray eyes narrowed as she glanced around the space. Though she had a wardrobe of gowns now, Ciara had noticed she still preferred the trousers she used to wear in the gold fields, where she'd grown up.

"Give me time," Ciara told her.

Callie held open the door to let her twin brothers in. Like Peter, Sutter and Frisco had piles of belongings up in their arms. They dumped them on the table.

"I'll fetch the crate," Callie promised, and Sutter promptly escaped.

Frisco lingered by the door. "You gonna have any cinnamon rolls soon, Miss Ciara?"

"Tomorrow morning," Ciara promised. "I'll save one for you and your brother."

His eyes lit, and he pelted out the door, likely to share the good news.

Callie shook her head, light-brown hair catching a stray sunbeam, as she returned to the house with a crate. "Wouldn't want to work any harder than they have to, those two." She set the crate on the table as well. "We brought you some clothes Mica outgrew for the new baby, and Levi will bring by the tall chair a little later. Be warned. It rolls."

Ciara was more interested in what crowded the crate. "Preserves!" she cried, picking up a jar of jewel-colored fruit.

"Plums, peaches, apples, green beans, and pickled beets," Callie said. "From last season, I'm afraid, but there will be more to come soon."

"I can hardly wait," Ciara told her. "If you're going picking, please include me."

She was stocking the treasures on the shelves in the kitchen when Rina, the local schoolteacher and wife to

Drew's brother James, came in the kitchen door. A pretty brunette with hazel eyes, she always held herself with the air of royalty, or at least how Ciara imagined royalty might hold itself.

"I wanted to apprise you of a theatrical the children will be enacting at the end of the week," she explained, brushing down her plum-colored skirts. Even after ten years living in Washington Territory, she still sounded as if she should be gracing some fine drawing room back East. "They have chores, but we needed something else to keep them busy while school is out of session."

"Are you looking forward to school starting again in September?" Ciara asked, setting a jar of ruby-red pickled beets on the shelf.

"Very much so," Rina confessed. "We have engaged the services of an excellent second teacher, who should arrive just before school is scheduled to start. That will make my work so much easier. Now, I should leave you to *your* work. I imagine a great deal must be done to turn this place into a restaurant for all to enjoy."

True. Ciara knew the challenge in her plans, but with friends all around, how could she fail?

By five, she had everything ready for dinner. That's the time Drew had said his men generally returned from work. She'd thought she'd spied Harry earlier, crossing the clearing, but he hadn't come in. As she kept the stew warming on one of the burners, she waited, listening. Surely they'd walk through the door any moment.

Only they didn't.

She grimaced.

She wandered out the back door and gazed at the rifle hanging from a strap on the porch roof support. She knew the basic functioning. Take the gun down, cock it, aim it, and press the trigger. She just couldn't make herself do it. With a shudder, she went back inside.

Harry, Mr. Willets, and Mr. Weatherly trickled in over

the next hour. Harry brought flowers he put in a porcelain pitcher on the table. She would not have thought he'd care about such things. Mr. Willets brought an armload of firewood so large she couldn't see his face over the top. Mr. Weatherly came last, carrying Grace, who was wearing a different dress and smiling a big, toothy grin.

"Someone had a good time with Nora," Ciara said, smiling at the baby. "And someone also received a number of presents today." She nodded toward the toys and belongings she'd piled up near the far wall to keep them out of the way.

"Where did these come from?" Mr. Weatherly asked, moving over to look. Grace reached for the pile, little fingers opening and closing.

"Various Wallins," Ciara supplied. She left him examining the things to go fetch the pot of stew.

Harry and Mr. Willets were already seated when she returned with it. The latter rubbed his hands on his trousers before taking up the silverware, knife in one fist, fork in the other.

"Dinner," she called to remind the third logger.

She brought out the cloth-lined bowl of bread, then waited for Harry to say the blessing before serving the food. Settling herself beside Mr. Weatherly and Grace on the bench, she started on her own dinner. But one touch of her fork to the beans, and she knew they were overcooked. The potatoes were like mush, breaking apart in the gravy. Could she have done any worse? What had made her think she could manage a restaurant?

Harry and Jesse were shoveling in the stew, and only a single piece of bread remained in the bowl, but Kit's plate was nearly full. He shoved in a bite before attempting another spoonful for Grace. As with previous attempts, she scrunched up her face and turned her head away.

Nora had said she'd been picky about eating up at the farm too. Likely everything was different from what Hannah's staff had served her. But Hannah was gone, and Kit was the only staff around.

Miss O'Rourke, seated beside him, took pity on him. "Sop the bread in a bit of gravy," she suggested. "It will be easier for her to chew."

"Thanks." He glanced up to find her own plate nearly full as well. "Sorry. I didn't mean to interrupt your meal."

She poked at the stew with her fork. "It's not a very good meal."

"Better than what we cooked," he told her. He reached for the last piece of bread and dunked a corner of it in the gravy to offer Grace.

"Much better," Harry agreed. "You have a rare talent, Ciara."

She raised her brows as if she doubted that, but she didn't contradict him. Instead, she turned to watch Grace nibble on the bread. "There. That's better, isn't it, Grace?"

The baby reached for the bread. Kit gave her a little at a time. "Maybe we'll finish dinner before breakfast."

"You're doing splendidly," Miss O'Rourke promised him. "You've only been an uncle twenty-four hours. I know men who have been fathers far longer who still don't know how to change a nappy."

Harry shuddered.

"I can change a nappy," Jesse announced.

She glanced his way. "Good for you, Mr. Willets. Where did you learn?"

"Sisters," he said, cheeks turning red as if he thought he'd shared too much. "Brothers. I'm the oldest of ten."

"Well, that would do it," she said with a laugh.

"You don't need to call us by our last names," Harry put in, sopping up the gravy with his own bit of bread. "You already call me Harry. You should call him Jesse."

Jesse dropped his gaze to his clean plate.

"Would that be all right with you, Mr. Willets?" she asked.

"Sure," he told the plate.

Harry hadn't included Kit in the conversation, but she turned to him, nonetheless. "And you, Mr. Weatherly? Should I call you Christopher?"

"Kit," he said. "That's what my mother and father called me."

"Well, since you will be my daily customers, I suppose it would be easier," she said. "Harry, Jesse, and Kit it is. And you may call me Ciara, as Harry already does."

"Thank you, Ciara," Jesse said slowly, as if trying the name on for size. Then, he grabbed his plate and cup and surged up from the table. "I'll just take these to the kitchen for you."

Ciara rose. "Not yet. I have a lemon pound cake for dessert."

He plunked back down in his seat, eyes lighting.

"I'll help you carry it," Harry offered, springing up.

"It's no bother," Ciara assured him. She headed for the kitchen.

"I'm not sure she knows you're trying to court her," Kit murmured to Harry.

"I'm working up to it," Harry snapped.

He and Jesse both stood again when she returned with the cake. She cut three generous slices and passed them around.

"I wouldn't give her any," she cautioned Kit as Grace started reaching for the plate. "Once she tastes sugar, it will be harder to get her to eat her vegetables. Why don't you put her on the rug? She might enjoy a little freedom."

Good idea. He swiveled on the bench and set her down at the edge of the colorful braided rug. Grace blinked, as if surprised to find herself out of anyone's arms. She glanced back at Ciara and nearly overset herself.

Kit reached for her. Ciara caught his arm. "Give her a moment."

Sure enough, the baby wiggled on the rug as if testing its stability, then scooted an inch forward on her bottom.

"Look at that," Jesse marveled. "She can move all on her own."

She could indeed. The success had clearly emboldened her, and soon she was scooting about the rug, Kit keeping watch between bites of the cake.

"This is really good, Ciara," Harry said. "You can make it any time."

Jesse nodded.

"Thank you," she told them with a smile. "When I have the restaurant open, I'm hoping to have a choice between two entrees and two desserts every day."

Jesse rolled his eyes heavenward as if thanking the good Lord.

"If they're all as good as this, you'll have no trouble filling the table," Harry predicted.

"If they're all as good as this, you'll need more tables," Kit agreed. "Jesse and I can help you there. Drew's been teaching us how to make furniture."

Once again, Jesse nodded eagerly. "Tables, chairs, chests."

Ciara tipped her chin toward Grace. "I think, Kit, you may find your hands too full to pay any attention to me."

His blood congealed. Grace had reached the stairs, pulled herself up on the first step, and was halfway up on the second, perilously close to the edge of the open stair. His fork fell with a clang of silver on tin, and he raced across the room to snatch her up. She frowned into his face, which was probably as red as her own, opened her mouth, and shrieked.

Other forks clattered. Something squeaked in the chimney. A log settled in the grate.

"Will you please teach her to stop doing that?" Harry demanded.

"I can't teach her anything at the moment," Kit said, turning from the wooden stairway. Why hadn't he noticed the thing was so dangerous? Someone—likely the Wallin father—had cut notches in the log wall of the house and inserted other planed logs to jut out. The stairs had no railing, no spindles. It was a miracle none of his children had fallen to their deaths!

He carried the baby back to the rocking chair and wrapped his arms about her. If Ciara had managed to put her to sleep last night, maybe he could do the same tonight.

Grace had other ideas.

She wiggled, she pushed, she pouted. Fat tears gathered in her dark eyes to roll down her chubby cheeks. She took a shuddering breath.

Kit felt like a great big bully.

"I'll help you with the dishes, Ciara," Harry offered, gathering up some of the plates from the table.

"I can dry," Jesse put in, reaching for the cups.

"Excellent," she said. "Harry, you wash and Jesse, you dry, and I can help Kit with Grace."

Jesse scowled at Harry. "That didn't work the way you wanted."

Harry shook his head and carried the dishes to the kitchen. Jesse trailed behind him like a massive forlorn pup.

"You didn't have much time to look through the gifts," Ciara said, dropping onto the chair beside his. "Levi brought a rolling chair that might keep Grace out of harm's way. But you should probably hold off bringing her up the stairs until you can rig a door or a barricade at the top to keep her safe."

"And keep my sanity," he agreed. "Thank you, Ciara. I feel like I'm saying that a lot, but I mean it. You've made it easier for Grace to accustom herself to these changes."

"Happy to help," she assured him. "Now, I better see to

the kitchen. I'm hearing a few too many bangs for my liking." She rose and hurried off.

He missed her immediately. Likely it was because she was so good with Grace. He wasn't sure how he would have made it through the last day without her help. But, very soon, her time would come at an even greater premium.

What was he going to do when she opened her restaurant?

CHAPTER SIX

CIARA MANAGED TO sleep in her own cabin that night. She was so tired from the day that the noises only kept her awake for a little while. And she was up in plenty of time to start breakfast.

The forest was silent as she slipped down the path in the predawn light, as if even its denizens slept at last. She tucked her red wool shawl closer over her blue flower-sprigged gown. The cool, moist air clung to her cheeks as she approached the big cabin.

Kit was lying on the floor near the fire as she came in, Grace sleeping in the cradle beside him. Dark curls swept their foreheads, and dark lashes fanned their cheeks. Both of them pursed their lips. Kit looked as if he was angling for a kiss. That fizzing sensation set off in her stomach again. Time to make breakfast.

She forced herself to turn for the kitchen. By the time she heard the thud of boots on the stairs, she had the table set and meat strips frying.

"Two more minutes," she called.

"Take your time," Harry called back.

"Why?" she heard Jesse ask, tone puzzled. "Drew will be here to fetch us in a bit."

She wasn't going to make any of them wait. She glanced out the archway in time to see Kit climbing out of his bundle of quilts, hair even more disheveled than the day before. He scratched his beard and stared down at the baby, who had just woken as well if the little fists flailing over the cradle's side were any indication. The poor man looked lost and worried and frustrated all at the same time.

Everyone needed a hand sometimes.

She went out long enough to lift Grace from her cradle.

"Go clean up," she said to Kit. "I have her."

"Are you sure?" he asked, gaze searching her face. "I don't want to interfere with your work. Harry and Jesse would probably have my head."

"And other parts of your anatomy," Harry warned, already seated at the table.

"It's no trouble," Ciara assured them all. She carried Grace back to the kitchen with her.

A short time later, she had porridge, meat, and cinnamon rolls on the table. The entire mass was scooped up and shoveled down in less than a quarter hour.

"Should I have made more?" she asked, glancing around at them all.

Jesse burped.

Harry frowned at him before directing his smile at Ciara. "That was plenty. Thank you. I can't wait to see what's for dinner."

Jesse nodded. But he brought her more wood before he left for the day.

Drew came to collect them, and Kit promised to catch up as soon as he'd taken Grace to Nora.

"There was a lynx on the path yesterday," Ciara warned him. "Nora said it had been prowling around."

"I'll keep an eye out," he promised her.

Grace waved a fist at her as he carried the baby out the door.

Ciara went to clean the dishes. Frisco and Sutter popped by in search of cinnamon rolls, and she sent them off with one each, encouraging them to tell everyone they met about the new restaurant opening soon. She also made up another batch of dough and set it to rising before gathering her basket and heading for the mercantile.

The Wallin Landing Trading Post and Post Office sat on the shores of Lake Union, with a dock sticking out into deeper waters. Plain, square, and weathered on the outside, inside it was crammed with all manner of goods, from fabric to writing paper to plows and tinned food. And, like a genii in one of the stories Maddie used to read them, James Wallin presided over his treasure trove.

"And how might I help Wallin Landing's newest business owner?" he asked from behind his counter at one end of the store. He wiggled brows as pale a blond as his fashionably combed hair.

"I don't own the cabin," Ciara reminded him, venturing closer. "I lease it from Drew by providing cooking services for his logging crew. I can't imagine that place being in anything but Wallin hands."

"There is that," he said with his charming smile. "Still, I doubt you have time for idle chat, though, if you did, there's no one better for miles."

"That, I *can* imagine." She glanced around at the many offerings. "I came to find out what you stock that I could use."

He waved a hand at his shelves. "Anything the mind can dream."

"Some people have big dreams," she warned, gaze coming back to his.

"And I am up to meeting them." His dark blue eyes, so much like his sister's, twinkled.

"Condensed milk?" she challenged.

"Yep."

"Confectioner's sugar?"

"Plenty. Rina has a sweet tooth."

She had a feeling the man in front of her had the sweet tooth. "Tinned pork?"

He wrinkled his nose. "Now, why would you want that?"

"A lady has to eat too, and sometimes she simply tires of cooking."

"Well, if you tire of cooking, you just come up to see Rina and me, and we'll feed you." He leaned closer. "Or better, go see Levi. He still makes the best biscuits in the family."

"I know," she said. "And I intend to steal that recipe from him."

"Ha!" He straightened. "You do, and your fame is assured. It will probably be assured anyway. You're Maddie's sister."

Her smile slipped. "I'll just look around. See what else inspires."

"Help yourself."

She ducked behind a stack of molasses casks. He hadn't meant to be hurtful. Of all the Wallin brothers, James was closest to her sister. Some had thought they might marry, until Michael Haggerty had come West with Ciara and Aiden. She should have expected he'd mention Maddie. That didn't mean her sister's shadow was covering her even here.

She heard the door open and glanced around the molasses to see a fellow approaching the counter. She couldn't tell the color of his hair under the broad-brimmed slouch hat nor his build in the worn flannel shirt and loose trousers. He couldn't have been very old, though, for his chin bore no sign of whiskers.

"Good morning, Miss McAllister," James said.

Miss McAllister?

"Mornin', Mr. Wallin," she said, voice husky enough for a young man as well. "You need anything done?"

"That calico still calling your name?"

Miss McAllister glanced toward the bolts of fabric standing upright along one wall. "It sure would be nice to have a dress again. If I can collect enough money, I could ask Mrs. Nora to help me sew it."

"No, you want to save your money," James told her. "There's going to be a restaurant opening soon." He grinned at Ciara.

The woman turned. She had a pleasant face, round-cheeked and open, with eyes the color of a summer sky. From this angle, Ciara could spy the honey-colored locks peeking out from inside the slouch hat.

For all she knew, this might be her first paying customer. She pasted on a smile and moved forward.

"Ciara O'Rourke," she said, going to join them at the counter. "I'm cooking for the Wallin logging crew right now, but I'm hoping to have the restaurant open in a few weeks."

"Katie Jo McAllister," she said. She stuck out a hand with nails worn down and blackened, then seemed to think better of the gesture and tucked it in a pocket. "I bet your restaurant will be real nice."

"Why don't you come back with me and have a cup of tea now?" Ciara suggested. "There's cake left over from yesterday evening and a cinnamon roll from breakfast."

Katie Jo's blue eyes widened, but she shook her head. "Appreciate the gesture, but I can only be away so long."

"The back room needs to be swept out," James suggested. "It shouldn't take you more than a few minutes. You'll still have time to visit with Ciara."

"Maybe next trip," she said. She ducked her head shyly.

"I'll keep some treats for you," Ciara promised. "Tell all your friends and family."

In answer, Katie Jo shuffled toward the storeroom behind the counter.

"Ask Rina," James murmured. "She'll explain."

Ciara nodded. "I was wondering, which of your brothers would you recommend to teach me to shoot?"

His fair brows rose to his hair. "You can't shoot?"

Said that way, she sounded deficient indeed. "I never needed to shoot in Seattle."

"Hart would probably disagree with you there."

Hart McCormick was the deputy sheriff and married to Beth. She liked him well enough, but he could be a little brusque. Not her idea of a teacher. "Hart and I disagree on a number of things," she allowed. "Now, who do you think would be willing to spare the time to teach me?"

"Harry would probably be happy to help," he suggested.

She had a sudden image of Harry with his arms around her. Her shudder must have shown, for James pressed his lips together a moment as if to keep from laughing. "Or Jesse or Kit," he said at last. "John's the best shot in the family, but he has his hands full with his farm at the moment. Callie's nearly as good, but she has music lessons to teach."

"I'll consider the matter," Ciara promised. "I'll take a sack of flour, a sack of rice, and a sack of dried beans."

James rocked back as if disappointed. "That's it? No raisins? No cinnamon sticks?"

"One stick," she added. "I have to be careful with costs until I open the restaurant."

"You could start an account and settle up later," James offered, pulling out a leather-bound ledger book. "I keep accounts for a number of folks. At least if you don't pay up, I know where to find you."

That's what she feared.

In the end, she let him convince her to take the raisins and a ham he had cured as well as the other things she'd requested. She decided to carry the smaller items and have him deliver the rest. Amazing how heavy a cinnamon stick and some raisins felt in her basket when they were weighted by the realization she might not be able to clear her debt. Maybe she could sweep, like Miss McAllister.

She barely managed a nod to the farmer who was pulling his wagon to a stop in front of the mercantile.

Something moved in the brush as she started up the hill. She quickened her steps, heart pounding, and came out into the clearing so fast she nearly ran into the woman standing beside the cabin. The silver of her hair was only a shade lighter than the fine gray wool traveling suit with its black soutache trim at the cuffs, neck, and hem. With a black feathered hat on her head, she was a picture out of *Godey's Lady's Book*. Beth would have been in alt.

Her lips thinned at the sight of Ciara, as if she were far less impressed.

"You there," she said in imperious tones. "I must speak to the leader of this hamlet at once. My granddaughter has been kidnapped, and I want her back. Immediately."

They were working below the bay that morning. Even if Kit hadn't been able to catch glimpses of the blue-green waters through the trees, he would have known by the pungent scent of tide flats. Drew liked to stay close to a creek or bay, so they had a shorter distance to haul the trees. Once in the water, the logs floated easily to Puget Sound, where they could be rafted together and sent down to one of the sawmills on Elliott Bay.

He'd heard of logging crews moving from acre to acre and cutting everything in sight. Drew had a different approach. He took commissions from the furniture makers and ship builders for specific types and sizes of wood, then located stands among the claims his family owned and picked the best trees for the job. He sometimes bid on clearing jobs for those just establishing their claims or seeking to expand their farmland. That was harder work, for not only did they have to clear all the trees from the property, but they had to uproot stumps as well. Still, they sometimes gained good timber from the effort that Drew used to make furniture.

Kit wiped the perspiration from his forehead with the back of his hand now, though the air was still cool. Three more spars, and they'd fill the order from the shipyards in Tacoma.

In the distance, a rifle sounded.

"Dinner?" Jesse asked, looking up hopefully.

They waited, counting off the seconds. No second shot came.

"Move," Drew said. "Now."

They moved.

They left the crosscut embedded in a tree, snatched up axes, and ran through the brush. They'd beaten a path to the location days ago and flattened it further with each trip, but the springy vines still clutched at their boots and tree limbs whipped their faces. Harry edged past Drew, until Kit beat him to the front. All he could think was that something had happened to Grace.

He shouldn't have left her with Nora. There was a lynx in the area. She wasn't eating well yet. She liked to climb stairs!

He careened into the clearing. Instead of Catherine holding his niece's lifeless body, an older woman in a fine gray dress stood beside a wagon, whose driver looked none too happy with his surroundings. Another woman, a maid by the black of her gown, peered up over the side of the wagon's bed, face pale.

Ciara and Rina lifted their skirts to climb down from the porch.

"What happened?" Drew asked, striding past Harry and Kit to meet them.

"Mrs. Virden believes her granddaughter has been kidnapped," Rina said as Ciara came to stand beside Kit. "She seems to think we might have her."

"Not you," Mrs. Virden said with ringing tones. "Him."

She pointed at Kit. "You are clearly Hannah's brother."

"You must be Rudolph's mother," he realized.

She put her pointed nose in the air. "You admit you've stolen his only child, then."

"Mr. Weatherly didn't steal Grace," Ciara put in. "When Mr. Yeager and I were traveling from Seattle to Wallin Landing, we met a man at the side of the road. He advised us to deliver Grace to him."

"So," Rudolph's mother said, turning to meet her gaze. "You are the accomplice."

Ciara drew herself up. Kit put a hand on her arm. He'd been dealing with the Virden arrogance ever since his sister had married into the family. She should not have to face it.

"Miss O'Rourke is new to Wallin Landing," he said. "She had no way of knowing Grace had other kin. Nor did she realize it was my brother's butler, Bottles, bringing Grace to me."

She sniffed. "The man should be discharged."

"I believe he already has been," Kit said. "I received a letter from a lawyer named Dixon Hitchcock. Do you know him?"

Her tone remained as cold as water off a glacier. "Mr. Hitchcock was in my son's employ. If I had the power, I would discharge him too."

"A shame," Kit allowed. "But his note says Hannah wanted me to take care of Grace."

His sister's mother-in-law shook her head, setting the iridescent black feathers in her hat to swaying. "Likely because she thought you had finally established yourself in a decent profession. She would not have wanted her daughter raised on a backwoods farm."

Drew stood taller, but Rina intervened before he could speak.

"Wallin Landing is one of the more prosperous

settlements outside Seattle," she said in her perfectly modulated voice. James Wallin had joked she was a princess, and Kit could see why. "We have the only school in the area, taught by women trained at the famed Boston Normal School, one of the finest in the country, with curriculum from Horace Mann himself. We have a mercantile, post office, library, and church. Furthermore, Mr. Weatherly holds a respected place in the community. He has already engaged the services of a nanny for your granddaughter."

Mrs. Virden's lip curled as she glanced at Ciara. "Nanny? Is that what you call her?"

Ciara flamed.

Harry unslung his ax and stepped forward. "We don't take kindly to our own being maligned."

"Men like you never do," Mrs. Virden sneered. She turned to Kit. "They can posture all they like. You know Grace was meant for more. Surrender her to me, and I will see that she is raised properly. She will attend the finest schools. She will want for nothing."

Except perhaps love. It was possible this woman had a heart under that tailored dress, but she likely had the same sorts of expectations her son had had. He'd lived under his sister's and brother-in-law's expectations long enough. He wouldn't allow Grace to grow up under the same restrictions.

"My sister must have known what you could give her daughter," Kit said. "She decided to send her to me instead. Grace stays."

Ciara's hand slipped down, clasped his tight. His chest swelled.

"We shall see about that," Mrs. Virden said. "Expect to hear from my attorney shortly." She picked up her skirts and swept to the wagon. The driver hurriedly dismounted to help her back onto the bench. Head high, as if she rode in a fine carriage, she suffered herself to be driven from the clearing.

Leaving her threats lingering in the air like dust.

CHAPTER SEVEN

"**W**ELL," RINA SAID as the sound of the wagon faded into the forest. "That was interesting."

Interesting was not the word Ciara would have used. In Five Points, where she'd been born, it wasn't unusual for some family members to turn on others, but never in her family, at least not until she and Aiden had argued. She couldn't imagine taking such a vicious attitude. What sort of person would Grace grow up to be living under that influence?

Kit clearly felt the same, for he hadn't hesitated to protect his niece.

"Can she do what she implied?" he asked now, glancing at Drew. "Can she take Grace without my permission?"

Drew rubbed his stubbled chin with one hand. "I'm no lawyer, and she'll find the best, but I suspect it all depends on what your brother-in-law put in his will."

"Was there a copy with Grace's things?" Ciara asked.

Kit shook his head. "Only that note, informing me that my sister wanted me to raise Grace. The lawyer said he would come tell me the rest soon."

"We may be able to learn more in the meantime," Drew said. "James will know where the will would be filed." He turned to Harry and Jesse, who were hovering as if unsure what to do with their axes or themselves. "No more work for today. We all have better things to do.

Take a minute, then go fetch the crosscut. You can have the afternoon off."

Harry saluted him with the ax handle. "You got it, boss." He tipped his head, and Jesse followed him up onto the porch and into the big cabin.

Rina looked to Kit. "The library has some books on territorial law. I will see what I can discover."

His smile rose for the first time since that woman had appeared. "Thank you, ma'am." As she hurried off, and Drew headed for his own cabin, Kit turned to Ciara.

"Thank you for alerting us. I'm sorry you had to deal with her in the meantime."

She shook her head. "I didn't alert you. Rina noticed us and came to intercede. She fired the rifle, and I'm glad she did. Mrs. Virden was fiercely determined to take Grace with her, no matter what anyone else thought."

"I suppose I can understand," he said, gaze going off down the road as if he could see his sister's mother-in-law even now. "It sounded like she was notified her son had died, showed up to take care of her orphaned granddaughter, and found her missing. Anyone might panic."

"Anyone might panic," Ciara agreed, turning for the cabin. "Anyone doesn't have to be thoroughly disagreeable about it." She lifted her skirts to climb up onto the porch. "I only wish I knew how to shoot that rifle, so I can alert you next time."

He joined her on the porch. "Well, why don't I teach you to shoot? You've certainly helped me the last two days."

She eyed him. Unlike Harry, who always seemed to be measuring the ladies around him for a wedding gown, Kit merely looked eager, dark eyes crinkled with his smile.

"It isn't just the shooting," she admitted. "I'm having trouble feeling comfortable here. Seattle is already a frontier town, and I spent half my life there. But this?"

She waved at the tall firs. "This is truly the wilderness."

He chuckled. "Don't let Rina hear you say that."

"She gave a spirited defense," Ciara allowed. "But she spends most of her time here in the clearing. How often does she have to venture out into the woods?"

"How often do you have to venture into the woods?"

"Every day!" She threw up her hands. "From my cabin to this one and back. Down the path to the mercantile. Up the hill to Nora's. All I can think about is what's waiting to pounce on me."

"Most of the big animals have moved farther out," he said, as if trying to encourage her. "We haven't seen a bear in months, and the last time they spotted a cougar was before I joined Drew's crew two years ago. Even deer know to avoid us most days. And if you look closely at these woods, you might find all sorts of things to put into your recipes."

She shook herself. "Edible food? Out here?"

He chuckled. "Don't sound so astonished. How do you think families fared on the Oregon Trail without a little foraging? How do you think the Natives lived for generations? I'll add that to the list too—teach Ciara to shoot and show her the beauty and plenty of the wilderness."

"That list is getting longer," she complained. "What exactly do you expect me to do in payment?"

As soon as the words left her mouth, she wanted to call them back. Harry would have probably asked for a kiss. Her gaze darted to Kit's lips and locked onto them, and her breath stuck in her chest.

"Simple," he said. "You help me learn how to take care of Grace. You've already done so much."

She licked her dry lips. "Deal."

Now his gaze dropped to her lips and hung.

Somewhere, a bird sang.

The cabin door banged open, and Jesse loped out. "More firewood," he said as he passed her.

Kit took a step back. "Think I'll take the time to clean up. We can work on shooting after dinner."

She nodded, and he took off around the house.

What was wrong with her? It had been a simple agreement, help for help. Nothing different than when she traded favors with Beth or Ada or even her brother.

But it didn't feel like trading favors with a friend. It felt like a relationship was being built, log by log, stone by stone, into something that would last. That was not why she'd come to Wallin Landing. She had work to do.

She came into the house to find Harry sweeping the floor.

"You don't have to do that," she told him. "I think Drew expects me to keep up the ground floor."

He finished with a flourish, then shoved his pile of dirt toward the door. "No trouble. Anything to help."

He opened the door and swept the dirt up and out.

Right onto Jesse.

The logs in his arms took the brunt of it, but the big logger coughed. "What are you doing, Harry?"

"Helping," Harry snapped. He stomped away from the door, and Jesse brought in the wood and dropped it onto the stack that was already halfway up the wall. They glared at each other a moment, then Harry slammed out the front door, and Jesse stalked through the kitchen and slammed out the back.

"I have no idea what's gotten into them," Ciara confessed to Dottie, when she stopped by the house late that afternoon. She had left Peter playing with Mica at the parsonage and now leaned back in Mrs. Wallin's rocking chair as if relishing a moment of peace. Harry and Jesse had gone to get the saw Drew had mentioned, and Kit had taken Grace's nappies to Callie to see about washing.

"I think I know," Dottie said, resting her hands on her abdomen and setting the chair to rocking. "Wood is how a logger says he's fond of you."

Ciara stared at her. "What!"

She nodded, setting her golden curls to bobbing. "When I first came to Wallin Landing, before John and I started courting, Harry and the other members of the crew at the time used to bring me fish from the lake and chop wood. Lots of wood. Kit and Jesse weren't in the crew then, but it wouldn't surprise me if they had the same idea."

"Well, it's a ridiculous idea," Ciara huffed, hugging the cup of tea she'd poured for herself.

"Not so ridiculous," Dottie maintained. "A man likes to show a lady his skills. They're good with wood."

"It isn't that," Ciara said. "I can see the attraction of a man who isn't afraid of chores and who's willing to provide. I'm simply not interested in courting."

Dottie blinked. "Whyever not?"

Ciara rose. "Because I have a plan for my life, and a husband would only get in the way."

"I doubt your sister feels that way about her husband, and she runs a business," Dottie pointed out.

Ciara raised her chin. "I am not my sister. Excuse me. I should check the pie."

She headed for the kitchen.

As always, the warmth from the stove was comforting, like greeting an old friend. This stove hadn't seen the delights her sister served. It wouldn't compare her to the marvelous Maddie. Here, she could just be Ciara. And that ought to be enough for anyone.

Kit shook the last of the water off his hair. On a warm July day, a dip in the cool waters of Lake Union was always welcome, particularly when he was the only one visible along the forested shores. Today, he felt as if the water had washed off the condemnation of Mrs. Virden's words.

She would not have wanted her daughter raised on a backwoods farm.

He shook his head again as he began pulling on his union suit. She didn't know the half of it. He felt as if he had done so little. Ciara and Nora were caring for Grace. Callie had agreed to wash the nappies with Mica's. He couldn't even give Grace a home. His belongings fit in a sea chest at the foot of the pallet he slept on in the loft. Traveling light had made sense when he'd moved from job to job, often living in cramped quarters. Now he had nothing to offer Grace, not even a bed.

Grace was meant for more.

Hannah would certainly have agreed. Rudolph would likely have done anything to keep his daughter out of Kit's hands. He'd seen Kit as unreliable, unstable. Kit could not be counted on to follow through. His patchwork collection of jobs was testament to that.

He shoved his arms into his flannel shirt. He'd have to make some changes. It didn't matter that he'd had no plans before now. Now he had a reason to plan, a reason to succeed. He'd talk to Drew. A few parcels of surveyed land to the north of Wallin Landing were still eligible for claiming under the Homestead Act. Maybe he could file a claim, prove it up by building a cabin and clearing the land. That would give Grace a home, at least.

He paused, hand reaching for his trousers. Proving up a claim could take five years or more. Didn't Grace deserve a home now? Should he move back to Seattle? Take a job at one of the sawmills or grist mills? The income would still likely only provide for a room or two in a lodging house. And who would care for Grace while he worked?

The options seemed narrowed, constraining. He could almost feel them wrapping around his wrists and ankles like shackles. That was one of the reasons he'd left the area the first time. Hannah and Rudolph had plotted his future, and he hadn't liked the destination. He'd felt trapped.

But his feelings didn't matter this time. Grace mattered. He had to find a solution.

He stopped by the mercantile on the way back to the cabin to talk with James. Several of the other farmers and trappers in the area were in the trading post, picking up supplies and wrangling over prices. Kit found himself waiting in front of the fabric bolts. It probably wouldn't take much to make Grace a new dress. He knew enough about sewing to fix a button or hem a frayed cuff. He'd learned to darn his own socks too. But a little girl's dress? Where would he start? Maybe Nora could teach him. She was an accomplished seamstress.

"And how can I help you today, Mr. Weatherly?" James asked after the others had cleared out. "Rattle for your new baby? Headache remedy?"

Kit ventured closer to the counter. "Should I expect Grace to have headaches?"

"The remedy is for you," James clarified with a grin. "I remember those nights when the crying didn't stop."

At least Grace hadn't given him one of those, thanks to Ciara. "Actually, I came for information," he told the shopkeeper. "Drew says you might know where wills are filed."

"Smart of you to write one now that you have a child," James said, leaning his elbows on the polished wood counter. "But I might consult a lawyer first."

"It's not for me," Kit said. "I want to see the particulars of my brother-in-law's will. Specifically, I want to know if there's a provision for Grace's guardianship."

"Ah." He straightened. "You'd have to go to the county offices in Tacoma. The Probate Court has the responsibility for wills and custody of minors. Insanity hearings too, but I will deny knowing that if anyone else asks."

Tacoma might be only thirty-some miles to the south, but he knew the difficulty in reaching it. Few roads had been built. He'd likely have to travel by steamer, then borrow a horse or rig from the livery stable as Mrs. Virden must have done. He'd have to spend the night as well before returning the next day, if there was a steamer heading north and the tides were favorable. He didn't want to take Grace into enemy territory, and he didn't like leaving her behind when she was just becoming accustomed to him. That didn't seem fair to her or anyone who might volunteer to watch her, especially Ciara.

He was still thinking about the matter as he came up into the clearing to find Rina waiting by the porch.

"All I could discover is that a family may designate a guardian for minor children," she told him.

"James implied the same," Kit said. "He thinks the will would have been filed in Tacoma. That's as far away as the moon right now. I have to hope Dixon Hitchcock arrives as he promised."

"I have heard he's one of the best lawyers in the territory," Rina offered. "His success in winning cases for his clients has been noted in the *Daily Intelligencer* often enough."

"Then maybe he's a match for Mrs. Virden," Kit said. He thanked her and excused himself to go fetch Grace from Nora's.

It was shortly before dinner when he brought the baby back into the cabin. The scent of cooking meat met him and set his mouth to salivating. Jesse and Harry must have thought the same, for they were already at the table, places set, and utensils in hand. He slid onto the bench with Grace, who was rocking in his arms as if even she expected a treat.

Ciara carried a platter into the room. Piled on top

were ham steaks, the pink flesh delicately seared. Harry stared at them, face awed. She followed the platter with a bowl of rice and another with gravy, along with peach preserves and pickled beets.

"This is so good," Harry said around mouthfuls after Jesse had asked the blessing with a simple, "Thank You, Lord. Amen."

"I'm glad you like it," she said, but she was regarding the food on her plate with a frown.

"You can't tell me anything is wrong with it this time," Kit murmured, offering Grace some of the peaches.

"It's fine," she said. "But it won't work for a restaurant. If I offered every customer a ham steak, I'd run through the ham in one serving. I'll have to reconsider."

Jesse volunteered to wash. Ciara looked ready to argue with him, but Harry took her hand.

"You've been working hard," he said, tugging her toward the rocker. "You should rest."

She rolled her eyes at him. "If I need to rest after serving only three people, Harry, I have no business running a restaurant." Still, she suffered herself to sit.

Grace, who had been scooting about on the rug, aimed herself in Ciara's direction.

Harry held up one finger, as if urging Ciara to remain in place, then ran up the stairs.

She shook her head, watching as Grace edged closer. Then she bent and scooped up the little girl. "What a big girl, moving about all by herself!"

"No, no, no, no, no," Grace chattered, gazing into Ciara's face.

Kit felt as if a swarm of mosquitoes nipped at his neck. What, was he jealous? That made no sense. He'd told Harry he wasn't interested in courting.

Why did some part of him want to argue?

CHAPTER EIGHT

K IT BARELY HAD time to shake off the odd feeling before Harry thundered back down the stairs, guitar in hand. He set himself up opposite Ciara and strummed a chord.

Grace stared at him, obviously fascinated. Kit couldn't look away either. His friend had said he was working up to courting. Apparently, he was launching a campaign tonight.

"The pale moon was rising above the green mountain, the sun was declining beneath the blue sea," Harry sang in a warm baritone. "When I strayed with my love to the pure crystal fountain that stands in the beautiful vale of Tralee."

Ciara leaned forward, as if she could imagine the idyllic spot he sang about. Once more, those mosquitoes bit as Harry's smile broadened.

"She was lovely and fair as the rose of the summer
but 'twas not her beauty alone that won me.
Oh no was the truth in her eyes ever dawning
that made me love Ciara, the Rose of Tralee."

She jerked upright and began shaking her head so hard some of the dark tresses fell from their pins to frame her face in long tendrils. That can't have been the reaction Harry had been hoping for, but he kept singing, undaunted.

"The cool shades of evening their mantels were spreading

and Ciara all smiling was listening to me.

The moon thru the valley her pale rays were spreading when I won the heart of the Rose of Tralee."

She sprang to her feet, raising a squeak from Grace. "I need to change her." Clutching the baby to her chest like a shield, she charged up the stairs and disappeared.

Harry lowered his instrument, gazing after her, shoulders slumped. "What am I doing wrong?"

"Nothing," Jesse said, lumbering out of the kitchen. "That sounded real good, Harry."

Harry shook his head and sighed.

Kit refused to smile, though everything in him wanted to crow in triumph.

"I should probably help with Grace," he said. He rose and edged around his friend, who was gazing at his instrument as if it had betrayed him.

Ciara had Grace on one of the pallets in the loft and was just doing up the ties on her nappy when Kit walked in. The rinsed ones he had yet to send to Callie hung on a line he had stretched across one corner of the space.

"I can do that," he offered.

"I know," she said, pulling Grace's gown back into place. "I just had to get away from Harry for a moment." She shook her head. "Rose of Tralee, indeed."

"Don't they call Irish lasses roses sometimes?" he asked, taking Grace from her.

"Oh, to be sure, they do. But there's a story behind the song, and I doubt Harry knows it. The man who wrote it came from a fine family, they say, and he fell in love with a common maid. They were parted for a time, but he came home intending to marry her, only to learn she had died. He wrote the song in her memory."

Kit stared at her. "Harry can't know. He's trying to court you."

"That's what I'm afraid of," Ciara said. "I'll have to speak to him, but not tonight. You can teach me to shoot tomorrow. For now, I just want my own cabin."

She ducked out of the room. He heard her steps on the stairs, then a curt goodnight to Harry and Jesse.

Irish rose. The Rose of Wallin Landing. Perhaps he was as fanciful as Harry, but it suited her.

And he could imagine defying his family, if he'd still had one, to claim her for his own.

They were mad, the lot of them! At least her concerns about Harry's courting kept her from paying much attention to the dark of the forest as Ciara hurried back to her cabin. They kept her from a good night's sleep as well, so she might have been a bit terse when she fed them griddle cakes with apple preserves and sent them on their way after breakfast. Grace waved at her as Kit carried her out.

Ciara was out on the porch, churning butter from the cream John had left her, when some of the area children started streaming past. The various blonds were likely Wallin children, but she spotted a few dark and red heads among the group. Frisco stopped long enough to eye her.

"No cinnamon rolls today," she told him.

He nodded and headed toward the lake, his twin in pursuit.

Rina came last, navy skirts swaying. With a smile to Ciara, she stepped up on the porch.

"We had our dress rehearsal this morning," she explained. "They seem a bit eager for the actual performance."

Across the clearing, three boys were chasing each other around the schoolhouse. One of the girls was attempting to scale the nearest tree, while four others cheered her on.

"They have a lot of energy," Ciara said, pausing in her cranking. "Maybe I should put them to work."

"Very likely they would be delighted, if their pay was one of your treats," Rina told her with a smile. "Would you like me to churn for a bit?"

"No, thank you," Ciara said, switching arms. At least the Wallins had a crank churn instead of a paddle. The older models had taken both her hands to plunge the wooden paddle up and down. "But James mentioned you might know the story behind a young lady I met, Katie Jo McAllister."

"Ah, Katie Jo." Rina seated herself on the edge of the porch. "She and her brother, Ezekiel, attended school for a time during the spring and fall a few years ago. Winter was too far a walk."

"Are they located so far out, then?" Ciara asked, stopping a moment to pry up the lid. A few globs of butter were already in evidence.

"About a half hour's walk north, along Salmon Bay," Rina answered. "But there were no roads until last year, and even now it's more of a track. She and her brother live with their uncle, who seems a bit set in his ways. I only met him twice, and neither time was particularly pleasant. He seems to think raising his brother's children cost him something, and it is only right that he should recoup his losses through their efforts to work on his claim."

She hadn't even met the man and already she didn't like him. "Maddie lost a great deal by raising me and Aiden. She might have stayed in New York, done well for herself there. Instead, she chose to come all this way and start a business in a frontier town. Then again, she met Michael here, and everyone sings her praises, so you might say it all worked for the good."

"For everyone," Rina agreed.

The sound of a wagon had them both looking toward

the south and the road from Seattle. A moment later, Beth drove into the clearing, Ada Rankin at her side.

Ciara straightened and waved as they came to a stop in front of the cabin, the very air seeming to sparkle. Drew's older son ran to take charge of the horses, and Beth and Ada gathered their skirts to climb down.

"Welcome back," Rina called, rising. "I would stay and chat, but I believe I need to rescue a young lady from a tree. Excuse me." She headed for the schoolhouse and the mass of children pointing excitedly at their classmate, who did indeed seem to have gotten stuck about halfway up the cedar.

Beth hopped onto the porch. "Oh, how I've missed you!" She enfolded Ciara in a fierce hug.

Ciara laughed as they disengaged. "It's only been a few days."

"An eternity, if you listen to Beth," Ada said with a smile, joining them.

The two of them couldn't be more different. Beth had the blond hair and deep blue eyes that marked most of the Wallins, while Ada's hair and eyes were a warm brown. Beth dressed in styles from *Godey's Lady's Book*. Today it was a striped pink with a white overskirt edged in flowered embroidery gathered back in a bustle. Ada's clothes tended toward the simpler, like the gray lustring fitted to her slender form. And Beth was enthusiastic. Always. Ada was more practical. Small wonder their friend, Scout Rankin, had fallen in love and married her.

"Go in and have some tea," Ciara offered. "I'll just be a moment."

"I remember how that churn works," Beth said. "We'll wait out here with you."

"Is there anything we can do to help?" Ada added.

"It's nearly done," Ciara said.

As she slipped the lid back into place, they spread their skirts and took seats on the edge of the porch, feet swinging. Beth cast her gaze out over the clearing she had called home for so long.

"So," she said, "which one do you like?"

Ciara frowned. "Which cabin? This one will work just fine. I already determined that before I proposed this arrangement to your brother."

Beth laughed. "No, not the cabin. The gentlemen—Harry? Jesse? Kit?"

Kit's face came immediately to mind, dark eyes alight with merriment, smile gentle. "None of them," Ciara said, resuming her churning with renewed purpose. "I thought you were up to your matchmaking, Beth McCormick. You can stop right now."

Ada spread her hands. "Might as well ask a bird to stop flying."

"Exactly," Beth said. "I favor Kit for you, myself, but I heard he's suddenly a father."

The story had obviously reached Seattle. "He is, though he's doing well in the new role. You should see him with little Grace."

"Oh, how nice," Ada said. "Is she a dear?"

"Well, she certainly has an opinion," Ciara said. "No is her favorite word. In multiples. And she has a piercing shriek. Kit has his hands full."

Beth's golden brows went up. "Kit, is it? Well, that's a start."

Ciara stopped churning and pointed her finger at her friend. "No."

"Your favorite word as well?" Beth teased.

Ciara gave it up and smiled. "I can feel the butter. Let me show you what I have planned for the restaurant. I assume that's why you came all this way."

Beth rose and shook out her skirts. "We came all this way to see how you were settling in. I know how challenging it can be to move. It took me a while to get used to Seattle, though I love it there."

"I'm still getting used to Seattle," Ada said, rising as well. "It's very different from Boston."

"And New York," Ciara admitted. Odd. Why was she suddenly homesick for a place that hadn't been home for more than ten years?

She dragged the churn into the kitchen, and her friends helped her press the butter into molds. After Ada put on the kettle, the three adjourned to the main room and talked for some time. Ciara felt as if someone had stolen her favorite pots when she at last stood on the porch and waved them out of the clearing on the way back to Seattle.

She had to remember she'd made this choice for a reason. It was time to move on with her dreams.

"Will you watch where you're swinging that ax?" Harry complained.

Kit grimaced and lowered the handle, the wood dampened by sweat and heated by the sun. "Sorry, Harry. My mind's somewhere else today."

They had felled one of the massive cedars and were hacking the limbs off the trunk to make it easier to skid to the bay. Harry and Kit had one side. The trunk's circumference was large enough that he couldn't make out Drew and Jesse on the other side.

"I know how you feel," Harry said, taking a moment to lower his own ax to the crushed vegetation around them. "I've tried everything I can think of—flowers, compliments, songs—and Ciara won't even give me the time of day."

"There's a little more to courting, I suppose, than compliments and gifts," Kit allowed. "You have to find commonalities."

"We both live in Wallin Landing," Harry said as if trying. "I work. She works."

"You both have dreams," Kit supplied, raising his ax once more. "She wants to start a restaurant. You want to farm your claim."

Harry lifted his ax as well. "I want a family. I never had that, growing up. My parents died when I was a boy, and my relatives kept passing me around to where I'd do them the most good—cleaning pots, mucking stalls, chopping wood." He swung and severed a limb in a single blow. "Now, I work for me."

"So do I," Kit said, hacking at another limb. "Or I did, until Grace."

"No shame in providing for your family," Harry said. "I just need to find a wife who feels the same way."

But it didn't follow that that wife should be Ciara. She had a gift and a dream of using it. It seemed wrong, somehow, to take her away from that, like separating a composer from his piano or an artist from her paints.

The work seemed to go on longer than usual that day, for all Drew called a halt a half-hour early. Kit trudged back through the forest, trying to cudgel his mind into action. He'd asked Drew whether anyone had a reason to go to Tacoma and could look into his brother-in-law's will, but his boss had shaken his head.

"From what James told me, until the will is formally entered into probate, it's unavailable to the public. I doubt the court will let any of us see it in the meantime."

Which meant he had to depend on this lawyer showing up soon. He also had to figure on a way to give Grace a home. The more he thought about it, a claim seemed too large. Would Drew or James be willing to sell him a parcel of land instead, just big enough for a house? There was still the cost of the land and lumber to consider, not to mention the furnishings, but it would be a start.

"She was a very good eater today," Nora told them when he picked up Grace.

"No, no, no, no, no," Grace told her, face serious.

Nora merely smiled. "I think she might have another tooth coming in, so you'll want to ask Catherine about teething powders."

Teething powders. Nappies. Food for babies. What did he know about any of those things?

Kit sighed as he carried Grace down the path to the clearing. He'd just have to keep learning. So long as he stayed one step ahead of the growing baby, they'd be fine. He came through the cabin door determined to follow the path that had been given him.

But the sight of Ciara and Harry, seated at opposite ends of the table, stopped him in his tracks. By the red on the back of the logger's neck, their conversation wasn't to his liking.

"So, you see why I cannot court at this time," Ciara finished.

Oh. That. Every instinct told him to tiptoe out, pretend he hadn't heard. But he couldn't seem to move from the doorway.

"I see why you're bent against it," Harry allowed. "But a husband doesn't have to be a hindrance. I could help."

She cocked her head, chocolate-colored braid bumping one ear. "You'd really want your wife cooking other men's meals?"

Harry shifted on the chair. "Well, no, not when you put it that way. I want a wife to be waiting for me when I come home. But I'm a good provider. My wife wouldn't have to work."

She straightened and rose, settling her gingham skirts around her with a finality even Harry had to notice.

"Working isn't a *have to* for me, Harry," she told him. "I love cooking. I love serving food and watching folks smile over it. It's my way of putting a little more joy in the world. I'm not willing to give that up so I can wait for a husband to come home. Ask Beth to help you find the woman you want. It's not me."

She glanced up then and met Kit's gaze. Her own face flaming, she turned and continued to the kitchen.

Harry sank his head onto his hands on the table. "Why is it every gal that comes to Wallin Landing is either spoken for or uninterested in marriage?"

Kit lay a hand on his shoulder in commiseration. "Sorry, Harry. Better luck next time."

Harry snorted and straightened, then shoved back his chair. "I give up."

Jesse came through the kitchen and dumped another armload of wood on the pile. He frowned as if even he were surprised by the amount stacked against the wall.

"You can forget the wood," Harry told him. "She doesn't want to marry."

Jesse's frown grew as he glanced their way. "Why?"

"She prefers her work."

His face cleared. "Oh. Well." He dusted off his hands and lumbered toward the stairs.

Harry followed, shoulders once more slumped.

Kit could understand their reactions. He'd seen it so often over the years. There seemed to come a time in a man's life when he knew himself ready for a wife and everything that entailed—a home, family. Harry and Jesse were ready. They just couldn't find a wife.

And Kit was going about it in the opposite direction. Grace was his family. He was beginning to believe he could provide her a home. At some point, he should probably work on providing her with a mother as well.

Somehow, he thought his chances were even slimmer than Harry's.

CHAPTER NINE

T HE SUN WAS still slanting through the trees from the west when Ciara finished the dinner dishes. Neither Harry nor Jesse had offered to help tonight. While she missed the break, she could not be sorry for the reason. The sooner the two loggers realized she was not here to court, the better for all concerned. She hardly needed two frontier sweethearts.

Kit was sitting on the rug before the hearth as Grace explored the area. Ciara could see them through the kitchen archway. The baby would scoot toward the table, then the door, then the hearth, but always she came back to the stairs. And every time she pulled herself up and reached for the second tread, Kit was on his feet to redirect her.

"No, Grace," he said gently. "You can't go up there. Not yet."

"No, no, no, no, no," Grace complained as he carried her back to the rug.

Ciara wiped her hands dry on her apron, removed it to hang by the door, then came into the main room. "Perhaps we should wait for you to teach me to shoot until she's back at Nora's."

He scrunched up his face, making him look a little like his niece. "That seems unfair to you, not to mention

Harry and Jesse. I know they want to hear the moment dinner is served."

Ciara laughed. "I suppose they do. But I doubt either of them would be willing to watch Grace."

He glanced at the ceiling, as if considering his chances. Then he called. "Jesse?"

"Yup?" The giant poked his head out of the stairwell.

"Would you watch Grace for a few moments so I can teach Ciara how to shoot? That way, she can call us to supper."

"Sure." He came down the stairs at a clip Grace must envy, then held out his arms for the little girl.

Something of her doubts must have shown on Ciara's face, for he nodded to her as he tucked Grace closer. "Oldest of ten, remember?"

As if to prove as much, he went to the bench, took a seat, and positioned Grace on his knee. Then he moved it up and down, bootheel tapping.

"Ride a cock horse to Banbury Cross to see a fine lady upon a white horse," he rapped out.

Grace regarded him with a frown.

"Rings on her fingers and bells on her toes, she shall have music wherever she goes."

When he reached the end, he unbent his knee and Grace started to topple. Ciara rushed forward so fast she collided with Kit, who was doing the same. He caught her in his arms to steady her even as Jesse caught Grace and set her upright again.

Grace bounced her body, clearly begging for more.

"She likes it," Kit marveled.

Ciara barely heard him, so close was his body, so warm his embrace.

"Then," she managed with a gulp, "it's safe for us to go."

He must have realized his position, for he dropped his arms and stepped back, cheeks darkening above his beard. "Good idea. We'll be just outside if you need us, Jesse."

"Take your time," Jesse said. "They don't tire of this easily."

Grace chattered at him as if ordering him to get back to work.

Ciara led Kit out the rear door and pointed at the rifle hanging from its strap. He took it down, then set about inspecting it.

"This is a Spencer," he told her. He swiveled aside a black piece of metal on the butt of the polished wood stock and tugged out a long black rod with bullets standing like little soldiers inside it. "It carries seven rounds, here. You'll need to ask Drew where he keeps the ammunition to reload."

Ciara nodded. It was about all she could do. He offered her the gun, and she had to force herself to take it. The smooth stock warmed in her grip. The weight was less than her large frying pan, but it felt a great deal heavier when she thought about the potential consequences of using it.

Kit came around behind her. "Hold it with one hand under the barrel and the other on the stock, and tuck it high into your shoulder so the wood runs along your cheek."

His hands reached around her to position the rifle. Once more, she was all too aware of his body next to hers, lean, strong. The scent of mint drifted past. She hadn't put mint in the pie. She didn't even have any with her. Was that his cologne?

As if from a distance, she heard him say, "Good. Make sure you point it at something safe, like the ground. You wouldn't want to hit one of the cows or Frisco or Sutter as they run past."

She nearly dropped the weapon at the very thought. Instead, she lowered it carefully, until the barrel was pointing at the porch, and glanced back at him. "Isn't there some other way to call you in?"

He shrugged. "You'd have to ask Drew. This is a Wallin tradition, from what I understand."

Beth had said the same. "Maybe it's time we broke it," Ciara said.

"Likely it will have to be broken as more people move into the area," he admitted. "But until you find another solution, this is your best way to reach us, especially if there's an emergency." Something crossed his gaze, and she wondered if he was thinking about Mrs. Virden's visit. What would she have done if Rina hadn't come to call the men in?

With precise care, she turned and lifted the gun into place again. "So I hold it like this. Then what?"

He reached around her once more. "This curvy piece at the top is the hammer. You cock it back, like this."

The metal piece clicked as it rocked back. She felt as if it had rapped her spine.

"Then you drop the lever and bring it back up." He pointed to the larger curve of metal on the bottom. She swung it out until it too clicked, then shoved it back into place.

"Now, sight down the barrel, put your finger in the trigger, and pull. Try not to hit any rocks."

"What if there's a rock under the ground?" she asked, barrel wavering.

He reached under it to steady it. "So long as it's not sticking out, you should be fine. Ready?"

Not in the slightest. "Maybe."

"Ready?" he challenged.

She aimed the rifle with the barest patch of dirt she could find. "Ready."

"Shoot."

She pulled the trigger. The gun rammed back into her shoulder, and she fell into Kit. His arms held her gently.

"Good work," he said, voice a tickle in her ear. "Now

shoot again, before every Wallin in the area comes a-running to help."

Right. Two shots for food. She cocked the hammer, dropped the lever, and fired again. This time, she managed to keep her footing.

Which was oddly disappointing.

James poked his head out of the barn. "Dare I hope for cake?" he called.

Ciara laughed as she lowered the gun. "You're welcome to a slice any time." Then she turned to Kit. "And so are you. You cannot know how much you've helped. What can I do in return?"

With her standing there, smile turned up, cheeks flushed from her success, a number of thoughts flitted through his mind. His gaze dipped to those rosy lips, which looked as sweet as one of her cakes.

But a kiss was still out of the question. She'd made it clear she wasn't ready to court. And he was in no position yet to seek a wife.

"You're helping me with Grace," he said. "That's payment enough." He took the gun from her and hung it back on its peg. "Are you ready to head for your cabin?"

She nodded. "I'm done for the day."

"Then let me walk you home, and I'll point out a few things along the way. I promised to help you appreciate the wilderness, after all."

"You can try."

So much doubt! But he understood. The Plains had felt strange after starting his life on a farm. Their fields had been neatly hemmed with fences, the crops planted, tended, and harvested on a set pattern. The Plains had seemed to stretch into eternity, with few landmarks and no regulation. Truth be told, he'd preferred them. They'd felt like freedom.

He poked his head into the cabin to let Jesse know what was happening. His friend waved a hand before setting Grace to bouncing again.

"I hope all that bouncing doesn't mean she loses her supper," he told Ciara as they climbed down off the porch. "We worked too hard to get it into her."

Her skirts brushed his trousers as they started for the path through the forest. He could imagine tucking her hand into his arm, if they had been courting, or perhaps walking hand in hand. As it was, she moved to walk on one side of the wide path, and he ended up walking on the other. That didn't stop him from admiring the dark sweep of her lashes against her skin. And were those freckles across the top of her nose? The little dots looked like cinnamon from one of her rolls.

"Is there nothing worth knowing close to the cabins, then?" she asked.

Ah, yes, he was supposed to be teaching. "Fewer here, as there are many who might harvest them. But see that low shrub among the firs?"

She paused to peer into the shadows of the forest. "The one with the chains of pale pink flowers?"

"Exactly. That's salal. Those pink flowers will turn into deep blue berries. You can eat them right off the vine or make them into pies or jellies." He smacked his lips, remembering the tart taste. "But don't try the leaves. They're like leather. If you're looking for something closer to lettuce, ask Sutter and Frisco to bring you watercress from the lake."

"I'll do that," she said, straightening. "Thank you."

"There's more," he promised. "Look there. You'll want to gather those in the morning."

He stopped beside a fallen hemlock, the moss dripping thick and green along its sides, and she frowned down at the white puffballs clustered together as if for warmth. "Should you eat mildew?"

He laughed. "They're mushrooms and very tasty fried up. But this variety spoils fast, so I wouldn't pick them until you're ready to use them."

She slanted him a glance as he started forward once more. "How do you know all this? I thought you were raised in the city of Tacoma."

"I came West with my family on the Oregon Trail," he told her, pushing up a branch that was hanging over the path. Fir needles showered down, perfuming the air with their dry scent. "The wagon train boss taught all the children to be on the lookout for food, not that there was much left after the other wagons had come through. And after I got back from Japan, I picked hops in the Puyallup Valley one harvest. Tribes come from all over to work the fields. I was fortunate that a few members were willing to teach me there too."

A frown was gathering, scrunching the freckles together. "Your sister married a man who had money, and you picked hops?"

The question held more surprise than censor. "Hannah, my sister, and Rudolph, her husband, hoped I would make something of myself in the company he ran, but I wasn't the sort of man to be a clerk. I wanted to look at something more than four walls and a pile of paper. So, I signed on aboard a ship heading for Japan and never looked back. Now I'm a jack of all trades, master of none."

"Sailor, hop picker, logger." She shook her head. "Any other talents I should know about?"

"Ditch digger, trapper, track layer for the Seattle and Walla Walla Railroad, oh, and a brief stint as a dentist's apprentice." He flexed his hands. "It takes a lot of strength to yank out a tooth when the owner's determined to keep it."

She shuddered. "No wonder you decided to try logging."

They had reached her cabin. "Drew saw me laying track

and decided he liked my dedication to the work. He gave me something I hadn't had in a long time. Respect."

"I can understand that." She put a foot on the step, then glanced his way. "My sister is one of the most famous people in Seattle. There isn't a man, woman, or child who hasn't had one of her treats. It's easy for them to think I'm just her apprentice, that I'll never measure up."

"Your sister is known for what she bakes," he acknowledged. "I don't recall having one of her roasts."

"They're good," she said. Then she grinned. "But mine are better."

"Maybe you could teach me to cook," he said. "I'm going to need to know more than I do now to take care of Grace."

She lowered her foot and turned to face him fully. "You know what I think, Kit Weatherly? I think you *are* a master at something. Learning. Some people finish school or learn a trade and never bother to try anything else. There's something to be said for a man willing to keep trying. I'd be proud to give you lessons in cooking."

She leaned forward, pecked him on the cheek, then ran up into the cabin and shut the door.

Kit lay a hand on his cheek, the skin tingling against his fingers. His sister had known him his entire life, Rudy for the better part of seven years before he'd lit out. They'd harped and harped at him for his unconventional ways.

Why was it Ciara O'Rourke could know him three days and see something even he had missed?

CHAPTER TEN

CIARA BRACED HER back against the cabin door, face so hot she might have fried a griddle cake on it. What was she doing, kissing him like that? It had only been in thanks for his help. Truly. But she'd already fended off Harry's attentions, and through him, Jesse's. Would Kit think she was setting her cap at him instead?

She stayed mostly in the kitchen Friday morning after serving a breakfast of biscuits and gravy. She thought she heard a grumble that her biscuits weren't as light as Levi's. Whose were? But at least she'd nudged them off the subject of courting.

She stopped by the parsonage as soon as the breakfast dishes were washed and the bread baked for the day. It was a little ways from the big cabin, up on a promontory overlooking the lake. Callie was out on the porch on a bench, dressed in her usual trousers. Her sewing basket sat beside her as she worked at darning a sock.

She smiled as Ciara approached. "Good morning! Come to beg watercress?"

Ciara paused in the act of lifting her green gingham skirts to climb the wooden stairs. "No. Why would you think that?"

"Frisco said he saw Kit Weatherly this morning, and he mentioned you might be looking for local food to cook. Don't be surprised if my brothers flood you with offers.

They can't get enough of your cinnamon rolls."

Ciara laughed as she sat beside her friend. The youngest of the Wallin brides, Callie was only a few years older than Ciara, and she too had traveled to reach Seattle, having followed her prospector father through gold camps from California in the south to the British Territories in the north.

"Well, they are welcome to stop by any time," she said.

Callie lay her needle in her lap to bring her finger to her lips. "Shh! Don't let them hear you say that. They'll be at the cabin every day." She dropped her hand. "So what *did* bring you to the parsonage? I don't imagine you have much time to visit."

"I don't," Ciara confessed. "I'm here to steal Levi's biscuit recipe."

Callie huffed, reaching for the sock she'd been darning. "You and everyone who's ever tasted them. I don't know how he does it."

Ciara sat beside her on the bench built from two carved stumps and a slab of timber. "Nothing different in the dough?"

"Not that I can see," Callie said. "But I was more used to cooking over a fire than in an oven when I came here. You could have skipped my biscuits across Lake Union like stones."

"I'm baking over one of the best stoves in Washington Territory," Ciara said. "And I understand I still can't match him."

"Let me guess," Callie said. "Harry said that."

"I can't be sure because I was in the kitchen," Ciara admitted, "But I think so."

"Probably sour grapes," Callie said, giving the sock a good jab with her darning needle. "I heard you decided against him courting you."

Ciara stared at her. "That's going around already?"

Callie shrugged. "It's Wallin Landing. Everything that

goes around comes around. So, is it Kit or Jesse?"

Once more, Kit's face came to mind, eyes wide and awed as she'd drawn back from kissing his cheek last night.

"Neither," Ciara said firmly. "I have a restaurant to establish."

"A lady can do both," Callie offered. "Cook and court."

"Not this lady," Ciara insisted. "Aside from my brother-in-law, Michael, I don't know many men who would allow a woman to work unless it was for them."

"The men of Wallin Landing might surprise you," Callie told her. "Catherine runs the dispensary. I don't hear Drew complaining. Rina teaches. James couldn't be prouder. Nora takes care of the little ones with Simon's gratitude. I teach music. Levi knows what it means to me. About the only one who doesn't have an extra job is Dottie, and she helps John with the library. Besides, she has Peter and soon a baby to tend to herself."

"You just accounted for the Wallin men," Ciara pointed out. "That doesn't mean the other fellows in the area think the same way."

"And it doesn't mean they don't."

She decided not to argue. Instead, she rose. "Tell Levi I want him to show me how he makes biscuits, first chance he gets. I'll send home cake or cinnamon rolls in exchange."

Callie laughed. "One word about that, and Frisco and Sutter will have him there in minutes, even if they have to truss him up like a Christmas goose."

"Whatever it takes," Ciara said with a grin. "And I look forward to what your brothers can find that I can use in the kitchen—watercress, fresh trout, berries."

"You may get more than you bargained for," Callie warned.

"If they bring more than I can use, I can share it with others," Ciara reasoned. With a wave, she headed down the road to where John and Dottie Wallin had their farm.

The trees closed in around her, walls on either side, nearly touching above. Something set the ferns to rustling, and she tried not to tense. Kit said the forest held more wonders than danger. She ought to look for it.

Weren't those mushrooms growing along the fallen log, like white cottages on the green of the moss? And there, blackcaps, a patch of bushes thick with the little deep-purple berries! She could just envision the preserves, pies, and sauces she could make with them. She should bring her basket back this afternoon. She hastened her steps.

John and Dottie had a house of planed wood with a big attic overhead. It sat on a sweep of lawn that ran down nearly to the road. Goats were contentedly cropping the grass as Ciara came up the drive. Several raised their heads and bleated, as if in greeting.

The couple was also out on the porch, enjoying the cool morning air, while Peter ran back and forth, galloping a stick horse his father must have made. John and Dottie both listened as Ciara explained her goal.

"I can bring you any extra meat I hunt," John said. The fourth Wallin brother, he was the only one to have inherited both their mother's reddish-brown hair and green eyes. "And I'll talk to Simon about any extra produce from the farm. His is a lot bigger than ours."

Dottie slid her hand into his. "Because he can devote all his time to it. You have the library."

He smiled down at her. "Which is only well organized because of you."

Something tugged at her heart. For all she'd foresworn courting, she had to admit it would be nice to have someone who encouraged her, who appreciated her accomplishments. Someone who thought she was valued, important.

More important even than the famous Maddie O'Rourke Haggerty.

Drew let his crew off a little early that afternoon. "We all have the theatrical to attend," he said, his dark blue gaze spearing each of his crew in turn.

"I can't mind," Jesse said, ax up on his shoulder as they trudged for home. "Even if I don't have children in the play."

"And not likely to at this rate," Harry grumbled. "Just once, I'd like to meet a gal as interested in me as I am in her."

Jesse nodded.

Kit's fingers went to his cheek, and he hastily dropped his arm. It was probably best if neither of his friends knew that Ciara had kissed him. The fact still amazed him. He kept telling himself it had only been in thanks, but the memory brought a smile to his lips every time he thought of it. Harry likely wouldn't take kindly to Ciara giving Kit any kind of attention.

He came into the cabin to find the table set and Ciara in the rocking chair with Grace. The ax slipped from his fingers to thud against the floor.

"Is she all right?" he asked, rushing forward. "Did she fall? Get sick?"

"No, no, no, no, no," Grace sang out, waving happy fingers.

"She's fine," Ciara assured him. "Nora had her hands full helping the other children into their costumes, so she asked if I would mind taking her for a bit. Grace and I were having a lovely conversation." She peered down at the little girl, whose pale pink muslin gown barely covered her stockinged toes. "Grace, do you think lace is going to be in fashion for trim this year?"

"No, no, no, no, no," Grace said obligingly.

"Ah, what about pearls? Perhaps around the neck?"

Ciara traced her collarbone with the fingers of her free hand.

Grace considered her a moment with a frown. "No?" she asked.

"I'm doubtful as well." Ciara grinned up at Kit. "You try."

"Grace, is it time for dinner?" Kit asked.

The baby looked straight at Ciara expectantly.

She laughed. "I'll take that as a yes."

Jesse came up to them and held out his arms. "Grace, want to play horsey?"

Grace reached for him eagerly.

The logger went to perch on a chair and start their favorite game. "Ride a cock horse to Banbury Cross…"

Kit followed Ciara into the kitchen to wash up for dinner. One sniff of the air, and his grin widened.

"Is that trout frying?"

"Courtesy of Frisco and Sutter," she told him, laying another fillet on the frying pan with a sizzle of butter and herbs. "Mashed potatoes are ready, and there's a nice mushroom gravy to go with them." She winked at him. "You were right. Wallin Landing has its own wealth when it comes to food."

He could hardly wait. He splashed water on his hands, toweled them off, and hurried to take his place at the table. Jesse handed him Grace before going to do the same.

"Are you all home early because of the theatrical?" Ciara asked, bringing in the bowl of potatoes.

"Drew expects everyone to attend," Harry warned her.

"I wouldn't miss it," she told him before going back for the gravy and trout.

Kit glanced down at the baby in his lap. Grace's gaze had fastened on the potatoes. "What do you think, Grace? Should we go to the theatrical tonight?"

Grace wiggled her fingers at the potatoes.

"Ha!" Harry barked. "You better feed her before you ask her any more questions. Even I can interpret that."

Kit laughed.

It was a merry meal. The conversation flowed, and the food was so good. Harry and Jesse even offered to clear the table and wash the dishes so Ciara could change for the evening. Kit took a moment to change Grace as well. The baby still tried to wiggle off the bed, but he worked fast enough that she didn't have too much of an opportunity. She pouted as he carried her back down.

Harry must have dunked his head in the kitchen sink, for the waves in his dark hair were more pronounced, and drops of water speckled his shirt. Jesse had donned a fresh shirt. Kit ran his fingers through his hair and decided that would have to be sufficient.

Ciara popped back inside. "Good enough for the theatrical?"

Harry gaped. Jesse visibly swallowed. Kit hadn't paid all that much attention to what she'd been wearing previously. Most of the ladies in Seattle favored the practical gingham or cotton print gowns cinched in at the waist with an apron that covered them from neckline to hem. Tonight, her gown was fitted down the front with jet buttons, and black piping adorned the caped sleeves and cuffs. The green leafy pattern offset her dark coloring, as if she were the queen of the forest.

"Good enough for the territorial governor," Kit told her. He offered her an arm. "Grace and I would be glad to escort you."

"No, no, no, no, no," Grace said enthusiastically.

Ciara offered him a smile, then directed it at the other two loggers as well. "Why don't we all go together?"

Harry and Jesse crowded forward even more enthusiastically than Grace.

Disappointment nipped at him. Why? It was the

sensible thing to do. She was making sure none of them felt singled out. He understood.

He just couldn't convince himself he liked it.

Ciara sat in the church hall with Kit and Grace on one side and Harry and Jesse on the other. All three of the men kept casting each other glances, as if trying to see whom she favored more. Apparently, her talk with Harry hadn't taken root. But she wasn't about to change her dress or hide her dreams just to please them.

The hall was crowded. A long building with windows that looked out onto the forest, the table that usually ran down the middle had been moved against the opposite wall and chairs and benches set up on either side of a center aisle. At the head of the room, a makeshift stage stood ready for its young thespians. Voices murmured all round, and the warmth of so many bodies was rising. So were the scents—lavender and rose, likely from the ladies, vied with leather and cedar shavings.

This was the first time she'd seen all of Wallin Landing turn out in recent years. Besides the brothers and their families, she counted at least a dozen husbands and wives as well as another dozen bachelors. Not everyone would come for such an event, so she could assume more in the outlying areas. Plenty of people to patronize a restaurant.

She could also see why Rina was looking forward to a second teacher. The Wallin Landing School had grown from three students to more than thirty, ranging from six to sixteen, and the number of babies, like Grace, in the audience attested to the fact that more students were on the way.

Rina and Catherine stood in the wings at either side of the stage. A tall boy in an old-fashioned blue coat with big brass buttons, strode to the front.

"Welcome," he called. His voice cracked, and he

coughed into his fist before squaring his shoulders, cheeks pinking.

"Welcome to the Wallin Landing School summer theatrical," he said, earnest voice carrying to all corners of the hall. "In this, our country's centennial year, we bring you the story of its founding. Picture the moment, Boston harbor, December 1773." He bowed and backed toward the rear, avoiding several crates that had been stacked in the middle of the stage.

Frisco climbed up past Rina, and several other children followed like beads on a string. They lined up on either side of the crates.

"King George wants us to pay taxes, but he won't give us a voice in government," Frisco said. He looked pointedly at the boy next to him.

"We'll show him," he piped up.

They seized the crates and tipped them off the stage with a crash that made Grace jump.

"That's for your tea!" one of the girls in the group cried.

"Down with tyranny!" another shouted.

One of the boys moved to the edge of the stage, hands wringing in front of his coat. "It's not really tea, Ma. I wouldn't waste it like that."

"Clever lad!" an older man called from the crowd. Ciara couldn't help thinking it must be the boy's father.

More scenes followed—the first Continental Congress argued over language for the Resolves; Patrick Henry, played by Sutter, passionately declared, "Give me liberty, or give me death!" Paul Revere rode on Peter's stick horse to alert the minutemen the redcoats were coming.

She was almost afraid of the ensuing battle between the students and James and Drew, who were dressed in red coats, so fierce were the children's faces. But they managed to drive the British off the stage with no real bloodshed and quite a bit of impromptu celebration from both the cast and the audience. Finally, the Continental Congress met again to sign the Declaration of Independence.

Once more their host stepped to the front of the stage. "And so we, in the words of President Abraham Lincoln, brought forth a new nation, conceived in liberty. Will you stand and join us in singing America?"

Ciara stood. So did Kit. His voice blended with hers.

"My country, 'tis of thee,
Sweet land of liberty,
Of thee I sing;
Land where my fathers died,
Land of the pilgrims' pride,
From ev'ry mountainside
Let freedom ring!"

Freedom. Wars had been fought for it. Every breast yearned for it. She would finally feel she had achieved it when she opened her restaurant.

But she could start contributing now.

"Next time you plan to hold one of these," she told Rina after the children had taken their bows to great applause, "let me know a month in advance. I'll sponsor a pie feed afterward."

"Excellent idea," Rina agreed. "Thank you."

"Thank *you*," Ciara countered. "The more folks who know about the restaurant, the better."

"We may have other ways for you to partner with the school," Rina said, eyes narrowing. "Let me think on it."

Harry and Jesse insisted on walking her home. She thought Kit looked resigned as he carried off a drowsy Grace. She should probably demur, but dark had fallen, and in truth she didn't mind a strapping fellow on either side, between her and the forest.

"I can come fetch you in the morning," Harry offered as they all stopped at her cabin.

"I get up pretty early," Ciara told him. "But thank you anyway, Harry."

"What about church on Sunday?" Jesse put in. "I can walk with you."

"That's very kind of you, Jesse," Ciara said. "But I'll need to freshen up after cooking breakfast. I wouldn't want to make you late. Good night, gentlemen."

She ran into the house and shut the door soundly. And she could only hope she could continue to deter them come morning.

CHAPTER ELEVEN

SATURDAY, THE MEN only worked a half day. Ciara had a feeling that might mean she'd find them underfoot. She did not want to give Harry or Jesse the option of claiming a moment of her time. So, when she had finished cleaning up from breakfast, she gathered her basket and left to go pick berries.

After days of sunny skies, clouds hung heavy over the treetops, and the road out toward Dottie and John's was a tunnel of cool shadows. Catherine, sweeping the steps of the dispensary, stopped long enough to wave and call a greeting. Ciara waved back.

But the farther she went from the main clearing, the darker the lane became. She had put her shawl around her shoulders. Now she hitched it up and clutched her basket closer. The ferns on her right swayed with a dry rattle, as if something was scurrying through them. At least it seemed to be scurrying away from her.

"They're probably more scared of you than you are of them," she told herself aloud. And she did her best to believe it.

She had the basket a quarter full when Dottie and Callie approached from opposite ends of the road. Dottie was wearing a faded gown, and Callie had on her trousers and a flannel shirt that might once have been Levi's by the way it hung on her, as if they both wanted to keep the blackcap juice from staining any good clothes.

"It seems we all had the same idea," Dottie said, lifting a large metal bowl.

Callie had a wooden one. "Frisco spotted these the day before yesterday. It was all I could do to keep him from eating them before I had a chance to pick."

"There's more than enough to share," Ciara assured them.

With grins, they waded in beside her.

"If you need more, there's another patch farther along the road," Dottie confided as her sure fingers plucked off the pebbly little berries. "They should be coming on in the next week or so. Plenty for preserves."

"The huckleberries closer to the lake will start to ripen soon," Callie said, brushing a branch from her cheek and leaving a telltale purple streak behind from her fingers. "There's a good patch right behind the big cabin. I'll let you know when to start picking."

"If Frisco and Sutter don't get them first," Dottie said with a smile.

"They won't go after the huckleberries," Callie predicted. "Too tart. They like them best with plenty of sugar in a pie or baked into griddle cakes."

Ciara stared at her. "That's brilliant! I'll add them to the menu."

She had hoped she'd stayed out long enough that the loggers would have given up waiting and found other ways to occupy their time, but Harry and Jesse were lounging in the main room of the cabin when she came back. They popped to their feet at the sight of her.

"Can't chat," she said, making for the kitchen. "I have a pie to bake."

Harry took a step as if to offer help, and Jesse put a hand on his arm. "We don't want to get in the way of that."

Apparently not, for they made no more forays in her direction.

She was putting the pie in the oven when Kit wandered in. From the other room, she heard Jesse chanting, "Ride a cock horse…"

Kit inhaled audibly. "That smells good."

Ciara shut the door and straightened. "It's just the scent of the oven heating, but you should be able to smell the pie shortly."

A lock of hair drifted past her eyes. Before she could blow it back, he reached out and brushed it behind her ear.

They both froze.

Grace shrieked. A cup slipped on the sideboard shelf with a chime of tin on porcelain. The wood settled in the firebox. Ciara shuddered.

"Kit!" Harry bellowed.

He grimaced. "I was looking for another washcloth."

Ciara took a step back, out of reach. "In the basket under the sink."

Face turning red, he headed in that direction. As soon as he was out the door, she tidied her hair. Why were her fingers shaking? Between the picking and the baking, she probably looked a fright. But his touch had been so sweet, so warm. And the look in his dark eyes….

She wasn't seeking a husband, much less a husband with baby in tow. She threw herself into making dinner.

Harry and Jesse made appropriate noises of appreciation when she brought the chicken noodle soup and rolls to the table a short time later.

"The soup might be a little hard to get into Grace," she told Kit. "I mashed some of Callie's canned beans, and the rolls should be soft enough for little bites."

He smiled his thanks as she sat beside him.

"Dear Lord," Harry said, clasping his hands together,

"we thank Thee for the beauty of Your world, especially when it sits down to dinner with us. Amen."

Jesse frowned at him.

Ciara ignored him and focused on the food. The soup needed a little more spice. Perhaps rosemary next time. But the rolls were light and fluffy, just the way Maddie had taught her to make them.

Would she be proud of Ciara? Would she ever understand why this restaurant was so important? Ciara had only a little left in her savings. She had to make this work.

"I'd be happy to help you in the kitchen, Ciara," Harry offered after devouring two slices of her blackcap pie.

"Me too," Jesse put in, leaning back from his empty plate.

Kit opened his mouth as well, and she held up her hand.

"No need, gentlemen. I appreciate your kindness, but I need to prepare a few things for tomorrow, so I'd prefer the kitchen to myself."

Jesse sagged.

"But you could bring your things to the sink," she allowed.

Chairs scraped as Jesse and Harry leapt to their feet. They jostled each other as they went through the archway to the kitchen.

"I can take that," Kit protested as Ciara reached for Grace's bowl as well.

She frowned down at the green paste. "She didn't like it."

"Not much," he admitted, gaze going to the baby in his lap. Grace smiled happily up at him.

"We'll try something else," Ciara promised. "Did she at least eat some of the rolls?"

"The better part of one," he said. "Sure you don't want help in the kitchen?"

She glanced to where Harry and Jesse were glaring at each other as they stood by the sink. "No, thank you. I have a little too much help at present."

Kit positioned Grace on the carpet and lay out some of the brightly colored blocks John and his family had given her. Harry settled back into his seat at the table and opened a book to read. Jesse pulled a chair closer and began whittling, wood chips falling softly to the plank floor. He made whistles and wooden animals for the Wallin children. By the way the two of them kept glancing up, they had positioned themselves to keep an eye on Ciara, working at the sink. He could hear the splash as she pumped water, the tinkle of porcelain against porcelain.

With a thud, Grace sent the blocks sprawling. He tensed for a shriek, but she grinned at him as if she had accomplished something grand.

"You like knocking them down better than stacking them," he realized.

"They know the power they have over us from a young age," Harry muttered.

Shaking his head, Kit began building a tower.

A short time later, Ciara stepped out of the kitchen. Jesse's head came up. Harry kept his head down over the book, but Kit saw his gaze dart to the pretty cook.

She dropped onto Mrs. Wallin's rocker. "Done."

"You need someone to walk you home?" Jesse asked.

"Jesse and I would be happy to oblige," Harry added.

Jesse cast him a dark look. "I asked first."

"Thank you, gentlemen. I'll consider the matter." She turned to Kit. "You're doing well with her."

"No, no, no, no, no," Grace warbled, fingers grasping the air as if to encourage him to keep building.

"I'm trying," he told them both. He swiveled so he

could keep his niece and Ciara in sight. "I've been meaning to ask you. How often do you change their clothes?"

She blinked. "More than once a day, very likely. They usually spit or dribble or do something to get them dirty. A bib might help. There should be some among the things Callie brought. Are you still short of clothing?"

"I have several changes," he acknowledged. "But they all look so dainty. Will they stand up to lye?"

"Talk to Callie," she said. "She'll know how to wash them. She's had to do it for Mica and probably for her brothers, under much more difficult circumstances. If she says you don't have to do anything special, I can throw in some of Grace's clothes when I wash my aprons on Monday, if you'd like."

"Thank you."

The words must have sounded as relieved as he felt, for she smiled. "What are friends for?"

"Friends." Harry said the word as if it tasted bad. "Would you happen to have any *friends* who might be looking for a groom?"

"Harry," Jesse growled, glancing up from his whittling.

"It's all right," she said. "I know how hard it is to find a lady around Seattle. What is it, eight and a half bachelors for every unmarried woman in the Territory?"

"More like twenty to one around Wallin Landing," Harry said. "I know. I've looked."

She cocked her head. "Have you? Because I met an unmarried lady just the other day."

Jesse dropped his knife with a clatter. "Who?"

"Her name is Katie Jo McAllister," she supplied. "She seemed very nice."

Harry shook his head, frown gathering. "Never heard of her."

"Me either," Jesse confessed.

She looked to Kit, who shrugged. Truth be told, he

hadn't paid much attention to the females around Wallin Landing, until Ciara had arrived.

"Maybe she doesn't come into the Landing very often, then," she allowed. "I'll look for her at church tomorrow and introduce you."

Jesse's grin hitched up.

Harry and Jesse walked her home. She wished she could have found the courage to go alone, but the woods still seemed dark and shadowy, capable of hiding untold danger. Harry was also out in front of her cabin when she opened the door at the hour of five, and he insisted on walking her to church after a quick breakfast. At least she convinced Jesse and Kit, with Grace, to accompany them, which did not seem to please Harry.

As soon as she entered the Wallin Landing chapel, she cast about for Katie Jo. The church wasn't large—two sets of bench pews flanking a center aisle with stained-glass windows on one side and a simple wooden cross at the altar. The pews were nearly filled that Sunday with families and bachelors from around the area, but she didn't catch sight of Katie Jo until Levi had finished preaching and the congregation had risen to leave. Even then, she had to shoulder her way to the door to catch the lady, who clearly hoped to escape unnoticed.

"Wait!" she called, picking up her skirts to dash after the woman before she could disappear into the forest again.

Katie Jo glanced back, eyes wide, as if she thought Hart McCormick and a posse were on her tail. Then she stopped and let Ciara catch up to her.

"Miss O'Rourke," she said with a nod. She was still dressed in the flannel shirt and trousers, but she'd pulled off her slouch hat to reveal thick tresses bound around her head in braids that gleamed gold in the summer sun.

"Miss McAllister," Ciara greeted, trying to catch her breath. "I was hoping you'd be at services."

She cast a wistful glance at the steeple. "I come when I can."

"Well, I'm glad you came today," Ciara told her. "There are two gentlemen interested in making your acquaintance."

She took a step back and held up one hand as if prepared to fend them off. "Ain't no man in these parts that would want to meet me."

Her distress was so real, Ciara hurt for her. What had she done! She'd scolded Beth just the other day for trying to play matchmaker, and here she'd gone and tried it herself.

"It's all right," she said. "You don't have to meet them. But you're welcome to join us all for dinner in the hall. I'm sure the Wallin family won't mind."

"Mighty kind of you," she said, "but I should get back. Maybe another time." She shoved her hat onto her head and pelted into the trees.

Ciara almost went after her, but the sound of wagon wheels had her turning. Most of the others streaming out of the church had stopped as well, as Beth drew her wagon up in front. Ciara's smile of welcome faded as she sighted Mrs. Virden next to her on the bench, with Hart riding alongside, deputy's badge sparkling on his chest.

Kit had stopped to ask Catherine about why Grace might keep tugging at one ear when the wagon pulled up to the church. He had grown used to Beth's happy smile and bubbly nature when she'd served as Drew's cook. Now her deep blue eyes were narrowed at the woman beside her, as if she'd brought his sister's mother-in-law under duress. Mrs. Virden kept her head high as Hart swung down from the saddle.

"Weatherly," he called. "A word."

Kit hitched Grace closer. He started toward the wagon, and Drew, Catherine, Rina, and James converged on him. Ciara wasn't far behind. Together, they approached the wagon.

Hart tipped his head at the waiting matron, who was looking down at them all, lips curling.

"Seems there's an issue between you and Mrs. Virden," Hart said.

Kit's grip tightened on Grace. The baby was regarding them all with a growing frown, as if she couldn't tell whether this was a friendly meeting.

"There's no issue on my side," he told the deputy. "My sister left me custody of Grace. I'm trying my best to raise her."

"And doing a fine job," Catherine put in. "As a nurse, I can attest to his care."

"And as a teacher, so can I," Rina added.

"Ridiculous," Mrs. Virden snapped. "Deputy, do your duty."

Hart glanced back at her, gunmetal-gray eyes narrowed as well. "As the sheriff told you in Seattle, ma'am, our duty isn't so clear in this case." He returned his gaze to Kit. "Would you show me the papers that came with Grace?"

"Certainly," he said, stomach knotting. "It was a single note. It's at the old family cabin."

He barely noticed Simon, Nora, John, Dottie, Levi, and Callie joining them, along with Harry and Jesse, but they made quite a parade moving from the church to the house. The Wallin children ran ahead, and the wagon trailed behind, as if Beth was doing all she could to hold off Mrs. Virden.

"Tell me where to find the note," Ciara murmured to him. "I'll fetch it down."

"The sea chest against the wall," he murmured back. "It isn't locked."

She hurried inside.

Mrs. Virden must have requested help, for Hart was lifting her down. The moment her feet hit the ground, she shook out her black silk skirts and advanced on Kit.

"I made inquiries in Seattle," she announced, as if relishing her audience. "You haven't held any job for longer than eighteen months before coming here, and most were positions of a common laborer. You don't have a home. You don't have a wife. In short, you are no kind of father for Grace. You cannot hope to raise her alone. Return her to me this minute."

She held out her arms.

"No, no, no, no, no," Grace scolded her.

Everything in him rebelled, yet how could he argue? He'd been wondering what he had to offer Grace since the moment Ciara had handed the baby to him.

"You're wrong," Ciara said, voice ringing as she stepped out onto the porch with the note in one hand. "Christopher Weatherly is a fine man, respected by all who know him. He has the makings of an excellent father. And he isn't alone." She marched up and aligned herself next to him. "We have an understanding."

Kit stared at her, as stunned as if she'd clubbed him with her frying pan.

"What's this?" Mrs. Virden cried.

The Virden family had always measured him and found him wanting. Oh, to feel superior for one moment. To shake their expectations and topple their pretensions, even if he had to pay the price later.

Kit slipped one arm about Ciara's waist and glared at Rudolph's mother. "Yes, yes we do. This talented lady and I have an understanding."

CHAPTER TWELVE

CIARA ALMOST THOUGHT she'd announced a run for territorial governor, so great was the outcry. James threw his hat in the air. Callie stuck her fingers in her mouth and whistled her approval. Catherine and Rina exchanged delighted glances. Frisco and Sutter jumped up and down and set most of the children to doing the same, even though they probably had no idea of the reason. Harry groaned, and Jesse grinned.

"I don't believe it," Mrs. Virden said. "This is a ploy to keep my granddaughter from me."

Ciara met her gaze. "Are you calling me a liar?"

Bodies stilled. Silence fell. Every gaze was on the older lady, and she had to notice not one of them was kind.

"I don't know you, young lady," she said, nose in the air. "But if you threw in your lot with this man, I can only question your sanity if not your intelligence and honesty."

"Oh!" Beth cried, slapping down the reins and setting her horses to fretting. "Apologize right now, or you can find your own way back to Seattle!"

"No need," Ciara said, anger licking up her like flames to kindling. "I always preferred action to words when it comes to showing people my intentions." She shook off Kit's arm from her waist, reached over Grace to take his face in her hands, and kissed him.

Her anger had heated her blood, but this? This was like fireworks on the Fourth of July, lighting up the night. Like finding the ring among the raisins in Maddie's báirín breac and thinking herself the luckiest girl alive. Like sitting down with a cup of tea and a scone and knowing herself home.

She dropped her hold and stared at him.

He stared back, color climbing in his cheeks. Even Grace looked stunned.

"Well, that's enough for me," Levi said, stepping forward. He met Mrs. Virden's shocked gaze. "I'm the local minister, Levi Wallin. And it will be my pleasure to marry these two at their earliest convenience. You are welcome to attend the wedding."

"Over my dead body." She whirled and stalked back to the wagon. Hart wasn't the only one ready to help her up.

"Wonderful!" Beth cried, beaming. "Oh, Ciara, I am so happy for you! And Kit, I know you will appreciate what a treasure you are marrying! One down, two to go." She winked at Harry and Jesse.

"Not courting, huh," Harry muttered to Ciara.

"You can see why," Jesse said, nudging him hard enough he staggered. The giant logger turned to Kit. "Congratulations!"

Kit nodded, but he looked just as unsteady on his feet.

As Hart remounted his horse, Arno, and Beth clucked to the horses to begin turning the wagon, all the other members of the Wallin family encircled Ciara and Kit, echoing their good wishes. Faces broadened with smiles; hands patted her shoulder.

"I still have your measurements from when I made the dress for Ada's wedding," Nora said to Ciara. "What color would you like your own wedding dress?"

"Don't you even think about cooking for the reception," Catherine warned. "We'll see to that."

"Have you shared the good news with Maddie yet?" Rina asked.

Maddie. Ciara nearly groaned aloud. She looked left, right, trying to see through the crowd, but the wagon had already entered the tunnel of trees.

Beth would spread the word in town. What would her sister think? Ciara had left with head high, claiming she wanted to do everything on her own. She'd lived here less than a week, and already she was engaged. What had she been thinking!

As if he noticed her concern, Kit spoke up. "We haven't told anyone about our intentions until now. We need to work out a few details before we make any arrangements. Now, if you'll excuse us, Grace needs changing. Ciara?"

To the sound of more cheers and chuckles, she clung to his arm as he entered the house.

"I'm sorry!" she blurted out as the door closed behind them. She dropped her hold of him. "I shouldn't have said anything. I just couldn't stand there and listen to her slander you."

"Thank you," he said, setting Grace down on the rug. "That's the first time anyone has stood up for me in a long time." He faced her fully. "So, what exactly is this understanding we have?"

Ciara flushed. "I think we both agree that Grace isn't leaving with that woman."

He nodded. "Absolutely. But you don't want to marry me."

He sounded so certain that something in her had to argue. "Why not?"

He shrugged, slowly, as if the gesture pained him. "I thought Mrs. Virden said it very well. I have no skills beyond being a common laborer, I have no home to offer you, and I come with an encumbrance." He left her for a moment to pull Grace down off the stairs.

"No, no, no, no, no," the baby protested as he carried her back to the rug.

"Quite right, Grace," Ciara said. "Your uncle obviously doesn't see his own value. But you and I do."

Grace righted herself on the rug and nodded, setting up a chatter as she frowned at Kit.

"It seems I stand corrected," he said with a bow to the baby. "But I'm still not convinced that Miss Ciara wants to marry me." As he straightened, his gaze met hers in challenge.

She swallowed. "You're a fine man, Kit Weatherly. Any lady would be proud to marry you."

He waited.

She threw up her hands. "All right. No, I don't want to marry you. I don't want to marry anyone. But Mrs. Virden doesn't have to know that, does she?"

"Maybe not," he allowed. "But I doubt we've seen the last of her, regardless. She just spent the past few days digging into my life. I imagine she's going to spend the next few days digging into yours."

Ciara rolled her eyes. "She won't find anything worthy of complaint. Born in New York, traveled through the Straits of Magellan to live with my sister, learned a trade, and came out to Wallin Landing to ply it. I don't see anything shocking in any of that."

He closed the distance and took her hands in his. "Good. Because I don't know how I'd react if she started in on you too."

She dropped her gaze. A shame. The acceptance that had been written there had swept over him like warm water from a bath, relaxing every muscle, calming every thought. He'd wanted to float in it for a while longer.

Years had passed since his father and mother had died, and he'd finally come to see a ghost of that look from the employers he'd encountered along the way. Now he had friends; he had a family of sorts with the Wallins. He encountered goodwill on a daily basis.

But never such understanding. It was as if she'd looked deep down inside him and saw someone worthwhile.

The experience was unsettling, for all it was welcome. He'd made it a habit to keep others at a distance with an easy smile and a friendly manner that invited no confidences. The closer anyone grew, the more flaws they were likely to find and pick at. His wounds felt raw enough as it was. Mrs. Virden's assessment of his character had only flaked the scabs off anew.

He'd never understood why he hadn't been able to settle into the life his sister and brother-in-law had wanted for him. Any man might count himself fortunate indeed to have been given entrance to such a position, with an entire career plotted out for him. Yet when he'd looked ahead, to the pinnacle he was being groomed to reach, the top had seemed bleak indeed—long hours, pressure to do more and be more, and expectations of social prowess. That wasn't him.

He didn't want it to be him.

"You lack any sort of ambition," his sister had complained. "How can you simply settle for less?"

"Why do you always have to have more?" Kit had countered. "There has to be such a thing as contentment."

He'd thought he'd found it. But to keep Grace, he might have to lose it.

Now he gave Ciara's hands a squeeze before releasing her. "You don't have to marry me, Ciara. No one will be surprised when you change your mind."

She raised her chin. From that angle, he could see that it had a decided point. A determined chin, his father might have said.

"The important thing is that Grace is safe," she told him. "Let's just focus on that."

He would have been happy to, but the rest of the residents of Wallin Landing had other ideas.

Sunday afternoons, dinner for the Wallin family and their workers was generally held at the hall next to the church. Every family brought something to share, and there was always more than enough food for visitors. Kit, Harry, and Jesse usually contributed by helping wash the dishes and ferrying them to and from the big cabin.

Ciara, however, had two blackcap pies and a salad of lettuce, fresh peas, and zucchini slices. After carrying the place settings up to the hall, Kit and the others each took a dish, leaving her to carry Grace.

Jesse raised the salad closer to his nose and took a sniff so deep Kit was surprised the peas didn't pop up. "Smells good."

"Thank you," Ciara said. "I used some orange zest to dress it and added some mint Frisco and Sutter found. And I know you like my pies."

He licked his lips as if to prove it.

Harry leaned closer to Kit, slowing his steps. "How'd you do it?"

As Ciara and Jesse continued toward the hall, which was located near the church on the promontory overlooking the lake, Kit frowned at his friend. "Do what?"

"Get Ciara to agree to marry you."

Harry didn't look mad. More like hopeful, as if Kit had some skill he lacked. The entire idea was laughable, but he'd never make the mistake of laughing at Harry.

"It was more her idea than mine," he said. "And I'm not sure where that's going to leave us in the end. But if there's one thing I've learned, Harry, it's that you have to look for the unexpected. You never know what's around the next bend."

He straightened, nodding thoughtfully. They both quickened their steps to catch up to the others.

Kit always enjoyed Sunday dinners. Everyone sat

wherever they liked at the big table that ran down the middle of the hall. Before and after the food was served, some kept the children busy, while others took a much-needed break and found some adult conversation. He'd learned his first lessons in tracking from John at that table, had long philosophical discussions with Rina about the works of Henry David Thoreau and the poets of an earlier age, like Wordsworth and Everard. And he'd eaten his share of good food from the tables that stood by the windows looking out onto the forest.

He hadn't even set one of Ciara's pies on the loaded table today before Drew came up to him and tipped his head to one side. Kit laid out the salad, then followed him to a quiet corner of the hall, if there was such a thing between the laughter of the children and the discussions of the adults.

"You've been working hard," his boss said, linking his thumbs into the belt loops on his Sunday best trousers. "Keep it up, and there will be a bonus in your pay every month."

"Thank you," Kit said, unable to think of anything more suitable.

Drew nodded. "A man needs to be able to care for his family." He clapped Kit on the shoulder and ambled over to where Catherine was settling their three children, Hans, Mary, and Davy, ranging from nine to six, at the table near their cousins.

Kit started for the table to join them, and Simon Wallin stepped into his path.

The second brother, he had shorter hair, a light shade of brown, and eyes like spring grass. He was also the only one who matched Drew and Jesse in height, for all his frame was leaner.

"You might be aware that the cabin where Ciara lives used to be mine," he said in his logical voice. "I would be willing to sell it to you for a small price. Or you could simply live in it until you've staked your own claim."

"Thank you," Kit said, knowing the words utterly inadequate.

But Simon didn't seem to expect more than that, for he nodded and strolled off to join Nora and their children Lars and Hannah.

Kit finally made it to the table, but the spots on either side of Ciara and Grace had been taken, so he had to content himself with sitting across from them. But the same sort of pattern presented itself all afternoon. James offered the use of the oxen to help Kit clear land, if he wanted to lay claim to some. John advised him how to design a cabin for a growing family. Levi offered to help him build that cabin.

Between bites and words of gratitude, Kit kept glancing across the table at Ciara, who still had Grace in her arms. Every lady in the room had stopped by, and, by the blush on Ciara's cheeks, not simply to gush over the baby. What sorts of things were they offering her?

And how would they feel when they learned Ciara didn't intend to marry him after all?

CHAPTER THIRTEEN

EVERYONE WAS SO kind. Several times that afternoon, Ciara felt tears pricking her eyes. From Catherine to Callie, they all wanted her to have the most beautiful wedding and to equip her well to start her marriage. From the look of things, the Wallin men were making similar offers to Kit.

One of the brothers went even further.

"I understand you're interested in how I make biscuits," Levi said, stopping beside her. He had the deep blue eyes and light golden hair of his sister, but the latter curled in wild abandon about his lean face, as if he had never entirely tamed the rascal he had been, despite his calling as a minister.

"Very interested," Ciara said. "I hear they're the best around. How do you do it?"

He leaned closer, and she would have sworn every lady stilled to hear his answer.

"First," he said, eyes twinkling, "lay them in the baking pan with their sides touching. It keeps the edges from browning and helps them rise."

"Clever," Ciara said, feeling unaccountably breathless. "And second?"

"Get the oven hot," he supplied. "Hotter than what you normally use to bake bread." He straightened. "That's it."

"That's it?" Nora asked beside her. "Why, I could do that."

So could Ciara.

"It's not hard," Levi allowed. "Not nearly as hard as choosing the right spouse. I'm glad you and Kit found each other, Ciara."

She felt like an imposter.

She was only glad that Grace fell asleep a short time later, giving her an excuse to leave the hall. She had barely reached the path down to the big cabin before Kit fell into step beside her.

"Everything all right?" he asked. He held out his arms, and she transferred Grace into his keeping. The little girl tucked her head into his shoulder with a sigh, thumb going to her mouth. For a brief moment, Ciara envied her.

She forced her gaze down to the rocky path, picking up her skirts to keep them from getting any dustier.

"They're so happy for us," she told him. "I simply couldn't keep smiling another minute."

"I know," he said. "Drew offered me a raise, Simon a house."

She cast him a glance. His head too was down, those broad shoulders sagging, as if the gifts were another burden he must bear.

"I told Catherine and Rina that I wasn't willing to talk about the wedding until after I had the restaurant going," she said. "That ought to buy us some time."

"How did they take it?" he asked with a glance her way as they came out on the flat of the clearing. The only occupants were the cows in the pasture, and James's two horses, Lance and Percy, contentedly munching in the fenced field.

If only she could find that contentment.

"The Wallin ladies were clearly disappointed," she told him. The memory of the look in their eyes made her cringe. "We'll have to make it up to them somehow."

"How long do we have before we run out of excuses?" he asked as they approached the cabin.

"I could probably stretch out the time for weeks," she allowed, climbing up on the porch. "But my funds are getting lower all the time. I came here to start a restaurant. I don't want to wait. I had hoped to open for dinners on Fridays and Saturdays, just with those closest to Wallin Landing, by next Friday."

"Then keep to your plan," he said. "Don't let me and Grace get in the way."

Easier said than done.

It was hard enough not responding to Grace's needs or her little smiles. She still wasn't eating as much as Kit and Ciara would want, and Ciara spent part of each meal coaxing her with new recipes. Catherine and Nora offered suggestions as well.

"We just need a routine," Ciara told Kit when the canned peaches they'd tried failed to find favor. "A simple set of nutritious dishes we know she'll eat."

"I only wish she'd come with some kind of instructions," Kit lamented as Grace reached for a roll.

"At least she likes bread," Ciara allowed with a laugh.

Then there was Kit. Harry and Jesse might have resigned themselves to her engagement, but she caught Harry watching her from time to time, head cocked, as if he was trying to see why she'd chosen Kit instead of him. She made a show of favoring Kit, serving him first, walking home with him each night arm in arm. It was only to further the story that they were betrothed. But it felt awfully real.

Kit seemed to be doing all he could to prove the story true as well. He held the bench for her whenever she sat. He gave Grace to Jesse so he could help Ciara wash and put away the dinner dishes. And he brought her gifts, as only a logger could: wildflowers from along the bay, mushrooms from the deep woods, and lots of wood for the fire. He'd asked Jesse to teach him to whittle, and his first project was a wooden rose, which he presented to Ciara with a bow. One night, he even sang the Rose of Tralee to Grace, though his gaze kept wandering to Ciara. When Kit sang it, she forgot the sad association and just hugged his warm voice close, like one of Mrs. Wallin's quilts.

She didn't forget her promise to teach him to cook. He often was up in the morning when she came in and stayed with her in the kitchen as she talked through her actions. Those dark eyes missed nothing. Whenever he was home before she shot the gun announcing dinner, he'd apply what he was learning to help her with the final preparations for that meal too.

She'd shared a kitchen with Maddie most of her life, and often spaces much bigger than this one. Having Kit beside her felt different, as if a part of herself had peeled off and was there to support.

"Why do you look at me that way?" he asked one evening as he was chopping parsley to garnish the soup.

Ciara blushed as she bent to retrieve rolls from the oven. "What way would that be?"

"I don't know," he said. "Almost as if you think I'm going to sprout wings and fly out the window."

Ciara laughed. "I don't expect you to fly, Kit. But I am amazed by how quickly you learn. It took me years to master the way Maddie made gravy, but you managed it in two tries."

"I had a good teacher," he told her with a smile.

She thought it more likely the skill of the student, not the teacher. He was something special. A shame he didn't seem to see that.

Every moment that wasn't spent on him, Grace, or her duties as logging crew cook, Ciara spent preparing for the opening of her restaurant. She'd asked the Wallins to spread the word. James would speak to all those who stopped by the mercantile, Catherine with anyone who dropped by the dispensary, John and Dottie to those who frequented the library, and Levi and Callie to any parishioners they might see during the week.

She had already planned what she would serve the first few times she was open, but she tested each of the meals on Harry, Jesse, and Kit. Jesse's face said it all, even when he didn't do more than grunt and give her two thumbs up before gulping the food.

She also honed her supply process. She provided a list of what she needed to whoever was driving or riding into Seattle for mail and tried not to gulp as she shelled out the pennies. Frisco and Sutter continued to bring her trout, mint, and peppergrass. Some of the other children were emboldened to offer berries, mushrooms, and even quail eggs. Her little pile of coins was dwindling, and she could only hope that she would bring in enough to replenish them.

Otherwise, it would be the shortest restaurant opening ever.

On Tuesday, she decided to take a few moments and check the garden on the side of the big cabin. The clearing was quiet as she stepped out. Catherine and Rina had taken all the children up to the farm with Nora, and Callie and Levi were out calling. Any other wagon or horse that had passed through had headed toward the mercantile. The garden patch looked almost lonely.

Mrs. Wallin had tended it so lovingly, growing herbs, fruits, and vegetables for the house. She'd even planted a few flowers. Ciara found a rose climbing the side of the cabin and cleared the grass away from its roots before harvesting the rose hips left over from the last bloom. The limbs of the nearby apple tree nearly touched the ground, so thick were the apples growing on it. A few were ready early, which she plucked, but they'd have quite a crop in a month or so if she could keep the animals and Frisco and Sutter away.

Still, bindweed and thistle had crept in since Beth had left, choking the plants that had seeded. She yanked out as much as she could to discover a few ripe zucchini and a couple heads of cauliflower. She'd have to plant more next year.

Next year. Because her restaurant would succeed. The thought inflated her chest and raised her head.

That's when she noticed the tall ferns at the side of the garden chattering as they waved. She stared at the offending plants. No, she wasn't going to give in to fear. It was likely a chipmunk or rabbit, attempting to remain hidden from her. She bent to cut off the last head of cauliflower.

The lynx stepped into the clearing and stared at her with baleful eyes. From the fields beyond, James' beloved steeldusts trumpeted a warning.

She already knew the danger padding toward her.

Drew rested his ax on the well-trod ground and nodded up the hill where they were working. "There's a clearing at the top. Good place for a cabin."

Harry raised a brow but wisely said nothing.

It was the third time that week their boss had taken the trouble to point Kit toward likely claims.

"A little far from Wallin Landing," Kit said before lopping off another branch from the cedar they'd downed. A monarch of the forest, the base stood taller than Jesse's head by a good two feet.

"An easy walk on a clear day." Jesse's voice drifted up from the other side before an ax cracked against bark.

A shot rang out in the distance. Everyone paused. The forest lay silent, waiting as well.

Kit was running before Drew barked, "Move!"

He hurled himself through the forest, leaping fallen trees, ducking under low branches. Before, he'd been terrified something had happened to Grace.

Now all he could think about was Ciara.

Had Mrs. Virden returned to torment her?

Had the stove caught fire?

Had an outlaw ridden into Wallin Landing?

What Jesse had called a good walk went surprisingly slowly even at a fast run. Kit was panting as he careened into the clearing. There was no sign of Ciara or whoever had fired that shot, though the flash of movement through the trees closer to the mercantile said that James was heading that way as well.

Kit jumped up on the porch and shoved through the door. Ciara rushed at him, throwing herself into his arms. He held her close, a wave of thanksgiving swamping him.

Harry and Drew followed him, Jesse bringing up the rear.

"What happened?" Drew demanded, ax at the ready.

Ciara raised her head from Kit's shoulder, her whole body trembling against his. "Lynx. I yelled at it, and it ran, but I didn't like it that close to the house. It came out of the woods by the kitchen garden."

Drew tipped his head to Jesse. "Go tell Simon. Harry, tell James. I think I saw him as we were approaching. I'll fetch John. It may circle back. We don't want it going after the stock."

"Right," Harry said, heading out the door with Jesse behind him.

Drew looked to Kit. "Stay here. If John's amenable, I'll have you go with him, see if we can drive it out of the area."

Kit nodded, and his boss strode out.

Ciara dropped her head back onto his shoulder with a shudder. "It was only a few feet away."

He rubbed her back with one hand, the cotton of her

gown soft against his fingers. "They don't usually attack full-grown adults. But I'm glad you called us in. It's prowling too close for comfort."

Her chest expanded against his as she must have taken a deep breath, and all at once he was aware of how close she was, how warm she felt in his arms, how well she fit against him. As if she noticed too, she took a step back.

"Thank you, Kit," she said, though her gaze appeared to be on his dusty boots. "I'm fine now. I should finish getting dinner ready." She hurried for the kitchen.

He nearly went after her, to do what, he wasn't sure, but the door opened, and John came in, rifle up over his shoulder. "I was already heading this way when Drew found me. It sounds like we need to do some herding. Ready?"

"Give me a moment," Kit said before going for his rifle.

"I don't want to kill it if we don't have to," Drew's brother confessed as they headed away from the cabin a short while later. Kit glanced back to find Ciara watching through the kitchen window. He raised a hand, and she pressed her fingers to the glass as if to clutch him close.

"As far as it's concerned," John continued as they neared the garden, "we're the interlopers in the neighborhood. But we can't have it going after the stock or, God forbid, one of the children."

The thought was like a bucket of rainwater dumped on his head, leaving him chilled. "Understood. So, what do we do?"

John stopped to crouch at the far edge of the overgrown garden. "We track it, we find it, we scare it out of the area." His fingers traced a rounded print in the dirt. "This way."

Kit had talked with John often enough about how to track. The fourth Wallin brother was the acknowledged expert in the family. Following him now, Kit began to see the forest from a different vantage point. That four-toed print in the mud at the edge of the lake, the break in a small branch where something bigger had passed quickly enough to snap instead of bend it. A momentary scent, blown on the breeze, of something that wasn't plant. Even the quiet that settled over the woods as they approached a pile of rock tumbled down from a wooded cliff.

The lynx was crouched near the top, body stiff and tail lashing.

John brought up his rifle. "Shoot below it. Push it up and over the top. And shout. As loud as you can."

With a nod, Kit brought up his rifle as well.

"Git!" John shouted. "Go on! Git!" The bullets zinged as they ricocheted off the basalt.

The big cat snarled.

"Yah!" Kit shouted. "Go on! Git!"

His shot sent the cat pelting away. As John had predicted, it went up and over, and Kit heard a clatter of stones as it must have run off.

"Is that enough?" he asked, lowering his rifle.

John shouldered his. "Possibly. We'll have to watch and tell the neighbors to do the same. If it keeps coming back, we may have no choice but to kill it."

He sounded sincerely sad as he turned for home. Kit knew the feeling. There was something proud, powerful by the way the animal had stood its ground.

"So," John said, retracing their steps through fern and grove. "You're going to marry Ciara."

Kit nearly stumbled on the narrow path. "We have an understanding," he said, feeling a little craven about not elaborating.

John held up a branch for him to duck under. "I remember when I first met Dottie. Beth thought I wasn't making enough progress in finding a wife, so she sent for a mail-order bride for me."

Kit shook his head, certain he must have misheard. "She sent for a wife, without your agreement?"

"Agreement or even knowledge," John confirmed. He hopped over a creek winding its way toward the lake, and Kit splashed after him. "I was ready to send her home, until I saw she had Peter. She needed someone to come alongside her, help shoulder her burdens, and the more I grew to know her, the more I wanted to be that person. It seems to me that Ciara feels the same way about you and Grace."

Kit chuckled. "Well, she noticed I need help all right. I don't know how I would have gotten through the last week without her. But that's no reason to marry a man."

"It's not the help but the person who needs the help," John insisted, squeezing through a stand of close aspens.

As if John took his silence for doubt, he glanced back. "You and I have several things in common, Kit. We both love to learn, we both like trying new things. And we don't talk about ourselves much. I've been told that last one makes it harder for someone to know a person. I'm glad Ciara took the time to know you."

But she hadn't. That was the entire problem. And he couldn't shake the feeling that once she did, she'd be turning tail faster than that lynx.

CHAPTER FOURTEEN

CIARA PACED THE plank floor, the swish of her skirts sounding as loud as a blowing wind. Clouds were gathering outside; she could see them crowding up over the hill every time she passed the window. Her own nerves seemed piled as high.

"They aren't that big, lynx," Jesse said helpfully from where he sat whittling by the hearth. "Not like a cougar. It shouldn't be a problem."

Oh, how she wanted to believe that! At least she'd put on a stew tonight, testing a new set of spices and vegetables, including the mushrooms Drew's son Lars had brought her. That could simmer right along with her fears.

"Would you like help setting out the plates?" Harry offered from where he'd been reading at the table.

Ciara shook her head. Better to keep busy. She made herself gather the cups and plates from the sideboard and began doling them out, gaze darting toward the window.

Harry's hand covered hers a moment, and she looked at him, startled.

"I know it might seem like I eat a lot," he said with a smile. "But I only need one plate."

She glanced at the three in front of him to the two cups at Jesse's usual place and sighed. "Sorry, Harry. Maybe I need your help after all."

"Always happy to oblige a lady," he said. He lay aside his book and started setting the table to rights.

Her gaze locked onto Kit's as he walked in the door. His hair was more mussed than usual, and fir needles stuck to his flannel shirt and trousers. But she couldn't spot any injuries.

"Taken care of," he told her with a smile. "Is that dinner I smell?"

"It will be on the table by the time you get back with Grace," she promised him, body feeling surprisingly light.

"And so will your plate," Harry said with a wink to Ciara.

She had the stew served and biscuits in a bowl within a half hour. The biscuits wouldn't be as light as Levi's, for she'd had no mind to try his hints. Kit had returned from Nora's with Grace, and the two sat in their spot on the bench. She wasn't sure why she sat, fork in hand, watching as he ate. He had graceful hands for a man given to hard labor. The fingers separated the biscuit almost reverently, as if she'd made something fine.

"You know what they say about cooks," Harry threw out from his place at the foot of the table. "Them that don't eat their own food aren't worth trusting."

Ciara flushed and forked up a mouthful.

"We already know Ciara's worth trusting," Kit said with a look Harry's way.

"But she needs to eat," Jesse protested. He picked up the cloth-lined bowl of biscuits and shoved it toward her. "They're real good."

She smiled her thanks as she took the bowl. "But not as good as Levi's?"

His smile slipped.

Harry snorted. "Nobody's biscuits are as good as Levi's. If that man wasn't a minister, he ought to be the one opening a restaurant."

"Well, he told me the secret on Sunday," she said. "I just

haven't had the opportunity to use it. But you'll see. I'll manage it."

"If anyone can, you can," Kit said.

"No, no, no, no, no," Grace added with an enthusiastic nod.

With Kit home safe, Ciara hoped to turn her mind to other things than that lynx. She whipped up enough batter for two cakes the next day and carried one to Dottie and John in appreciation. Avoiding the shortcut behind Drew's house and through the woods, she took the long route by the road.

"Did you run all the way?" Dottie asked after Ciara had knocked at the door of the farmhouse and offered the cake.

Ciara fought to calm her jittery breaths. "Just in a hurry, I suppose."

Dottie smiled as she accepted the cake. "And you took the time to bake for us? That was so kind!"

"Well, I wanted you and John to know how much I appreciate what he did with that lynx," Ciara told her. "I kept expecting it to jump out of the trees."

"I was frightened when I first came to Wallin Landing too," Dottie told her. "Every noise, every flash of movement made me think something was out to get me. I'd been raised in cities and villages. What did I know about the wilderness? John helped me realize there's a great deal of beauty to be had here."

"Kit's doing the same for me," Ciara admitted. "I've spent most of my life in towns too. How did you accustom yourself to the differences?"

"I suppose I never did," Dottie said with a laugh. "But I'm not scared anymore. I know I can look to the people around me for help. I'm not alone."

The words kept repeating in Ciara's mind as she started back for the cabin. She wasn't alone either. Kit had proven he'd come at a run when she called. Harry and

Jesse weren't far behind, despite the fact they understood she wouldn't be marrying either of them. And she knew from experience she could rely on Drew, his brothers, and their wives for anything she needed.

The woods looked different this time as she strolled along the road. Sunlight picked out branches of dusky green fir. Birds flitted here and there. The air was cool and scented by the moisture of the lake. That patch of blackcaps Dottie had spotted were nearly ripe, promising untold riches. She'd be stupid to forget the dangers, but Kit and Dottie were right. She'd be equally unwise to forget the beauty.

Something larger moved among the trees, and she cocked her head. Deer? Elk? Not a moose! Once more, fear beckoned her closer. She squared her shoulders and walked on, but her gaze kept darting toward the trees.

Horse!

She nearly laughed aloud at the realization. A rider was making his way south, closer to the lake, on the back of a dappled gray. She couldn't make out his face. Was this someone new to the area? Maybe she'd see him at dinner when the restaurant opened.

In two days!

Now the haste in her steps had nothing to do with fear, or at least not fear of anything in the forest. She still had a lot to do to be ready.

The cabin furnishings had been designed to feed eight people, and Mrs. Wallin's china service was large enough for a dozen. Ciara had brought her own service, a rose-patterned porcelain that would serve another dozen. She could safely feed eighteen before having to wash, with a few settings left over for the next batch of customers, even though the tables she planned to use only sat twelve. Would she have half that number on the first night?

She was in the middle of fixing dinner when she heard the main door open.

"Hello, the house!" She recognized James' voice. "You have a visitor."

"We don't have to bother her." That was Katie Jo. "I can jaw at her some other time."

"Not at all!" Ciara wiped her hands on her apron and swept through the archway into the main room. "I'm so glad you came! Thank you, James, for escorting her."

"Always delighted to do a good deed for fair lady," James said with a bow. He waggled his eyebrows at Ciara. "And if I hadn't, she might have bolted."

"No such thing!" Katie Jo insisted. "I wanted to see Miss Ciara. I just didn't think we should interrupt her work."

"Your timing is perfect," Ciara assured her. "I just put an apple and pork pie in the oven, and I have at least a half hour before it has to come out and cool. Sit with me."

James winked at her before whisking himself out the door. Katie Jo went to perch on one of the chairs so carefully she might have thought it would break. She pulled off her slouch hat, and whisps of her honey-blond hair stood on end.

"You sure?" she asked.

"Absolutely," Ciara said, taking a seat in the rocker. "How are you faring?"

"Middling," she said, setting the hat on her knee as a man would have done. "My brother took sick, but he seems to be getting better."

"Rina mentioned you have a brother," Ciara said. "So do I. Older or younger?"

"Younger, by a fair bit."

"Mine's four years younger. We didn't always get along when we were children, but he's tolerable now."

Katie Jo smiled. "They grow into themselves, don't they."

"They do indeed. Would you like something to drink?"

Her smile faded. "Who told you I drink? I'm more of a temperance kind of gal."

"Lemonade," Ciara clarified. "I made a fresh batch this morning."

She dropped her gaze and fiddled with her hat. "Sorry. I'm used to folks assuming the worst."

"It's that way for the Irish too, sometimes," Ciara said. "Why don't I bring us each a glass? And I have a cake. I have to save most of it for the gentlemen this evening, but there's enough for us each to have a slice, if you like."

She nodded. "That would be real nice."

Ciara bustled into the kitchen. It took two trips, but she had the lemonade poured, cake sliced and plated, and everything back to the table in short order. Katie Jo took a seat in Harry's usual chair.

"I hear your claim is quite a walk from Wallin Landing," Ciara commented as she passed the lady a plate.

"'bout a half hour's walk through the woods in good weather."

"You're a lot braver than I am. Just walking up to Nora's gives me the shivers."

She handed a glass to Katie Jo, who hesitated to accept it.

"It's good," Ciara promised.

She ducked her head as she took the glass. "I believe you. I just don't want to hurt the fancy glass."

Plain glass fancy? She'd seen crystal in Seattle. "Well, it's a celebration when someone comes to see me, so I can use a fancy glass if I like," Ciara said. "I'll be the one having to wash it, after all."

Katie Jo's sky-blue eyes flickered up, then focused on the cake, and she forked up a mouthful so fast she might have thought Ciara intended to pull back the plate.

"I hear you're getting married," she said around the cake as Ciara slipped onto the bench.

She grimaced. "Maybe. We're still figuring that out."

Katie Jo eyed her. "Is it all that hard to figure?"

"Sometimes," Ciara said with a shrug. "He has a niece to raise. I'm trying to start a restaurant. The timing isn't good." Did Katie Jo hear those for excuses? Ciara did.

"Oh, well. If you need anything, just holler."

"That is so kind of you," Ciara said. "It's nice to have a lady here abouts who *isn't* married to talk to."

Katie Jo's smile finally returned. "I never had a gal friend before. Mostly it's just Zeke and me and Uncle Cole."

"My parents are gone too," Ciara confided. "My sister raised me. And now I'm here on my own, though I was thinking today that I'm not really alone. There are lots of people here to help. Like you."

Katie Jo raised her glass. "Here's to friends. I can't wait to see your restaurant and your wedding."

Ciara raised her glass too, even though she knew at least the wedding wasn't going to happen anytime soon.

Kit kept an eye out for the lynx the next couple of evenings. He knew the Wallins were doing the same, but no one reported seeing the soft-footed beast. On Thursday morning, when he was patrolling around the cabin, he surprised a rider, but the older man merely tipped his broad-brimmed black hat and rode off.

"Is there someone new in the area?" he asked Drew as they were heading out to the work site, to the south of the main clearing this time. "Fellow with a dappled gray horse?"

"If there was, James would have mentioned it," Drew said. "Though a couple new homesteads were built at the tip of the lake. We should probably go down and say hello at some point, invite them to see the school and library."

If his boss, the acknowledged leader of Wallin Landing, couldn't be concerned, Kit reasoned he shouldn't be either. Besides, he had his hands full with Grace.

He'd wanted to travel to Tacoma and check his brother-in-law's will, for surely it might have been filed by now, but there simply hadn't been time. Every day, his niece challenged him, from eating to dressing to trying to crawl. Ciara was a Godsend. Any question he had, she answered. She'd been the one to suggest pulling his sea chest into the doorway of the loft to keep Grace from the stairs. Now the little girl slept in the cradle next to his pallet, and he could actually close his eyes without worrying she was going to take a tumble while he slept.

He'd also rigged a swing on the porch out of leftover pieces of board and twine. He could slip Grace into it, and she could move it just by kicking her legs. She delighted in it, and he had his hands free to chop wood or do other chores.

"That looks like fun," Frisco had said, leaning against one of the other porch supports and watching Grace bounce. "I wish I had something like that. For the little ones," he hurried to add, as if he feared Kit would think him childish.

Kit eyed the contraption, then the big cedar near the schoolyard. By this morning, with Rina's permission, he had set up two swings from the branches, and the children were taking turns.

He kept listening for gunshots calling them back from work, but none came except the call for dinner. Ciara seemed to have accustomed herself at last to her new home, even if she still asked his escort to walk her to her cabin in the evenings. Still, the closer they came to the restaurant opening, the more tense she seemed.

"You're worried," he said the night before her opening.

She glanced up from where she had been setting the table for dinner. "Is it that obvious?"

Kit rose from playing with Grace on the rug and came to her side. That one lock of hair persisted in coming free from her bun whenever she had been working particularly hard. He tucked the strand behind her ear and tried not to glory in the soft silk or the soft look that crossed her face at his touch.

"Yes," he told her. "And only to be expected. Everything you've done will be tested tomorrow."

She closed her eyes. "Heaven help me."

"He will," Kit said. "He promised."

She opened her eyes. "Thank you for the reminder. Please say you're coming. Harry will probably make faces at me all night, and Jesse will hide. He already asked if he could take a plate up to the loft."

Kit chuckled. "Wise man. There's going to be a crowd."

"Maybe," she said. "Hopefully."

He caught her hands, which were starting to rub together in front of her apron. "I'll be there, Ciara. And so will most of your friends."

"I know." She forced a smile. "One more dish to try tonight. Jugged hare with onions and garlic."

He released her. "I can hardly wait."

She hurried back to the kitchen then, apron swinging over her gingham skirts. Something hitched in his chest, a longing, a need. He wanted to comfort and encourage and cheer while she soared.

Did that mean he was falling in love with his make-believe fiancée?

CHAPTER FIFTEEN

BY FRIDAY EVENING, Ciara was once more pacing, and she didn't know why. Everything was ready. She was wearing a clean green gingham gown with puffy sleeves and a fresh white apron with ruffles at the yoke and hem. Her hair had so many pins keeping the braid wound around her head she felt the weight, but the effort would be worth it if her hair didn't fall while she worked.

The cabin was likewise ready. She'd set the long table to accommodate eight bachelors or a family or two and positioned along the back wall two smaller tables she'd brought from her cabin and the loft. Those would do for couples or families. Fresh flowers, courtesy of Frisco and Sutter, sat in vases on each table. Silverware gleamed. Gingham napkins, a gift from Nora, sat waiting to grace laps and necks.

Kit had crafted a sign from a slice of timber to hang in the big window. One side said "Open." The other said "Family Only." She went to grab it, fingers stroking the painted wood. The last of the pork and apple pies were in the oven, the others cooling on the sideboard. Fish chowder simmered on a burner. Jesse and Harry had already taken their dinners and climbed the stairs to the loft. It was now or never.

She flipped the sign to Open.

Nothing happened.

She shook herself. Well, of course nothing happened. What, did she think the sign was magic? That one flick and customers would appear? She stepped away from the window with a sigh and headed back to the kitchen to check her pies.

As she closed the oven door, steam swirling about her, she heard the cabin door open. Heart starting to pound, she glanced out the archway.

Kit stood with Grace in his arms, surveying the room and making it seem brighter by his very presence.

"Welcome to dinner, Mr. Weatherly, Miss Virden," she called. "Sit anywhere you'd like."

He transferred Grace to one hip. "I was thinking maybe Grace and I could help you."

Stepping to the opening, she spread her hands. "There's no one to feed."

The door opened again, and Drew and Catherine walked in. His dark-blond hair had been slicked back, and he wore his Sunday best shirt. Catherine had a wide-skirted dress with daisies all over it, as if she were going to a fine tea rather than dinner in a log cabin.

Drew nodded around, as if she'd decorated the place differently. "Very nice. Two for dinner?"

"Right this way," Ciara said, moving to show them to one of the smaller tables. Drew held out the chair for his wife, who sat with a smile.

"We have two specials tonight," Ciara said, trying not to rush through the words. Why was she nervous? She'd known these two most of her life. "Fish chowder with brown bread or pork and apple pie, and I have lemon pound cake and Spotted Pup for dessert. That's a rice pudding with raisins, molasses, and cinnamon. Each of the dinner choices is fifty cents, including lemonade, with another ten cents if you want a dessert. What would you prefer?"

"I'd like to try the chowder," Catherine said.

"Make that two," Drew added. "We can figure out dessert later."

"Very good," Ciara said, backing away.

The door opened, and two men in rough denim and buckskin coats shuffled in, gazes darting about as if they thought a pack of wolves might be waiting. By the dirt under their fingers, Ciara guessed they were prospectors.

"We heard you were serving dinner," one said, rubbing his grizzled chin with the back of one hand.

"We are indeed," Ciara told them. "Take your seats at the long table, and I'll be with you shortly."

She hurried into the kitchen. Kit was already there, pulling down plates and cups with one hand while he bounced Grace with the other.

"Thank you," she said, and then she was too busy to say anything else.

They kept coming. A husband and wife from up the lake had ventured down to see what she might be offering. Three more prospectors showed up from across the lake. They had apparently paddled over in a canoe. When James and Rina arrived, she had to put them at one end of the long table, where James quickly had the other bachelors laughing at his wit. No sooner had the first two fellows finished and left, with belches and praise, then three more came to take their places.

She cut and served and stirred as fast as she could. She ran out of Spotted Pup within an hour. Kit asked Jesse to take Grace so he could pitch in to clear place settings and start the dishes.

Over the splash of water and the bubble of chowder, she heard the door again.

"How many more?" she asked, wiping steam from her cheek with the edge of her apron.

"Two more fellows at the long table," Kit reported from his vantage point at the sink. "One's got a claim next to

Simon's. I've seen him on the ridge. I don't recognize the other."

Ciara dusted off her hands and bustled out to meet them.

"Welcome to dinner, gentlemen," she chanted before reeling off their choices.

The thinner man nodded throughout her recitation. When she stopped, he just kept waiting.

"That's what we have tonight," she said. "Which would you prefer?"

"Can I have all of them?" He laid a gold coin on the table. "I can pay."

Ciara scooped up the coin. "Coming right up." She turned to the other man, whose face was as seamed as old leather. "What can I get for you, sir?"

He also laid a coin on the table, silver and shiny against the wood. "Information. I understand you're going to marry Christopher Weatherly."

His gravelly voice made her feel as if someone had opened the door and let in a blast of winter wind. "Information isn't on the menu," she told him. "I can get you fish chowder, pork and apple pie, or lemon pound cake. Which would you prefer?"

"Slice of cake," he said. "And maybe I can convince you to change your mind."

"Doubtful," she said. She didn't pick up the coin.

Instead, she went to the kitchen and positioned herself so that a stray glance wouldn't betray Kit's presence. "That stranger's asking for information about you. You might want to slip out the back. Now."

Kit shook water off his hands, watching as she opened the oven and heat and the succulent scent of baking pie wafted into the kitchen.

"Slip out the back?" he repeated. "What do you think I did, rob a bank?"

"I don't think you did anything wrong," she informed him, taking out the last of her pies and reaching for a clean knife to slice it. "But someone is hoping you did, and I'm betting Mrs. Virden hired him. It might be better if you just disappeared until he finishes eating."

Kit shook his head. "And leave you with this horde? I'll take my chances."

She frowned at him a moment, as if trying to see inside to what drove him. Then she pulled down a plate and began serving her pie.

He leaned back to catch another glimpse of the two newcomers. The one he hadn't recognized was sitting with his back to the wall, as if determined to remain aware of everything around him. Visible around the leg of the table, a holster sat heavy on one hip.

He couldn't be a lawman. Ciara was right. Kit hadn't done anything wrong. And Hart McCormick would have sent word if another deputy sheriff or marshal had been heading this way.

Ciara passed, balancing a plate on one hand and a bowl on the other.

Kit reached for one. "Let me."

"No," she said, swiveling fast enough she nearly swept the pie from the porcelain. "You stay in here."

She marched out of the kitchen.

It took her two more loads, but she had everyone served. She returned to the kitchen and leaned against the back wall as if she needed its support.

"Full house," Kit commented.

Her grin popped into view. "Better than I imagined."

Better than anyone had imagined, even with high expectations. Almost every diner left promising to return and bring friends and family. Several paid extra to take home slices of meat pie and cake. Others left additional coins in thanks. The stranger lingered for a while, then finally paid what he owed and departed. Ciara closed the door behind him and turned the sign to Family Only.

Kit came out of the kitchen, drying the last of the dishes. "That was a good night."

She eyed him. "A great night. I may need to hire help."

He put on a sad face. "And here I thought I was applying for the job."

"You were a gift from the Lord," she told him. "But I can't expect you to work every night, especially when you work during the day."

"It's only Friday and Saturday," he protested as he followed her into the kitchen.

"For now," she said. "I'm hoping to be open six nights a week by harvest time." She went to the stove and surveyed what little remained.

"I can cut up the cake and make trifle tomorrow," she said, hands on her hips. "I have enough strawberry preserves, and I can whip cream. That's one dessert."

"They loved the Spotted Pup," he said. "Grace even ate it."

"I told you to be careful with the sweets," she warned him. "And I'm out of raisins, and so is James, so it will have to be something else tomorrow." She sighed as she glanced at the kettle that had held the chowder. "And the fish chowder was too salty. Everyone who had it asked for extra lemonade."

"Maybe they just liked the lemonade," Kit suggested.

"I tasted it. Too salty. I'll know better next time."

Her shoulders rose and fell in another sigh.

Kit abandoned the dishes and came up beside her. "You must be worn out." He didn't know whether she would allow it, but he set his hands on her shoulders. She didn't flinch. He began kneading muscles that were tight under his fingers.

"That feels good," she murmured, tipping her head

to one side and threatening the braid that had stayed in place all evening. "I changed my mind. You're hired."

He laughed. "And here I thought you liked how I washed dishes."

She turned to face him, and his hands fell. "I like a great deal about you, Kit Weatherly."

Her lips were inches away. He remembered how they'd tasted last time, sweeter than any pie she might bake. He leaned closer.

"You done?" Jesse asked.

Kit straightened to find the logger in the archway, Grace up in his burly arms.

"No, no, no, no, no," Grace told Kit, face firm.

"She missed you," Jesse said.

"I doubt that," Kit said, but he went to take the baby from him.

"How did it go?" Jesse asked Ciara. "Sounded like a lot of people."

"Quite a few customers," she admitted. "More than I expected. It was a very good first night, Jesse. Thank you so much for watching Grace so Kit could help."

He glanced down at his feet, which were shuffling against the wood floor. "Wasn't any trouble."

"We'll think of an alternative for tomorrow," she promised.

He nodded and wandered back out.

Grace yawned, tiny teeth showing white, before tucking her head into Kit's shoulder.

"I should get her to bed," he told Ciara.

"Of course. Thank you again, Kit. I couldn't have done it without you."

Her smile saw him out of the kitchen.

The stranger was leaning in the open front door.

Kit stopped, stiffening. "The restaurant is closed."

"I saw the sign." The man strolled toward the table as if he owned the cabin. "Forgot to leave a little something for the cook. Best food I've had for a while." He laid a silver coin down on the wood.

Then he glanced at Kit. "Bit late for a little girl to be up, isn't it?"

"I don't see how that's any of your concern," Kit said.

He put two fingers on the brim of his hat. "My mistake. Just wanted to be of help. Must be hard for a bachelor to raise a baby."

"He's not a bachelor." Ciara's voice rang from behind Kit, and she came up to link her arm in his. "At least, not for much longer. Thank you for the consideration. I need to close up for the night."

He touched his hat again. "Ma'am." His spurs clinked as he walked to the door. It shut quietly behind him.

She released Kit and flew to the window.

"Dappled gray horse," she reported. "I saw him in the woods the other day."

"I saw him too," Kit said, cold crawling up his spine. "I think you're right. Mrs. Virden is watching me, looking for any weakness. A shame she's likely to find some."

CHAPTER SIXTEEN

"HOGWASH," CIARA SAID, turning from the window. "No one is perfect. I'll bet Mrs. Virden has a few things she's not proud of."

He snorted, and Grace startled.

"No, no," she began, only to lay her head back down on his shoulder with a thud even as her eyes drifted closed again.

Kit gazed down at the sleepy baby, smile softening. "The stranger's right, though. I should be more attentive to her."

Ciara crossed to his side. "You have to eat and sleep and work. You make sure someone else watches Grace when needed. I think you're doing brilliantly for a man who became a father only ten days ago." She dropped a kiss on Grace's head, the dark curls tickling her chin. "But yes, you should probably get her to bed. I'll see you in the morning."

"I'll put her to bed," he said, "but I'm not sleeping until I know that man is gone." He headed for the stairs.

Ciara cast another glance out the window, where twilight thickened until she could almost feel its velvet fingers. The barn was a shadow across the clearing. She could barely make out James closing the big doors for the night. Nothing else moved.

Squaring her shoulders, she returned to the kitchen. She

had to finish cleaning up and then confirm everything was ready for breakfast.

Kit found her just as she was banking down the stove. "Grace is asleep," he said. "Jesse and Harry too. Do you need any help?"

"I'm done," she said, and suddenly she wanted only to lay her head on his shoulder and feel his arms around her, like Grace had done. "Would you mind walking me to my cabin?"

"Not at all."

They came out the rear door, and he reached for the rifle hanging by its strap.

Ciara shivered, though the air was just beginning to cool. "Are you expecting trouble?"

"Doesn't hurt to be careful," he said, checking the butt for ammunition. As if satisfied by what he saw, he slid the lever back into place and held the rifle across his arms. "Shall we?"

They set out along the path. The rustling noises weren't nearly as concerning with him at her side. She glanced up and saw a bat glide across the light of a rising half moon.

"They'll give up," she told him. "This stranger and Mrs. Virden. Once they see how well you're doing with Grace, they won't have any other choice."

"Maybe," he said, gaze swinging from the shadowed forest on one side to the other. "But I can't help remembering how determined Rudy was to make me into a man he could admire, never mind what I found worthwhile. If he learned that determination from his mother, Grace and I could be in for a long ride."

"His mother may have determination," she said as they came out in front of her cabin, "but you have love. That's worth far more."

In the moonlight, she could see his smile. "You're just as determined to make me believe, aren't you?"

"Of course. I remember what it was like living with strangers after my mother and father died in the tenement fire." Just saying the words would once have caused her to cringe. "Aiden and I were so alone, and we'd just become accustomed to living with Maddie, when she decided to up and go with Mr. Mercer to Seattle! It was ten long months before we saw her again. Mrs. McNeilly, who ran the children's home, was very kind, and it was fun having other children around us, but it didn't feel like home. That's what Grace deserves—a home with someone who loves her."

"That's what I want for her too," he murmured. "But I remember the lean years, before Hannah married. I don't want Grace to suffer because of choices I made. Mrs. Virden can give her so much more."

"If she's that worried about Grace's financial wellbeing, she can set up a trust," Ciara said. "Or offer to buy you a house. It doesn't have to be a choice between love and income."

He chuckled. "Wise words, Miss O'Rourke. Why do I think Mrs. Virden will see things differently?"

"She might see things differently now," Ciara allowed. "But she'll come around when she realizes how happy her granddaughter is here. Now, I should let you get some sleep. Tomorrow will come early."

"Earlier for you," he said. "Good night, Ciara, and thank you."

He leaned closer, and her heart fluttered like the wings of a hummingbird. She held herself still as his lips brushed hers, softly, gently.

He was only thanking her. She knew that. But as he withdrew, it felt like so much more.

Saturday was even busier. Ciara made Kit and the others a hurried breakfast of Johnny cakes and applesauce, then shooed them out the door to wait for Drew so she could start working on dinner. John had offered her some choice venison that would make excellent pie, and she wanted to soak the beans for a ham and bean soup. Then there was cobbler to make and cream to whip. And she wanted to try Levi's way of making biscuits. The work took the better part of the day, but at least she could say nothing was overcooked or too salty.

By the time she flipped the sign from Family Only to Open, eight bachelors were waiting on the porch. Another dozen filed in during the three hours she served dinner. She ran out of venison pie and trifle, and she had to save the last scoop of blackcap cobbler and a dollop of whipped cream for Jesse, or they would have gone out too.

Harry had taken one look at the throngs and offered to watch Grace so Kit could help.

"You're welcome to help too, Harry," Ciara had teased, and he had beat a hasty retreat with the baby up the stairs, where Jesse had already gone into hiding.

She and Kit danced around each other all night as she took and plated orders and he cleared and washed. As soon as one diner finished, Kit had the place set for another. When two argued over the last slice of venison pie, his look from the archway made them quiet and speak to her more respectfully. He stirred the soup while she whipped more cream. And always with a calm and a smile that kept her focused.

"I had no idea," she told him when they'd chucked the last diner out the door around eight. As he turned the sign to Family Only, she dropped onto the bench at the table and tipped back her head, stretching the muscles in her shoulders. "This is madness. A lovely madness, but still. And everyone praised the biscuits!"

"I'm not surprised," he told her, gathering up the last of the dirty dishes. "You're a great cook, and most of these men haven't had someone make them dinner in years."

She eyed him as he ferried the dishes toward the kitchen. "So you think it's the novelty? This tide will ebb?"

"They came for the novelty," he called back. "They'll return for the food."

She could only hope.

He ventured back through the archway and took Jesse's chair at the head of the table. "Are you still considering hiring permanent help?"

"Yes." She straightened. "But what I cleared last night and today wouldn't pay a salary for two, not with the cost of supplies."

He cocked his head. "It would if you had more tables."

She glanced around the room. There was plenty of space; Lars Wallin had built this cabin for his growing family, after all. "I suppose I could see if TP Freeman has any at his second-hand emporium. But it might take a while to get them here."

"I could build you some."

Her heart thudded, and she put a hand on her chest. "Oh, Kit, that's so kind. But you have enough to do."

"Wouldn't take that much," he mused, glancing around as well. "Drew has been teaching Jesse and me how to build furniture. Jesse already volunteered to help when I mentioned it earlier. Harry, Drew, and John would probably pitch in too, for that matter. I'll ask them tomorrow after services." His gaze came back to hers, soft and warm. "Will you walk to church with me and Grace?"

That would probably be expected, given that everyone thought she and Kit were betrothed. And she was surprised how much she wanted to go with him, regardless.

But this was another kind of dance. She'd tried hard not to encourage Harry and Jesse. She shouldn't make Kit think she wanted their engagement to become real.

Yet he had been a good friend to her and was even now helping to make her dreams come true.

She must have taken too long to answer, for his smile slipped off like butter on a griddle cake. She forced a smile.

"Of course," she said. "Anything for Grace."

For Grace. Of course. He shouldn't read anything more into Ciara's actions than friendship, even though at moments, something more than friendship felt as if it were simmering, as warm and sustaining as one of her stews.

"Thanks. Shall I walk you home?"

"I think I'm fine tonight," she said. "I'm so tired I probably wouldn't notice if a circus elephant crossed the path in front of me. Good night, Kit, and thanks."

"Good night, then," he said, watching her hurry out the door.

Even after two nights of hard work, however, she was up and in the kitchen before he brought Grace down Sunday morning. Kit had wrestled the baby into one of the frillier of the dresses Callie had provided, with a matching cap trimmed in lace on Grace's dark curls. Grace hadn't shrieked about the matter, but he caught her muttering her favorite word under her breath as they approached the kitchen.

Ciara was also dressed for church, in the fancy green gown trimmed in black she'd worn to the children's theatrical. She'd wisely covered it in one of her voluminous aprons, cinched at her waist.

"Griddle cakes ready in a moment," she said, flipping one in her frying pan. She blew a dark lock of hair out of her eyes and grinned at him.

"I'll set the table," he offered.

He had the places lined up, even while balancing Grace

on his hip, when Harry and Jesse loped down the stairs a short time later. They too were dressed in their best, with clean shirts, string ties, and combed hair. By the reflection in Jesse's boots, he must have spent some time polishing them.

Ciara made a point of walking with all of them, but as they approached the church, she latched onto Kit's free arm. He felt as if he'd grown two inches.

"It's not often a man can walk into church with the two prettiest ladies in the area on his arms," he said to her.

She beamed.

Every male gaze darted their way as they stepped into the Wallin Landing chapel. Drew and his brothers nodded respectfully. Others gaped so hard Kit wouldn't have been surprised if they started salivating. He recognized a number of the men she had served at her restaurant the last two days. Indeed, nearly every pew was filled. Kit found a spot behind James and Rina and settled in for the service.

Callie played the opening hymn on the piano in the corner, with Simon accompanying her on his violin. Voices, this time predominantly male, rose in chorus. A few were decidedly rusty, but it was the heart that mattered.

When it came time to take the pulpit for the sermon, Levi raised his brows as if surprised by the number of people gazing back.

"Good to see you all today," he said with a smile. "Our community is growing by leaps and bounds. That's why I thought it might be a good time to talk about loving your neighbor."

Half a dozen glances arced toward Ciara. Kit edged a little closer.

He stayed close when the service ended and everyone began wandering toward the exits. Harry and Jesse fell in behind them.

"Lots of fellows sniffing around our gal," Harry muttered, sending a frown toward one of the older prospectors, who hastily put his hat back on his head and scurried off.

Ciara cast him a glance. "I wasn't aware I was your gal, Harry."

"You know what I mean," Harry grumbled as Jesse's cheeks turned red. "You came here to cook for us, and now they all expect you to cook for them too."

"I can do both, you know," she informed him as they stepped out into a misty morning.

"And she just proved that," Kit reminded him.

Harry tugged up the collar on his shirt. "Just making sure no one impinges on your time."

Kit turned to Ciara. "Would you take Grace a moment? I want to talk to Harry and Jesse."

She regarded him thoughtfully, but she accepted the baby and headed for the big cabin.

"You're betrothed, I know," Harry said. "You don't have to remind us."

Jesse nodded.

"It's not that," Kit said, guilt tugging. "Ciara's restaurant could use a few more tables, preferably by next Friday. I was hoping you two could help me build them."

Jesse grinned. "Happy to. Right, Harry?"

Kit thought the other logger might refuse, but Harry nodded as well. "Right. The more who can eat, the quicker the crowds can leave."

Kit had a feeling the crowds would only grow.

But Harry and Jesse weren't the only ones ready to lend a hand. By the time they'd finished dinner with the Wallins in the hall that afternoon, Kit had convinced John and Drew to help as well.

Catherine, who had been sitting beside her husband when Kit approached, nodded her approval. "That's an excellent idea. It gives Ciara room to expand."

"Room that will be needed sooner than later," Drew predicted. "We can take a couple hours off early every day this week to work on them. I have some timber stored in the barn we can use, and we'll need to think about chairs as well."

"Perhaps Ciara can borrow them from the hall, for now," Catherine suggested. "Then you all can finish them as time allows."

"Thank you," Kit said. "I know more tables and chairs will make a world of difference."

"And now that we know the restaurant will be a success," Catherine said, "I hope that means you'll let us start planning your wedding."

Her voice carried sufficiently that every lady at the table looked his way, gazes as bright as her smile.

His gaze focused on Ciara, whose eyes had widened.

"Maybe not just yet," he demurred. "We still have a lot of things to work out first."

Ciara sagged. Had he relieved a burden?

Or was she disappointed by his answer?

Did that mean she wanted to marry him after all?

CHAPTER SEVENTEEN

KIT WAS HOLDING off the Wallins' kind suggestions to plan a wedding. Ciara ought to be glad. She wasn't ready to jump into marriage. She had her hands full, and so did he.

So why was she so disappointed in his answer?

As it was, she'd been having a lovely afternoon. She'd brought another lemon pound cake and a salad to contribute to the dinner table, but it was awfully nice not to have to do more. The last few days, she hadn't cooked so much at one time in her whole life! But she couldn't regret the progress. Her dream was coming true.

Still, she had a ways to go if she wanted to open six days a week by harvest, about six weeks away now. The venison pie had gone over well, but she couldn't count on having a haunch handy every weekend. With the numbers she was serving, trout wouldn't be smart either. Frisco and Sutter would have to fish for days to bring her enough for one night, and where would she keep them fresh in the meantime?

But she couldn't rely on salted meats. Many of her customers would have been living off the stuff anyway. Her restaurant had to be better than that if she wanted to keep them coming back.

"Stews, soups, and chowder are the order of the day," she told Grace Monday evening as she was skimming the stock she'd had simmering all day. One of the farmers nearby had offered her three chickens in exchange for two dinners at the restaurant. She'd already treated Kit and the others to dinner of fried chicken, mashed potatoes, and gravy, with biscuits and honey. She'd combined the remaining meat and bones with carrots, onions, parsley, rosemary, and thyme.

Grace nodded wisely from her tall chair. It had wheels on the bottom, so it could be rolled from location to location, and a tray in front for food or toys. Grace preferred to drop either on the floor then scold until someone brought her more. The glowing smile seemed to be enough to keep most folks at the game.

"What's that?" Kit asked, coming through the archway. He and Jesse had been measuring the front room to see how many tables they might be able to fit and what sizes.

"The menu," Ciara explained, turning to position her wire strainer over the mouth of the storage crock. "Stews, soups, and chowders. I can do two each night in rotation and add in other specialties as the supply allows."

He nodded, lower lip sticking out. For some reason, her gaze latched on it, and she had to remind herself of her task. She lifted the kettle and began pouring the rich chicken stock into the crock.

"You'll need a lot of biscuits," he pointed out as he watched. "But I prefer your molasses oat bread. With butter and honey?" He closed his eyes a moment and inhaled, as if savoring the taste.

"Excellent suggestion!" Ciara straightened. "I can do some kind of bread each night too—báirín breac, oat bread, scones."

"What's barmbrack?" he asked, mangling the Irish word.

Something her sister specialized in, but he didn't need to know that. "A heavy bread made with tea and raisins," she supplied. "Very filling. And I ought to focus on that aspect of the menu as well. I want my customers leaving feeling as if they'd had enough."

"No, no, no, no, no," Grace argued. Then she peered over the edge of her tray and looked up at Kit expectantly.

He bent and retrieved the block she'd dropped. "So long as you keep having two desserts a night, I don't think anyone is going to complain. Even Grace."

As if to prove it, Grace took the block he offered and pulled it toward her mouth.

Ciara took it from her before she could chew on it. "This needs a washing."

"No, no, no, no, no," Grace said with a deep sigh.

Over the next few days, Ciara tried various combinations on Kit and the other loggers. It was hard to find a set of vegetables to pair with the ham without the stew or soup tasting too salty. But the fish chowder always went down with big smiles. And Kit was right—none of them ever refused another slice of her molasses oat bread. She also made more stock, until she had crocks for chicken, venison, and vegetable stock stored in the cold cellar beneath the kitchen.

Life settled into a routine of cooking, helping Kit with Grace, and the familiar chores of laundry, churning, and sewing. Callie agreed to let Ciara collect the eggs one day a week from the chicken run in the main clearing. Simon and John had chickens of their own. Ciara let everyone know she'd be glad to take any eggs they didn't need. Not only did they improve some of her recipes, but they made a good breakfast.

Her heart couldn't help swelling as Kit, Drew, Harry, Jesse, and John began moving the tables they'd built into the main room of the cabin on Wednesday. Each table was a solid plank on carved legs and could seat four to six. Besides the tables she had, there were now two more next to the stairs, another on the back wall, and a larger one in the middle of the braided rug. They'd also fashioned a few stools to augment the chairs from the hall.

"It really looks like a restaurant," she marveled.

"A restaurant that deserves a name," Kit teased. "I can make you another sign. I just need to know what to put on it."

Her mind was a blank. "I'll think about it and let you know. Thank you."

"And who's going to be helping you serve these tables?" Drew asked, setting a leg into place.

"At least I have an idea there," Ciara said. "But I may come begging if she refuses."

"She?" Kit asked as the other men left. "I thought the Wallin ladies were fairly busy."

"She isn't a Wallin," Ciara clarified. "And I don't know whether I can convince her, so I'd rather not say anything further until I know."

She could only be thankful again when James Wallin brought Katie Jo to visit Thursday morning. Her friend glanced around at all the tables, and her honey-colored brows went up.

"Your restaurant must be doing good," she said. "Wish I could have come for the opening."

"I wish you could have too," Ciara assured her, beckoning her to take a seat on the rocker, which still held pride of place next to the hearth. "And I wondered. I know you were hoping to work at the store to earn money for a new dress. I might have another way to earn some money."

"What's that?" Katie Jo asked with a frown as she settled on the chair.

"I need help at the restaurant," Ciara explained, pulling one of the stools from the table on the rug and spreading her skirts to sit. "It would only be on Fridays and Saturdays for now. You wouldn't have to serve the tables or cook. I'd take care of that. But someone needs to watch the stove and wash the dishes. Maybe even clear off tables between servings. I'd pay you fifty cents a night."

Once more her brows shot up. "That's a mighty good wage. Only I don't see how I could get home before dark, especially as the days get shorter."

"You could stay with me Friday and Saturday nights," Ciara offered.

Her sigh raised the shoulders of her flannel shirt. "I'm highly tempted, Miss Ciara. But my uncle wouldn't approve of me being gone for so long, and I don't like leaving my brother alone."

"Bring him too," Ciara told her. "He can sleep with Kit and the others in the loft."

She smiled. "You think of a way around every problem, don't you?"

"I try," Ciara said. "If I need to send you home with pie for your uncle to sweeten the deal, I can do that too."

She wiggled her lips. "I'll ask. But you should probably have someone else in mind when the answer is no."

Friday afternoon, Drew let Kit off early again, in case Ciara needed help with the restaurant. He walked back through the forest, ax on his shoulder and mist swirling about him. It was one of those Seattle days when the sun never managed to burn through the clouds, leaving everything gray. Even the lake glinted silver through the trees as he made his way south.

He was passing the track that led up over the hill toward the Sound when another fellow came out of it. His slouch hat was pulled down to shadow his face, and his hands were shoved in the pockets of his dusty trousers.

"You headed to Wallin Landing?" he asked in a high tenor.

"Sure am," Kit said. "Are you coming in to dinner at the new restaurant?"

"I'm working at the new restaurant," he said proudly, falling into step beside Kit.

Odd. He thought Ciara had said she was hiring another woman. Maybe she'd had to settle for a young man instead. At least this one had fairly broad shoulders and a height just a few inches shorter than Kit's six-foot frame. He should be able to do the work. But he likely could have been clearing timber for better pay.

Then again, who was he to tell a fellow where he should work?

"Do you live out this way?" Kit asked.

He nodded. "Uncle has a claim along the north of the creek before it empties into Salmon Bay. I get in to the Landing a couple times a week for supplies and mail. Miss Ciara thought I might want work. I'm hoping Mrs. Nora can sew me a new dress."

A dress!

He tried to catch a better glimpse of his companion, but the slouch hat was an effective barrier. Maybe it wasn't just those shoulders that widened that chest. He hastily looked away, face flaming. Then he thought of another way he might know for sure.

"I'm Kit Weatherly, one of Drew Wallin's loggers," he said, offering his hand. "Nice to meet you."

"Katie Jo McAllister," she said, grasping his hand in a firm grip and giving it a shake. "Nice to meet you too. You're going to marry Miss Ciara, I hear."

So, his companion *was* female. And it seemed the gossip had gone all the way up to the homesteads along the bay. "We have an understanding."

"Must be nice," she said wistfully.

"No sweetheart for you?" he asked.

Pink worked its way into her cheeks. "Naw. I have better things to do with my time than chase after a feller."

Ciara had said something similar. His sister would have been shocked. In her mind, the greatest accomplishment a lady might have was to marry and marry well. Which left him out.

He fell silent, and his companion did not seem disposed to talk. In fact, she didn't say another word until they came out at the edge of the main clearing. Then she pointed at the horse tied up along the porch rail. "Someone beat us to it."

So early? Ciara couldn't have started serving yet. The sign in the window clearly said Family Only. Had Beth come out to visit? The black horse could be Hart's.

Then again, some of the strangers who had arrived in Wallin Landing hadn't come for a friendly visit.

Kit lengthened his stride, and Miss McAllister matched him as if she sensed his urgency. They hopped up on the porch at the same time, and Kit just managed to open the door before she barreled through.

Ciara looked up from where she was serving tea to another young lady at the table. "Oh, good. You're here."

"You bet," Miss McAllister and Kit said in unison. Then she blushed and wiggled in behind him as if embarrassed by the outburst.

"Miss Virden, this is Mr. Weatherly," Ciara said, setting the teapot down on the table. "Kit, Miss Virden says she's baby Grace's aunt."

Rudy's sister? He didn't recall meeting her, but some of his brother-in-law's family had remained back East. Kit came around the table. Thick lashes fluttered over gray eyes as misty as the Seattle day as Miss Virden glanced up at him. Golden blond hair cascaded down behind her, and enviable curves swelled the navy riding habit she wore.

"Mr. Weatherly," she said in a soft voice. "I'm sorry we must meet under such trying circumstances. How is our dear niece, Grace?"

"Fine," Kit said. His legs felt unaccountably shaky, so

he dropped onto the chair nearest her. "Are you here on behalf of your mother?"

Her rosebud lips turned down. "No. My mother can be a difficult person. She and I haven't spoken for the last five years. But when I heard Rudolph and Hannah had passed, I knew I had to come and see how Grace was faring. From the sound of things, she's in very good hands." She smiled prettily.

"Our stranger with the dappled gray horse apparently works for Miss Virden," Ciara put in. "He's down at the mercantile right now, arranging for a letter to go back East."

"I apologize if he troubled you," Miss Virden said. "I know Mr. Dullard can seem very stern, but I've found him invaluable. Being a woman alone, in a strange town, I didn't know who to trust. You understand." She appealed more to Ciara than him.

"Of course," Ciara said. She glanced at Kit. "Miss Virden brought papers to prove her identity. I thought you might want to see them before fetching Grace."

"Yes, Grace's location appears to be a well-kept secret," Miss Virden said with a tinkling laugh.

He hadn't intended it that way, but he was glad Dullard and the Virdens weren't sure where the baby might be. And he didn't know what to think about Miss Virden. He excused himself and rose to join Ciara in the kitchen. Miss McAllister shuffled after them.

"I'm so glad you decided to come, Katie Jo," Ciara said. "Thank you. Give me a moment to explain things to Kit, and then I can show you what I'd like you to do."

Miss McAllister cocked her head to peer out the archway. "Happy to help, but I'm not so sure about that lady out there. Who's this Grace?"

"The daughter of my deceased sister," Kit explained. "I've been made her guardian." The fact sounded more legal than it felt. He glanced to Ciara. "You've had a moment to talk with her. Do you trust her?"

"I suppose I must," she said, handing him a sheath of papers from the sideboard. "She came prepared to plead her case."

"And what is her case, exactly?" Kit asked, perusing the closely written correspondence from lawyers and prominent Tacoma businessmen offering condolences and assistance to a Miss Elodie Virden.

"She says she wants to see that Grace is protected," Ciara supplied. "But I suspect she'll soon offer that protection herself."

Possibly. Yet Hannah had to have known of Rudy's sister. She seemed a lady his sister would have admired. Why choose him over her for Grace's upbringing?

Miss McAllister was just as skeptical. "Why didn't she come sooner?" she asked. "If one of my kin had passed and I knew a baby was left, I'd have been there yesterday."

"Rudolph's family lived in Philadelphia," Kit replied. "It's possible someone sent her a telegram."

"Then she came pretty far in about two weeks," Ciara said. "The train might have taken her to San Francisco, but she'd still have to catch a steamer up to Seattle, and that's a week in itself."

Kit lowered the papers. "There's no way we can confirm these are legitimate without going to Tacoma or at least sending telegrams from Seattle. In the meantime, I suppose it's all right for Grace to see her, so long as I stay close."

"Good idea," Miss McAllister said with a nod. "That way, if she tries to steal the baby, we can all jump her."

CHAPTER EIGHTEEN

MISS VIRDEN COULDN'T have come at a poorer time. Ciara needed to train Katie Jo and finish the preparations for dinner, but she also wanted to be on hand to help Kit, who was clearly torn as to whether to trust the newcomer. He'd gone up to Nora's to fetch Grace. The best Ciara could do was keep an eye on their visitor while she showed her friend what needed doing.

"I've got gingerbread in the oven," she explained to a rapt Katie Jo. "And batter for carrot fritters ready to go in the frying pan if they're ordered. They cook fast. When they're done, we need to squeeze on a little juice from an orange and scrape a little sugar on top. Are you comfortable doing that?"

Katie Jo visibly swallowed. "Maybe you could show me how much the first time. Then I can copy you."

"Good idea." She turned for the sideboard. "We have enough dishes to set each table once and about half the second time. But as soon as someone's finished, I need those dishes washed and the tables reset for the next diner."

Katie Jo nodded. "Easy. There's even a pump inside here. We should keep a big kettle of water heating on the stove."

"Yes, please. Fill it up and add it back as you use it."

Ciara put her hands on her hips and glanced out at the

main room. "Oh, and sweeping after a table is cleared. You wouldn't believe the mess some of them leave."

"I have to take care of my brother and my uncle," Katie Jo said. "I know messes."

Ciara couldn't help it. She wrapped her arms as far as she could around Katie Jo's bigger frame. "Oh, I am so glad you're here!"

Her friend was blushing as Ciara disengaged. "If I do something wrong, you just tell me," she said. "I may not know much about restaurants, but I learn fast."

"Good," Ciara said, turning for the door. "Because I have a feeling we're both going to need to learn."

She came out into the main room to find Miss Virden still sitting patiently at the long plank table.

"I'm sorry," Ciara told her. "I have to open the restaurant shortly. Please wait for Kit on the porch."

She rose, gloved fingers knitting together in front of her riding habit as if she was about to offer a prayer. "Perhaps I should inquire at the local inn about rooms for the night for me and Mr. Dullard."

Ciara shook her head. "There isn't an inn at Wallin Landing. The closest hotel is in Seattle." Though it might not be a bad idea to consider adding that to her plans. A restaurant with a few beds upstairs could be even more valuable to the growing settlement.

Just then, Kit came through the door with Grace. A half dozen faces peered hopefully behind him, but he shut the door on them.

"You've got a line already," he told Ciara. "And I spotted Harry and Jesse headed this way."

"I'll feed them first," Ciara said. "Take Miss Virden out the kitchen door. She and her man are hoping to stay in the area. I explained there's no place around like that."

"If you see Frisco or Sutter, ask them to take word to Levi," Kit told her. "He may know of a place."

Grace reached out chubby arms, fingers wiggling. Ciara

brightened, until she realized the baby's gaze wasn't on her. It was on Miss Virden.

Whose face was melting.

"Oh," she murmured, her fingers pressed to her lips. "Those eyes! She looks so much like Rudy."

From the first, Ciara had thought Grace resembled Kit. Perhaps Rudolph Virden had been dark-haired and dark-eyed as well.

"Grace," Kit said, "this is your aunt Virden."

Grace shrieked.

The window rattled. Miss Virden reared back. Katie Jo strode out of the kitchen, spare frying pan up and at the ready.

"You stick a pin in that baby again?" Harry complained as he came through the door, Jesse on his heels. His gaze swept from Grace to Kit to Miss Virden, and he stopped in his tracks. Jesse bumped into him.

Harry turned his stagger into a bow. "Ma'am. Welcome to Wallin Landing. Is this feller bothering you?"

"This is Miss Virden," Kit gritted out. "She's the sister of my brother-in-law."

"Family, eh?" Harry couldn't look more pleased. "Well, Miss Virden, I'd be happy to show you around."

"Right now, I'll settle for you showing her out the door," Ciara said. "No offense, but I need to start serving."

"Of course," Miss Virden said graciously. She turned to Harry, who was offering his arm with a big grin, and lay her slender fingers on the dirty, sweaty flannel. "I am at your disposal, Mr...?"

"Harry Yeager," he told her. "But I'd be honored if you would consider calling me Harry. This here's Jesse Willets, another fine gentleman of Wallin Landing. Come along, Kit. We wouldn't want Miss Virden to lose out on an opportunity to visit with her sweet little niece."

Katie Jo stepped aside to let them out the kitchen door. Then she dove out of sight behind the stove.

Ciara went to turn over the sign.

She took six orders before hurrying back to the kitchen to put the food on the plates.

"So that's the sort of gal men like, huh?" Katie Jo asked, gently squeezing a slice of orange over the carrot fritters as Ciara had shown her. "All prim and fussy like?"

"Some men prefer the helpless sort," Ciara agreed, ladling pork and cider stew into a bowl. "But I think you'll find most of the men who came to Seattle value a lady who can work beside them. It's not easy taming the wilderness all by yourself."

Katie Jo sighed as if she wished she could believe that.

They were so busy over the next three hours that Ciara had no time to spare to think about Miss Virden. It was such a blessing to have her friend beside her. Katie Jo washed and dried the dishes and had each table reset before Ciara could greet the next customers. And when a miner showed up drunk and disorderly, Katie Jo grabbed him by an arm and showed him to the door.

"That's some gal you got there," one of the prospectors said to Ciara, nodding in obvious admiration.

"See?" Ciara told Katie Jo when she mentioned the compliment. "There are plenty of men who like a lady who acts assertively."

"So long as I'm not assertive with them, I'll bet," she countered, but she was grinning.

Ciara didn't know where Harry, Kit, and Jesse ate, or Miss Virden for that matter, for they hadn't returned by the time she flipped the sign to Family Only that evening. After checking that the fire was banked for the night and everything was ready for breakfast in the morning, she led Katie Jo to her cabin.

"Here's your first pay," she said, pressing two silver quarters into the woman's hand. "You certainly earned it."

"Weren't nothing," Katie Jo demurred, but she fingered

the coins a moment before tucking them into her chest pocket.

"I didn't see you bring a valise," Ciara said. "Did you leave it on my porch?"

Katie Jo slapped her trousers. "Didn't see the need. I mostly just peel these off and sleep in my unmentionables."

Oh.

"I'd offer a nightgown," Ciara said, "but I don't think we're the same size."

Katie Jo barked a laugh. "That's for sure. Likely you take half the material I do for a shift and such."

"A few yards," Ciara allowed. Ahead, a tree swayed, as if blown by a breeze. She didn't feel a breeze. She moved closer to Katie Jo.

Who did not appear to be concerned in the slightest.

"I thought we'd share the bed," Ciara explained as she entered the cabin. "There's only one, but it's large. It's up in the loft."

She hadn't had to share a space since the children's home, but the cabin was nearly as big as Mrs. McNeilly's whole flat. Still, Katie Jo glanced up at the loft and shook her head.

"I'll just bed down by the fire, same as I do at home. Got a blanket you can spare?"

"Blanket and pillow," Ciara offered. "But it's a plank floor. There isn't even a rug."

"Never needed a rug afore."

Her mind boggled. She secured everything for the night in her cabin as well, then climbed the ladder to the loft and tossed down bedding to her guest. The look of Katie Jo in her red flannel long underwear, stretching out on the floor, tugged at her heart.

"If it's that bad at home," Ciara said, leaning her elbows on the railing that edged the loft, "why don't you just move in with me?"

"No, thank you," Katie Jo said. "My brother needs me.

The only reason our uncle let me go was the promise of that pie."

The more she heard about Katie Jo's uncle, the less she liked him. "He'll have it," Ciara said, "even if it sounds like he doesn't deserve it."

Katie Jo blew out the lantern. "He's not a bad sort," she said in the darkness that settled over them like a quilt. "He took us in when our parents died. But he can't do everything his own self, like you said. Me and Zeke have to contribute. Good night."

"Good night," Ciara called, recognizing a door being shut. She undressed in the dark, still wondering how she might be able to help her new friend.

She left Katie Jo sleeping the next morning, shoved her hair up into a bun, and pulled on one of her older dresses before dashing to the big cabin to finish breakfast. Porridge and applesauce were easy, and she knew Grace could eat both.

So, apparently, could Miss Virden, who showed up, eyes shadowed and pretty pink lips yawning, as Ciara was setting the table.

"Might I beg a cup of coffee?" she asked, sinking into the chair Harry usually used.

She ought to charge the woman but decided against it. Drew would likely expect her to extend hospitality. "Coming right up," Ciara told her.

Kit appeared in the archway a short time later as she was lifting the kettle of porridge from the stove to serve.

"Let me carry that," he offered, taking the handle from her grip.

She was almost afraid to ask the question that had been poking at her. "Where did Miss Virden sleep last night?"

"The teacher's quarters at the school," Kit said as she gathered her perforated tin cinnamon and sugar shaker. She had scraped the sugar cone and grated a cinnamon stick into it yesterday. "They haven't been used since

Rina married James, but John had repainted and Dottie redecorated for the new teacher, so the place was ready for an occupant. And Mr. Dullard said he was fine sleeping under the stars. James and Rina fed us all."

They came out of the kitchen together to find Harry bending over their visitor and Grace, wildflowers in his grip. Jesse dropped wood in the box with a crash.

The pattern was obvious.

"Smitten, both of them," she told Kit, after Harry and Jesse had declined breakfast to show Miss Virden around the area before they had to go to work. "Do they make such fools of themselves for every lady who shows up at Wallin Landing?"

"No, no, no, no, no," Grace said from her tall chair.

"You and Miss Virden are the first ladies to show up at Wallin Landing in a long time," Kit said, giving the baby some applesauce. "Not counting Miss McAllister." He lowered his voice. "They'd probably be chasing after her too, but I'm not sure they've figured out she's female."

"Well, they'll know soon enough," Ciara predicted. "And then I'll have to watch them make fools of themselves over her!"

Still, it wasn't just the men. She had to watch Miss Virden simper and smile at Kit for a good part of the morning as they sat with Grace in the main room of the cabin. Drew had excused him from work so he could spend the day with his newfound kin. Mr. Dullard had seemed content to prowl around the area like the lynx. She didn't like thinking who he considered his prey.

Kit didn't seem to have any concerns. He had pushed the extra tables against the rear wall to give the baby room to play on the rug. Miss Virden wouldn't deign to lower herself to the floor, but she sang to the little girl in a high, sweet voice and told her stories about her brother. Grace seemed captivated.

So did Kit. Ciara was highly tempted to march out

there, grab him by a dusky curl, and drag him to safety.

But they weren't really engaged, and she doubted Miss Virden, with her fine riding habit and delicate ways, would have wanted to remain in Wallin Landing.

Not even one more night, it seemed.

"I should return to Seattle," the lady told Kit that afternoon, as Ciara and Katie Jo were setting the tables for dinner. "Mr. Yeager and Mr. Willets offered to escort me and Mr. Dullard when they returned from work today. Just think about my offer, Kit. I'll just fetch my things from the school."

He nodded, and she rose to glide from the room.

Ciara set down her load of silverware with a rattle, feeling as if her own life had been as easily upended. "What offer, Kit?"

Kit ran his fingers back through his hair before turning to face Ciara. Her dark eyes were wide, and her fists were firmly planted on her calico-covered hips. Miss McAllister hurried for the kitchen as if she smelled trouble brewing instead of coffee.

"Elodie wants to bring Grace home with her," he said.

Ciara's brows rose. "*Elodie?*"

He shrugged. "She asked me to use her first name, since we're family of a sort."

"Of a sort," she drawled as he went to start tugging the tables and chairs back into place on the rug. "And where's home, exactly?"

"Apparently San Francisco. That's why she could reach us so quickly."

She took a step closer. "And you believe her when she says she's Grace's aunt?"

"No, no, no, no, no," Grace said.

He bent and picked up the baby. She regarded him solemnly, as if she was chiding him too.

"I don't know what to think. I don't remember Rudolph having a sister, but people were often surprised Hannah had a brother."

She crossed her arms over her chest. "And you're ready to hand Grace over because of a pretty face and good manners?"

He frowned. "I intend to make sure her papers are real. I'd hoped she might have a copy of Rudy's will, but he never sent one. But I must ask myself what's best for Grace."

She dropped her arms. "I thought we agreed it was best for Grace to be with someone who loves her."

"We are. Elodie loves her too. Her father left her an inheritance, so she need never want. And she can offer Grace things I can't—a home, a lady's guidance."

"So much guidance."

He knew sarcasm when he heard it.

"I didn't notice her offering to feed or change her," Ciara pointed out. "You know raising a baby is more than playing pat-a-cake."

"She can probably afford a nanny," Kit said, feeling compelled to defend the woman. "She can probably afford a lot of things I'll never be able to give Grace. How can I deny my niece those opportunities?"

She regarded him a moment, then shook her head. "Katie Jo's right. One look at prim and fussy, and your brains become addled." Even though there was a good half hour before it was time to open the restaurant, she marched to the window and flipped the sign.

And chaos reigned. Kit gathered up Grace and headed for the loft.

He came down again for dinner, Grace safely behind the chest at the top of the stairs. Ciara was taking orders from a group of eight men who had filled the long table. The other tables were also crammed. He slipped into the kitchen.

"Just fetching a plate for me and Grace," he told Miss McAllister, who was elbow deep in the wash tub.

"Bean and bacon soup and chicken and dumplings tonight," she told him. "Smells mighty good."

It did at that. "She sure can cook," Kit mused, ladling the savory dumplings onto his plate.

"She sure can. I hope you appreciate that."

He glanced up from considering the Spotted Pup that lay waiting, raisins gleaming like jewels in the white pudding. "I just said I did."

"And I hear you just spent the entire day mooning after that gal with the golden hair." She shook her head. "I don't think Miss Ciara liked that."

Had she been jealous? Why did that make him grin like a loon?

He finished loading his plate and left before he said something that might get him in more trouble.

CHAPTER NINETEEN

S UNDAY, CIARA WAS almost glad the restaurant was closed. Having Katie Jo working beside her had been a blessing, but both of them were tired. Her friend's slouch hat had sat even lower on her head as she'd prepared to start for home that morning. Ciara had counted out her earnings for Saturday night, plus a share of the considerations that had been left, then sent her off with a blackcap pie and the remainder of the Spotted Pup for her parsimonious uncle.

"I hope this rush didn't scare you," she said as Katie Jo stepped down onto the forest path. "I could use your help again next weekend."

Katie Jo shot her a grin. "I'll be here, but you'll see me afore then. I have enough for that material now. I need to talk to Mrs. Nora about a dress!"

"Maybe she could make you something prim and fussy," Ciara teased.

Katie Jo shuddered. "Where would I wear something like that? No, I'll just talk to Mrs. Nora and pick something sensible."

Sensible. That certainly wasn't the word Ciara would have used to describe Miss Virden. She'd left as well. Harry and Jesse had driven her in to Seattle with the buckboard wagon and James' steeldusts last evening, Mr. Dullard riding alongside as if he didn't trust them with their cargo. The absence of the two loggers would likely make the church feel a little less crowded than last week.

Finishing the other two pies for Sunday dinner had put her a bit behind that morning, so the clearing was quiet as she walked with Kit and Grace to the little chapel on the hill. The day was already warm. She was glad she'd worn her blue cotton print with the white daisies. With a silvery satin ribbon tied at her throat, she looked suitable for church.

Sensible.

She brushed her free hand along the skirts. There was nothing wrong with sensible. Like Katie Jo, she didn't need frills and furbelows to make herself feel like a lady. She *was* a lady. An accomplished lady, a cook. A business owner.

She must have been grinning, for Kit looked at her askance. "What's got you smiling?"

"Just thankful for my life," she said, giving her skirts a swish. "And for friends to help."

"Ah, friends," he said. Somehow, the word didn't sound so pleased coming from his lips. But she didn't have time to ask him what was wrong before they were through the doors of the church.

They slipped into place near the back as the congregation sang the opening hymn with gusto. Following the readings, Levi preached on being neighborly again. She'd listened to a couple pastors in Seattle who liked to wave their arms and use words with four syllables. His plain speaking suited her just fine.

"I've been hearing a few concerns about the number of people moving out our way," he began, glancing around at the miners, loggers, and farmers filling the church. A few shifted on the hard wooden pews or directed their gazes at the stained-glass windows. "I expect we'll see more as Seattle expands. I hear David Denny is already planning to sell lots for houses above the swale. How fortunate those folks will be to look down on grassland used for circuses and fairs and such."

Several grumbled. What, were they jealous of Mr. Denny's good sense in staking his claim along the base of Lake Union and up the closest hill, where Seattle was likely to grow? Or did they too wish they could build fancy houses overlooking a parkland?

"What is it we fear?" Levi challenged, spearing them with his midnight blue gaze. "Too few resources? Our Lord proved He could feed five thousand with only a few loaves and fishes! Of course, I'll bet He wished Miss Ciara O'Rourke had been there to help."

Ciara blushed as grins aimed her way.

Levi spread his hands. "Look around you, my friends. We have been blessed with more than we need. We shouldn't be afraid to give some to others. The blessings will only grow as they are shared."

"I like what he said," Ciara mused as she came out of services with Kit and Grace a short time later. "Blessings growing as they're shared. I certainly enjoyed sharing the work and the profits with Katie Jo."

"You both worked hard," Kit agreed as they headed for the cabin. "Why don't you let me make something for the family dinner this afternoon?"

Ciara laughed. "Too late! I already have two pies. But you can help by carrying the extra plates."

He sighed theatrically. "That's me—dish washer, dish carrier."

"Pie eater," she joked.

His smile trickled away. Grace must have spotted her swing, for she started bouncing in his arms. Whoops sounded from the swings he'd built by the school as the children went back and forth.

"You're not just a pie eater, you know," Ciara said, stepping up onto the porch of the big cabin. "You're an important part of Wallin Landing."

He avoided her gaze as he shifted Grace to his other arm. "Kind of you to say, but as far as I can see, the blessings have all been on my side."

"I don't think Drew, John, Frisco, and Sutter would see it that way," Ciara said. She reached out and tickled Grace under her chin, setting the baby to wiggling. "Grace certainly wouldn't see it that way. And neither would I. Everywhere I look, there's your handiwork."

He glanced around as if noticing it for the first time. "It's just a couple of swings and a few tables."

"Maybe," she said. "And maybe it's the encouragement we all needed. I know. At times, encouragement was few and far between. New York is a long way from Washington Territory."

He followed her into the cabin. "Your sister sent across the country for you. She must have wanted you."

"She did, and I will always be grateful. But Maddie has high standards, and there are times I fear I'll never live up to them. Not that she criticized," she hurried to add as they stopped on the rug. "I know my sister loves me and appreciates what I do. It just never felt good enough."

She glanced around at the homemade tables, the few crumbs left from Katie Jo's sweeping. "This feels real, like it's all mine. And it feels good."

"It should," he said. "You deserved every thank you and silver coin you made the last two weekends. You are amazing."

Her cheeks were heating as he took a step closer.

Grace wiggled between them. "No, no, no, no, no."

Ciara laughed. "Someone has a different opinion."

"Someone needs to be changed," Kit said. He headed for the stairs.

They played with Grace on the rug for a while, then took a stroll along the lake before returning to the house to retrieve the food and start for the hall. Others were making their way as well. Lars ran ahead of Drew and

Catherine, his little brother trying to keep up. Victoria walked with a high head beside Papa James and Mama Rina.

"I want to ask you something," Ciara said as they ambled in that direction as well. "What would you think about the cabin being used for more than a restaurant? Miss Virden proved that there's call for someplace to spend the night near Wallin Landing. I imagine there are others who camp in the woods. This could be an inn instead of just a restaurant."

He nodded thoughtfully. "Great idea." He glanced her way and grinned. "But you'll have to find something to do with me, Grace, Harry, and Jesse first. We're rather fond of our beds."

"I'll think on that," she promised with a laugh.

Suddenly, everyone stopped as the sound of horses' hooves heralded the arrival of a wagon. With a rattle of tack, Harry and Jesse pulled the buckboard up at the base of the hill.

Ciara stared. Kit's gaze went from her to the red-headed lady sitting on the bench between the two loggers.

"There you are!" her sister heralded even as Jesse jumped to the ground to help her down. Maddie strode to Ciara's side, forest green skirts snapping. "What's all this I'm hearing about you getting married? And why am I learning of it first from these two?"

Kit saw the change in Ciara. Her breath caught, and she raised her chin, as if ready for a fight. Her sister looked just as ready, brown eyes smoldering. He could see the resemblance in the delicate features, the dark sweep of their brows.

And the way those slender frames bristled like porcupines.

"Mrs. Haggerty," he said, stepping between them.

"I'm Christopher Weatherly, and this is my niece, Grace Virden. I'm so happy to finally meet Ciara's sister."

Maddie looked him up and down. "Tis happy I am to be meeting you both. Am I to take it you're the groom?"

Ciara latched onto him as if she would never let go. "Yes. He is."

Kit kept his smile in place. "Let's have dinner, and then I promise we'll explain everything."

"Maddie!" Catherine came hurrying down the hill, sky-blue skirts bunched in her fists. "I didn't know you were coming!"

"Sure-n, I didn't know it meself until these two stopped by the house this morning," she said with a jerk of her head toward Harry and Jesse, who were driving the buckboard toward the barn. "Would you be having room for one more at your table?"

"Always," Catherine promised. She linked arms and led Ciara's sister toward the hall.

Ciara slumped, as if she couldn't stand tall another moment.

Kit gave her arm a squeeze. "I won't leave you to face her alone."

She shot him a pale smile. "Thank you. Truly, I'm happy to see her. I just wasn't expecting it."

She was quiet through dinner, but that was to be expected. The Wallins were giving most of their attention to their guest. Though someone rode in for the mail every other day at least, there was always hunger for news of the city, the territory, and the wider world. Maddie could provide all three.

TP Freeman's store, which had burned down after the Centennial Celebration in July, was a loss, she reported, but the resilient businessman was already selling stock from his home. Front Street along the wharves was nearly impassable what with the new grading to level out the hills.

"And there's more calls for requesting admittance to the union," she told them all. "According to the *Daily Intelligencer*, the federal government will be giving Oregon more than one hundred thousand dollars to improve navigation on the Columbia River."

A murmur went around the table, likely at the astronomical number.

"Some are asking why we can't be given the funds to improve our own rivers," she continued. "And they're saying it's because we're only a territory."

"We'll be a state someday," Drew said, and his brothers nodded.

"The sooner the better," Simon agreed.

Maddie stuck her fork into the slice of blackcap pie Dottie had just served her. Kit recognized the fluting along the edges. That had to be one of Ciara's.

"Not soon enough for Michael and the Irish Brigade," her sister predicted. "They're talking of marching to Olympia and laying the case before the territorial governor." She picked at the crust and frowned.

Ciara rose in a flash of her flowered skirts. "More lemonade, anyone?" She all but ran toward the table along the wall, where the food and pitchers of water and lemonade stood nearly empty.

Callie had already appropriated Grace to play with her little niece, Mica, so Kit stood and followed Ciara to the table.

Her hands were trembling as she sloshed liquid into her glass.

"She didn't say she didn't like it," he pointed out quietly.

Her gaze brushed his and leaped away, like a deer startled in the wood. "She didn't say she liked it either."

"You didn't give her a chance."

She set down the glass. "You're right, but I couldn't bear to hear her say I'd failed."

He took both of her hands in his. "You haven't failed,

Ciara. Your restaurant is a wild success. Harry and Jesse and I have never eaten so well. You've made a place for yourself here."

"I want to believe that," she said. She raised her head. "Thank you, Kit. You know just what to say to calm my nerves."

"Then trust me to know what to say to your sister about this engagement."

She nodded, and they returned to the table with her glass. If they walked hand-in-hand, it would only support the ruse of their betrothal.

"Will you come home with us, Maddie?" Catherine asked as the ladies began gathering up what little remained of the food to return to the various houses. "We never used to run out of things to talk about."

"Sure-n I should spend time with my sister and Mr. Weatherly first," Maddie demurred with a pointed look in their direction.

"I'll take Grace for a nap," Nora offered.

And so Kit surrendered his niece to her and found himself walking along the lake again with a pretty lady on each arm.

The Wallins had cleared many of the big firs off a strip from the mercantile south for some distance to make the beginnings of a park. Drew had carved the benches that sat in the shade of the remaining trees. John had built the dock that ran out into the water. Frisco and Sutter were at the end, fishing poles in hand even though the day was likely too warm for the fish to rise to the bait. A cool breeze drifted across the blue-gray waters, and Mount Rainier rose in white and silver majesty in the distance.

"And now will you be telling me about this betrothal?" Maddie asked, tilting her head to see around him to her sister.

"It's not a true betrothal," Kit supplied. "We had a reason for claiming one."

Her sister drew herself up, but Ciara plunged in as if the words had been banging on her lips to escape.

"That's why I didn't come to tell you. Kit's sister and brother-in-law passed away and left him custody of his niece. Her grandmother showed up and demanded he give her over because he didn't have a wife. So, I pretended I was going to be his wife."

That wasn't the only reason Mrs. Virden had thought him a poor father, but Kit decided not to mention that at the moment.

Maddie shook her head, red hair catching the sunlight. "I can understand you wanting to protect that precious child. But will you be having no concern for your reputation, my girl?"

"Reputation?" Ciara snorted. "As if I need one. I could have had a dozen men in Seattle, more here!"

"And will they continue to be treating you with respect when they hear you're a jilt?" Maddie demanded.

"No one would dare to do otherwise," Kit said, feeling his own shoulders tighten at the very idea. "Not with the Wallins, Harry, Jesse, and me ready to lay into them if they tried."

Maddie chuckled. "Oh, I'm sure you boys would be terrible to behold." Her smile faded. "Still, I cannot be liking it, not when I can't be around to protect you."

Ciara bristled once more.

Kit stopped along the shore, the lap of the water softer than their conversation. "I won't let anything happen to her. I promise."

Ciara blinked, but her sister shook a finger at him even as she let go of his arm. "I'll be keeping me eye on you, Mr. Weatherly. You can promise all you like, but I'm thinking you'll have your hands full with that baby of yours."

Ciara must have expected him to say something more,

for she spoke up. "You aren't still thinking about giving Grace to her aunt, are you?"

"Aunt?" Maddie asked, glancing between them.

"Miss Virden showed up claiming to be the sister of Grace's father," Ciara explained. "She wants to raise Grace too. I can't help thinking we need to know more about her."

"She brought papers that verify her identity," Kit told them both. "Besides, she seems to know a great deal about his family. Certainly more than I did."

"So, you can't confirm the stories are true," Ciara pointed out.

"I suppose not," Kit admitted.

"Sometimes papers are only worth, well, paper," Maddie put in. "Why don't you be bringing them in to Hart McCormick? You can drive me home tomorrow. Sure-n someone here at Wallin Landing will put me up for the night."

"You're welcome in my cabin," Ciara said graciously.

"Good. That's settled." She rubbed her hands together. "Now, let's be seeing this restaurant I've been hearing so much about."

CHAPTER TWENTY

CIARA FELT AS if a skein of thread had tangled itself around her body, strangling movement, thought. She could barely walk into the cabin with Maddie at her side. She glanced around the room, trying to see it through her sister's eyes. Were the tables too rustic? Too close together? Had she made the wrong choice to keep to stews, soups, and chowders? Were her desserts too common?

Her gaze lit on Kit, who stood confident, comfortable, relaxed in his dark trousers and white church shirt. He'd been beside her at every step. He knew how hard she'd worked.

So did she.

"We started with the big table," she told her sister, "and a couple smaller ones along the back wall. But they filled too fast the first weekend, so Kit built me more."

"John, Drew, Harry, and Jesse helped," he put in.

Never one to brag, that fellow. "We still packed them in," Ciara said, "but I hired a new friend, Katie Jo McAllister, to help with the dishes and table clearing. That made a great difference."

Maddie wandered to the window and peered up at the sign. "And whose idea was this darling?"

"Kit's," Ciara said. "He thought I should have some

way to signal when I was serving folks outside the Wallin family and their crew."

She cast Kit a glance. "Clever fellow."

"Yes," Ciara said with a look to him. "He is."

He didn't argue, but pink was building above his beard.

She went on to show her sister her list of various dishes to include over time.

"Sure-n, you'll want to be watching the carrot fritters," Maddie warned. "I never could keep them from coming out too crisp."

"I remember," Ciara said. "I find adding a little cream makes all the difference."

Maddie glanced at her from the corners of her dark eyes. "Did you now? I'll have to be trying that."

Her, giving her sister advice! What was even more astonishing was that it sounded as if her sister might take it.

"Tis a fine place you have here," Maddie said as they came back out of the kitchen. "You'll be wanting a sign over the porch. Ciara's Restaurant?"

It was the logical choice, but it didn't sound right, as if someone had called her by the wrong name. "No. I haven't decided yet. It will come to me."

Maddie glanced around again, then met her gaze with a smile. "I think I'll be going up to visit with Catherine a wee moment. Will you come for me when you're ready to retire?"

"I will," Ciara promised. She walked her sister to the door and watched as she crossed the clearing.

"That went well," Kit ventured behind her.

"It did," Ciara said. The wonder of it curled around her, loosening the strands of anxiety that had held her tight. She turned to meet his gaze. "You're right, Kit. It's a fine restaurant, and it will only grow."

His eyes were warm and deep. "Yes, it will."

Words pressed against her lips. She'd been brave enough

to share her dreams with her sister. She should be brave enough to share them with him too, especially when more and more they centered on him.

But not just yet. It seemed too much, too soon. She'd already risked enough today.

"You should probably retrieve Grace," she said.

He nodded. "I'll see you in the morning." He started whistling a tune as he sauntered out the door. It sounded like The Rose of Tralee.

She stood at the window, watching him cross the clearing, hands in his pockets. There was a simple elegance about him, an ease of movement. He didn't swagger like Harry or lope like Jesse. He walked like a man who knew who he was and was content in that. A man that a woman could count on.

She finished setting the cabin to rights, then went to fetch her sister. At least Maddie wasn't opposed to sharing a bed with Ciara.

"I remember when you and Aiden and I had to crowd in one," her sister murmured as she snuggled under the quilt on the big bed in the loft.

"So do I," Ciara said beside her. "Those were dark days. You made them brighter."

Her sister's fingers brushed at Ciara's hair, as gentle as a dove's wing. "And you made them brighter for me, me darling girl. I've missed you, but I know why you came out here."

Ciara tensed. "I wasn't trying to leave you behind, Maddie."

"Sure-n, but I know that. You wanted something all your own, and you've done it. I hope you're as proud as I am."

Tears burned her eyes. "I am. I truly am."

"Good. Now, what about this young man of yours?" Humor underlaid her sister's tone.

"I told you, he isn't my young man," Ciara protested.

"And I'm thinking he could be."

She turned on her side. Her sister was another shadow in the bed, but she felt the warmth from her body. "Sometimes I think so too."

"And does that thought make you happy?"

"Yes," Ciara admitted. "But I haven't told him. I don't know whether he feels the same way."

"He has the look of it," Maddie said. "I saw how he watched you today, all pride and protection. Ready to sing your praises. Ready to ride in if I said something that might hurt."

"Friends do that too," Ciara pointed out.

"That they do. This seems more. But you'll only know if you ask."

And that would be her hardest task yet.

Ciara must have survived her evening with her sister, for both she and Maddie were in the kitchen when Kit brought Grace down the next morning. Jesse, who was on his heels, stopped at the bottom of the stairs and inhaled.

"Cinnamon rolls!"

"One of my sister's specialties," Ciara agreed, coming out of the kitchen with a cast-iron frying pan in her apron-covered hands. "And we have scrambled eggs and bacon to go with them."

Grace wiggled as if encouraging Kit to the table.

She needn't have bothered. He was moving as fast as Jesse.

Harry came down as they were taking their places. "Now, that's a breakfast." He straddled his chair and rubbed his hands together.

Ciara and her sister sat on the opposite bench, Kit said the blessing, and they all dug in.

"You working today?" Harry asked him around mouthfuls.

Kit grimaced. "Sorry. Drew said I could take Mrs. Haggerty back to town and pick up the mail."

Harry shook his head, but he didn't protest.

Nora, Catherine, and Rina were on hand to see them off. All three had come with Ciara's sister on Mr. Mercer's expedition ten years ago, Kit had heard. They hugged each other in the warm summer sun before he handed Grace to Nora and then helped Maddie up onto the bench. He turned to Ciara.

"Ready?"

She handed the sheath of papers Miss Virden had brought to her sister. "Ready."

He set his hands on her waist and lifted her up onto the bench. Easy to imagine holding her closer for a moment. Her cheeks were pink as she arranged her gingham skirts with her free hand. He thought his cheeks might match.

He checked the tack one more time, then climbed up onto the bench himself and set the steeldusts in motion. The Wallin ladies waved them out of the clearing. He thought he heard Grace shriek as the trees closed in around the wagon.

"So," Ciara's sister said in the shadowy path that smelled of the tang of cedar. "Tell me more about yourself, Mr. Weatherly. Would any of your family have been coming from Ireland?"

"Not to my knowledge," Kit said over the creak of the wagon. "My family had a farm outside Philadelphia for ages. My father told stories about relatives who fought in the Revolution. He decided to seek adventure elsewhere and brought us all West on a wagon train when I was a child."

"And *all* would be?" she prompted.

"My sister and I and our parents. Our mother died on the trail. Our father died after we had reached Tacoma. My sister was more than ten years older than me. She raised me."

She looked to Ciara. "So you have that in common."

"Yes," Ciara said, "though I get the impression you were a more tolerant older sister."

"Hannah had hopes," Kit allowed. "She ever only wanted the best for me. We just disagreed on what that meant."

"And what does it mean to you?" Maddie asked.

He thought Ciara was waiting for the answer as well.

"At first," he said, "it was about learning what lay beyond the horizon. Maybe my father's need to travel was in my blood. Then it was about trying to find the thing I was good at. Like you with baking and Ciara with cooking and running a restaurant."

"And what are you good at?" Maddie asked.

"Everything," Ciara answered before he could. "You saw the furniture he built and the sign he made. He built swings for the children too. He whittled me the prettiest wooden rose. He can wash dishes faster than anyone I know. He mastered your gravy on the second try. And he showed me all kinds of food, right in the forest!"

None of those things, with the possible exception of the furniture, seemed all that great an accomplishment to him. "I'm still looking," he told Maddie.

She nodded. "So long as you keep trying, there's no shame in that."

His sister would have disagreed with her.

But she asked him about the forest then, as if just as interested as Ciara in its bounty, and he spent the next little while pointing out plants and animals to them. Then the conversation moved on to the city and the territory and their plans for the future, including Ciara's idea of turning the cabin into an inn. Before he knew it, they had reached the edge of Seattle.

The city had grown the last few years, with houses pushing out to the north, east, and south and more docks stretching into the waters of Puget Sound on the west.

He guided the horses down the clear-cut hill to Second Avenue, where he knew Maddie had her famous bakery. As usual for that time of the day, there was already a line out the door.

Ciara frowned. "Who's on the counter?"

"Sure-n your brother offered to help," Maddie said as Kit set the brake. "Not that he wanted the job, mind you. I'm still looking for someone to my liking."

He climbed down and helped her off the bench.

"Thank you kindly for the ride, Mr. Weatherly. I expect I'll be seeing more of you."

"I hope so, ma'am," Kit said with a bow.

She laughed and waved a hand. "On with you, now. Make sure that sweet baby is cared for."

With another wave to Ciara, she swept into the knot of men, which parted as if they knew the true queen of the kitchen had arrived.

"Do you want to stay and visit your brother?" Kit asked, careful not to let his opinion show in his voice.

"No, thank you," Ciara said, facing front. "Aiden's made his thoughts known, and I'm not ready to hear them again. What I do want to hear is what Hart thinks about those papers."

Kit grinned. "I was hoping you'd say that." He climbed back up and set the horses in motion.

They located the deputy down by the docks. The latest steamer from San Francisco was in, and Hart appeared to be watching the newcomers as if suspecting more than one might be trouble.

Kit brought the wagon to a stop, set the brake, and handed Ciara the reins. Then he hopped down and came to take the papers from her. "Deputy? A word?"

The lawman turned to meet him as Kit came forward. "Problem, Mr. Weatherly?"

"Possibly." Kit went on to tell him about Elodie Virden's visit and showed him the papers.

Hart's face tightened with each word as his gunmetal-gray eyes scanned down the page. "I meet every steamer. Don't recall seeing an older woman come through recently, other than your sister's mother-in-law."

"She's a young woman, very pretty," Kit said. "Very pleasant too. Grace liked her."

"Sounds like a whole lot of people would like her." His eyes narrowed. "Can I hold onto these a while? I want to look them over more closely and send a telegram to the sheriff in San Francisco. He's been good about looking into folks for me."

"I'd appreciate it," Kit said. "If she is genuine, Grace may have a chance for a better home than I can give her."

Hart sent a glance toward Ciara. "Thought you were building a pretty good home."

"We have an understanding," Kit said lamely.

"Are you staying in town tonight?"

"No, we're heading back, as soon as the horses have a moment to rest."

"Then I'll ride out in a few days and tell you what I hear."

Kit thanked him again, then returned to Ciara. "Sure you don't want to see your brother? Lance and Percy could do with a rest before we start back."

She fidgeted with her skirts. "Let's go see Beth."

They spent an hour with the youngest Wallin sibling. Beth and her husband lived in a fine house up the hill from the Occidental Hotel. Every piece of furniture was well made and covered in fabric that looked too nice for the frontier town. Then again, Beth McCormick frequently looked as if she'd stepped out of the pages of the ladies' magazine she favored, *Godey's Lady's Book*. Kit's sister would have loved her.

He left Ciara with her friend and ventured down for the mail. He was coming out of the post office with a sack when a dark-haired young man barred his way. He wore a striped cotton shirt and gray flannel trousers, and there was something familiar about the way his dark eyes smoldered. When he put his hands on his hips and widened his stance, Kit knew.

"You're Aiden O'Rourke," he said.

Ciara's brother nodded slowly. "I am that. What's this I hear about you marrying my sister?"

Kit nearly groaned aloud. "Have you spoken with your other sister yet?"

His hands fell. "No. She's been too busy since returning from the Landing. But she said you and Ciara were in town. And you didn't bring her to see me. That told me all I needed to know." He put up his fists and set one foot in front of the other. "What have you done with my sister?"

Kit lowered the sack of mail carefully. "Nothing, I promise you. She's up at Beth McCormick's right now."

"Why should I believe you?" he demanded.

"I suppose you have no reason," Kit allowed. "You don't know me. But all you have to do is walk up the hill with me, and you'll see the truth of what I'm saying."

Once again, he dropped his arms. "I might do that."

"You *should* do that," Kit told him, feeling confident enough the boy wasn't going to swing at him to bend and pick up the sack of mail. "I think your sister would like to see you, if you can be pleasant."

"Pleasant," he spat out. "You don't know her very well, do you?"

But he fell into step beside Kit as he started back up Commercial.

"I think I know your sister fairly well," Kit said. "Enough to understand that family is important to her."

Aiden sent him a considering look. "Maybe, but Ciara and I don't always get along."

"My sister and I rarely agreed on anything," Kit said, leaning into the climb. "But she was generally glad to see me, at least so she could tell me how I should improve."

Aiden wrinkled his nose, reminding Kit of Ciara. "Oh, you had one of *those* sisters. Ciara's not like that. She doesn't fret over me or criticize my actions. Lately, she's more likely to forget I exist."

"I doubt that's true," Kit told him, breath coming harder from the climb. "Your sister is a very loving person."

He snorted. "With you, apparently."

They reached the house, and Aiden paused, glancing at the sturdy clapboard as if he thought it might tumble down the hill into the Sound at any moment.

"Come on," Kit urged him. He stepped up onto the porch and rapped at the door.

Ciara herself came to open it. She glanced from him to her brother standing in the street. Then she shoved past and launched herself at the lad.

CHAPTER TWENTY-ONE

CIARA DREW BACK at arm's length and took a good look at her brother. Aiden's dark hair had more than one cowlick in it. Like him, it was always swirling in multiple directions. But were those shoulders in the cotton shirt broader than she'd remembered? The look in his dark eyes wiser?

"I've missed you," she said.

He shook his head even as he shrugged out of her grip. "You have better things to do with your time than visit with me. You made that perfectly clear."

Guilt bit, and some of her sister's Irish brogue came out in her tone. "I wasn't after ignoring you, brat. Do you have any idea how hard it is to be starting a new restaurant?"

He rubbed a hand behind his neck as if it had heated with his cheeks. "No, but I'm beginning to have an idea of how hard it is to run one, what with me helping Maddie in your place. You've been missed as well."

"I told you you can always ride out to Wallin Landing," she reminded him.

He shook his head again. "I wouldn't have come here today if not for that man of yours. He talked me into it." He leaned closer, with a sidelong glance at Kit, who was keeping a distance as if to give them a little privacy. "He's remarkably reasonable. Not the sort I thought you'd end up marrying."

Ciara cuffed him on the shoulder. "Who did you think I would marry, then? Some fellow with sawdust for brains?"

"Nah," Aiden scoffed, straightening. "I thought you might be hanging after one of those poetic types the girls are always mooning over, like Vaughn Everard."

Ciara sighed. "Ah, but there is no one like Vaughn Everard, and he's been dead for more than twenty years!"

"There is that," Aiden allowed.

Beth came out on the porch then and waved a hand. "You needn't stand there talking. Come on in, Aiden. I have lemonade and some of your sister's gingerbread."

"Which sister?" Aiden asked, and Ciara cuffed him again.

Laughing, they all adjourned to Beth's parlor, where Aiden consumed far too many cups of lemonade and pieces of gingerbread while regaling Ciara and Kit about what had been happening in the city. Ciara kept glancing at Kit, who sat on one of Beth's fine chairs as if as comfortable there as on a stump at Wallin Landing. He wasn't as poetic as Vaughn Everard, or even Harry, but she was becoming more certain every day that he was the only one for her.

She just had to find a way to tell him.

It was getting late in the afternoon when Kit went to fetch the steeldusts from the paddock behind Beth and Hart's house. Lance and Percy came readily to his call, as if they knew he would be taking them home, and he set about putting them in harness.

"Good lads," he said as he settled the tack over their glossy hides. "It's not often you get to carry an Irish rose, I imagine."

As if cognizant of the honor, the team stepped lively as he guided them around the house for the front.

Aiden had already gone, and Ciara was saying her goodbyes to Beth on the porch.

"I hope the next time we see each other we can talk about weddings," Beth said with a look to Kit.

"Perhaps," Ciara said. But she lifted her skirts and hurried down the steps to the waiting wagon, climbing up onto the bench before he could offer to come around and lift her up.

Beth waved as Kit directed the horses out onto the street.

"We have to find a better way of explaining our situation," Ciara said as he drove them up the hill. "Sooner or later, they're going to expect us to marry."

"Sooner rather than later, if I had to guess," he said.

And the prospect gleamed brighter than the sun on Lake Union.

He nearly laughed aloud. He was falling in love with Ciara O'Rourke. He'd feared he had nothing to offer her, but he'd come to hunger for what she offered him— trust, respect, admiration. How could a man not love a lady who looked at him as if he'd hung the moon?

But could this amazing woman have come to care for him as more than a friend? He cast her a glance. Her gaze was steadfastly on the line of trees swiftly approaching.

All at once, the doubts were untenable. He navigated to the side of the road and drew the wagon to a stop.

"What's wrong?" she asked, leaning forward and tilting her head as if to study the horses. "Did one of them throw a shoe?"

"No," Kit said. "But I may have a better way to answer these questions about when we intend to wed. You told Mrs. Virden you preferred action. So do I."

He leaned over and pressed his lips to hers.

Like Fourth of July over Elliott Bay, like curling up in

front of the fire with a favorite book. Her lips hinted of the gingerbread they'd just consumed, and her hair was scented with roses. He had to force himself to lean back. He was fairly certain his smile was more crooked than Jesse's.

She stared at him. "Why did you do that? There's no one here to see us."

"I've been wanting to do that for days," Kit confessed. "I'm falling in love with you, Ciara."

She pressed her fingers to her lips, lips he had just kissed, lips he could still feel against his own. "Oh, Kit. I feel the same way."

He gathered her close then, her slender body trembling against his. A wave of thanksgiving swept through him, higher than an ocean peak. If more words and kisses were exchanged, only the forest gave witness.

At length, he drew back, but he kept one arm about her waist. "Nothing would make me happier than for this engagement to be real, Ciara, but I know I don't deserve you."

Her back stiffened, and she pulled away from him.

"Yes," she said, chin coming up and eyes smoldering like her sister's. "Yes, you do. But until you realize the truth of it, I'm not marrying you."

Oh, the maddening, wonderful, man! Ciara wanted to pull him close, run her fingers through that wild hair, and tell him again how much he'd come to mean to her. They were already partners in raising Grace, even in the running of the restaurant. She could see him beside her, friend, groom, husband, father of her children, if they were so blessed.

But if he could not appreciate his own worth, how could they build a future together?

"Ciara," he started, as if intending to argue with her,

but she arranged her skirts and faced front. With a sigh, he took up the reins and directed the horses out the forest road.

The sun was dipping toward the horizon. Long shadows fanned across the road, dappling Lance's and Percy's coats. The rattle of tack hid the quieter sounds of the woods, but she caught sight of a hawk crossing overhead. She rummaged in her brain for some way to make him understand.

"You saw me with Maddie," she finally ventured. "I was afraid of what she'd say about the restaurant. And then I realized it didn't matter. I'd built something fine and good, something that will grow even better with time and effort. What she thought of it was less important than what I thought of it."

He nodded, gaze out over the horses. "I'm glad you realized that. You are so talented, Ciara. You deserve to be recognized."

"So why," she challenged, "are your sister's expectations more important than your own?"

He started, and Lance and Percy obligingly picked up their paces. He let them canter for a bit, then slowed them down. Ciara waited.

"There's a difference between our situations," he said. "You know you have skills. You just had to step out from under Maddie's shadow. I'm in agreement with my sister. I'll never be the man she wanted."

"And why should you?" Ciara asked, frowning. "Why can't you be the man *you* want?"

"Because that man doesn't have a home for a wife and daughter nor skills to support them."

Frustration simmered in the admission. Ciara cocked her head. "I've seen the work you did with the tables and chairs. I've heard Drew praise your efforts with an ax. You are perfectly capable of building and supporting a home for a wife and family. Perhaps you don't have one merely because you haven't needed one until now."

His shoulders rose and fell in a deep sigh. "Or maybe I'm the useless sack of bones my sister claimed all along."

If his sister had been here, Ciara would have been delighted to correct her impression. What sister was so cruel? Then again, hadn't she said things to Aiden that had kept him from wanting to associate with her? Perhaps it was the way of brothers and sisters, always testing each other.

But she knew she could count on Aiden in a pinch. And Kit's sister Hannah had known she could count on him, or she would never have sent Grace to him.

"Bosh," Ciara said. "I know a useless sack of bones when I see one. Take Scout Rankin's father. You never met him, I know. He passed five years ago now. *He* was a useless sack of bones. He never proved up his claim enough to keep it. He used it more as a den of iniquity than a home. He made Scout cook and clean and fetch fresh victims to cheat at his card games. And his son went on to become one of the wealthiest, most respected men in Seattle. Despite him."

He cast her a considering glance, straightening. "So, despite Hannah, I can still make something of myself."

"You already have," Ciara insisted. "All you have to do is open your eyes and see it."

He was quiet most of the rest of the way to the Landing, as if she'd given him much to think about. He'd certainly given her plenty. He claimed to be falling in love with her, and she could believe it from the way he treated her, as if she were clever and beautiful and worthy of all praise. She'd told him she cared about him.

They'd pretended to be engaged. Did these confessions mean they were?

He reined in at the porch of the big cabin, then came around to help her down. As she stood in his embrace, he lifted a hand to her cheek. "I want to be a man you can be proud of, Ciara. You deserve no less."

She held his hand against her skin, allowed the warmth to seep into her. "You already are, Kit. Please, believe that."

His smile said he was trying.

While he returned the wagon to the barn, took care of Lance and Percy, then went up to fetch Grace, Ciara started dinner for the three of them, Harry, and Jesse. She hadn't wanted to leave the stove going with no one to watch it, so she had to build up the fire. While the oven warmed, she put together a quick hash from ham and potatoes, grated some carrots, and made up the batter for fritters. Harry and Jesse came in as she was setting the table.

"Good news from town?" Harry asked, pausing at the foot of the table. Jesse stopped to hear the answer as well.

"Deputy McCormick will look into the matter," Ciara told them. "That's all we can do for now."

Jesse sighed.

Dinner was more challenging than usual. Sitting beside Kit at the long table, she had never been more aware of him. The moment he reached for the pitcher of lemonade and his arm brushed hers. When he turned to say something to Harry, and his leg bumped her skirts. And when he forked up a fritter and grinned, sugar sparkling on his lips, it was all she could do not to lean over and kiss it off. Oh, but she had it bad!

Harry glanced out the window. "At least an hour of daylight left. Would you two be willing to help me with my cabin? I just about have the porch on."

Jesse nodded. Kit looked to the baby in the tall chair beside him. "I should tend to Grace."

"I'll watch her," Ciara offered. "Harry's hoping to go courting soon. He'll want a house ready for his bride."

Harry grinned at that, but some of the air seemed to have gone out of Kit's lungs, and she chided herself for reminding him of what he had yet to achieve.

The three men helped clear the table, then headed out. Ciara wheeled Grace's chair into the kitchen and positioned it near the tub of dishes.

"We can certainly fend for ourselves," she told the baby, handing her a wooden spoon, which she happily waved, as if conducting a fine orchestra.

By the time the dishes were washed, dried, and put away, Grace's little head was bobbing. Ciara picked her up and rocked her in the chair. The words Harry had sung to her when she'd first come to Wallin Landing came to mind, only it was Kit's voice she heard as she sang it to Grace.

"The pale moon was rising above the green mountain.
The sun was declining beneath the blue sea,
when I strayed with my love to the pure crystal fountain
that stands in the beautiful vale of Tralee."

The door opened, and Kit paused in the doorway, gaze tangling with hers. Warmth bathed her, as if she'd opened the oven door to find her cake the perfect height and color. He came to her and bent, lips brushing her heated skin.

Grace sighed happily in her sleep. Ciara knew the feeling.

With a chuckle, he retrieved the baby. "Shall I walk you home?"

"Please?" Ciara said, rising. "If you think Grace can manage a few more moments."

"It's more of a question as to whether I can manage without you," he said.

Harry, who had been coming in with Jesse, stepped aside to let them exit. Ciara was sorry for the sad look in his eyes, as if he envied what she and Kit had discovered.

She could only hope he would find the right lady for him soon.

And hope that Kit would realize he was truly all she needed in a husband.

CHAPTER TWENTY-TWO

KATIE JO ARRIVED at the big cabin the next morning before any of the menfolk were down.

"You must have risen early," Ciara told her friend as she stood by the stove, flipping griddle cakes.

Katie Jo nodded, rubbing her side with one hand. "Gave myself a stitch I walked so fast. But I wanted to ask you a favor. Would you watch Grace this morning so Mrs. Nora can take the measurements for my dress?"

"Of course," Ciara agreed. "Grace and I are old friends. We get along fine."

Thumps on the stairs heralded the arrival of the three loggers. "Stay for breakfast?" Ciara asked, settling her cakes with the others on a platter.

Katie Jo shook her head so hard her hat slipped on her hair. "I'll head up to Mrs. Nora's," she said, backing toward the rear door. She had whisked herself out of sight by the time Harry poked his head into the kitchen, brows up in question.

"Coming," Ciara promised him, picking up the jar of preserves with her free hand.

She explained the change in plans to Kit as they ate.

"Happy to help a friend," he said. "If you're sure you don't mind."

"Not in the slightest," Ciara assured him. "I want Katie

Jo to get that dress, sooner rather than later." She nodded toward Harry.

As if he'd noticed, the logger frowned. "This Katie Jo, is she the gal you mentioned in the area?"

"She is," Ciara promised him. "And I think you'll see her clearly once Nora has her dress done."

"Must be some dress," Harry muttered before attacking his griddle cakes again.

They left a short time later. Kit glanced back more than once before disappearing among the trees. Ciara wasn't concerned. With the lynx gone, the clearing didn't feel nearly so dangerous. Or perhaps she was finally starting to feel at home.

Grace, unfortunately, did not seem nearly as pleased with the sunny morning. Ciara had placed her in her swing so she could start a load of wash in the big tub in front of the cabin. All the napkins had to be cleaned and bleached, and her aprons were beyond needing cleaning.

"No, no, no, no, no," Grace scolded her, as if she thought Ciara was putting too much soap in the water.

Ciara straightened. "Well, you can do it your way when you're old enough. This is how I do the laundry."

Grace pouted.

Ciara spotted Catherine coming across the clearing, practical brown skirts gathered in one hand and basket on the other arm.

"Callie says the huckleberries behind the cabin are coming on," she reported to Ciara as she drew closer. "Dottie is watching all the children at the farm. Rina and I are going to help Callie pick. Would you like to join us?"

Ciara pointed her wash stick at the tub. "I really should get these done. Another time? But if you have any extra, you know I'll take them."

"Of course." Catherine paused to tickle Grace before moving around the cabin. A short while later, Rina and

Callie passed by as well. The latter must have noticed Ciara's glance at the gunbelt around her hips, for she patted the revolver.

"Just in case the lynx comes calling," she said.

Ciara shared her grin.

She kept working. Maddie had been employed as a laundress before leaving New York and when she first arrived in Seattle. It was hot, heavy work. She could see why her sister had wanted more.

She heard the hoofbeats a moment before a dappled gray horse appeared between the trees. She recognized the rider a moment later, but not the two men at his back. One was a beefy fellow with a fierce black mustache. The other had sandy scruff on his chin and a crooked nose. The three cantered into the clearing and set their horses in a half circle around her, for all the world as if they intended to come in and set a spell.

She shoved an apron deeper into the wash tub with her stick. "Restaurant's only open Friday and Saturday evenings, gentlemen. If you want supplies, I'd recommend the mercantile by the lake."

"We didn't come to eat," Mr. Dullard said, leaning a fist on the pommel of his saddle. "We came for Grace."

Fear flashed through her like lightning before the thunder. She backed up until she was standing in front of Grace, shielding the baby from his view.

"That's against the law," she said, hating that her voice shook along with her legs. "You have no right."

"You probably heard that might makes right." He nodded, and his two men swung down from their saddles.

Ciara turned and snatched the baby up into her arms.

Grace shrieked. Loud. Long. Until Ciara's ears were ringing. The two men fell back. Their horses shied. Lance and Percy trumpeted from the pasture.

Ciara only wanted more noise.

"Help!" she shouted. "Help us! Villains! Brigands!"

"That won't do you any good," Dullard said calmly. "I've been watching. Your menfolk are gone. The loggers are up north, the farmer on the hill, the merchant down by the lake, the preacher out being neighborly, and the one on the road headed for Seattle for the mail. You're alone."

Panic was as tight as her grip on the baby, but the cock of a rifle sounded as loud as Grace's shriek.

"There, you would be mistaken," Rina said, gun up and at the ready, as she came around the cabin, Callie and Catherine right behind.

The leader chuckled. "You're the schoolmarm. You ought to be able to figure the odds. We may be even numbers, but only one of you is armed."

"Make that two," Callie said, drawing her revolver.

"Still two to three," he said as his men drew their guns as well.

Ciara could hardly catch her breath, her heart was pounding so fast. Grace snuggled closer with an uncertain whimper.

Rina aimed the gun out into the clearing. The two men hesitated. Looking grim, she fired. The sound echoed across the fields, likely across the lake.

"You can't even fire that thing right," Dullard sneered.

But Callie and Catherine were smiling, and Ciara knew why. One shot—sure to bring every Wallin man at a run. Kit would be here soon, with Harry, Jesse, and Drew. Likely Simon was already heading down from the farm and James up from the mercantile. She ran her hand over Grace's back and sent up a prayer.

Dullard's men must have decided Rina's gun posed little threat, for they started forward again.

"Into the house, ladies," Rina said, rifle now aimed their way. "Ciara, you first."

Somehow, she made her legs obey, backing for the door behind her.

"No, no, no, no, no," Grace scolded the men.

Callie and Catherine followed her, and Rina came last, shutting the door. Callie and Catherine dragged the big table over to block it.

"Now what?" Ciara asked, jiggling Grace even as the scruffy-chinned fellow peered in the window, then ducked out of sight.

"Up the stairs," Rina advised. "They'll find the kitchen door soon before we can barricade it."

The women gathered their skirts and climbed the stairs. The kitchen door crashed open as they all reached the top.

They had invaded Ciara's kitchen.

Her kitchen.

She straightened, then nodded toward the trunk set against the wall. "Kit uses that to keep Grace from climbing down. Maybe we can use it to keep them from climbing up."

Callie and Catherine positioned it, then Callie and Rina hunkered down behind it, guns trained on the stairs. Catherine drew back a little way with Ciara.

"We only have to hold them off a short time," the nurse said in a calm voice Ciara could only envy.

She nodded.

The man with the black mustache appeared at the foot. He raised his gun and aimed it at the blond heads sticking up over the trunk.

Ciara stiffened.

"I wouldn't do that if I were you," Catherine called. "Ride away now, and you might escape. Harm one of us, and there will be no safe place for you to hide."

"Folks around Seattle don't take too kindly to ladies being threatened," Callie agreed, the hammer on her revolver clicking into place. "Even little ladies."

He lowered his gun and glanced toward his leader for

direction. Dullard and scruffy-chin joined him at the foot of the stairs.

"They're bluffing," Dullard said. "Go get the baby."

Catherine stepped in front of Ciara like a shield.

"Hello the house!" James's voice called from outside. "Everything all right in there?"

Ciara counted off the seconds to the thudding of her heart. If Rina called her husband in, he would walk into an ambush. If she didn't, Dullard might succeed in taking Grace.

Dullard must have figured his own odds, for he jerked his head toward the kitchen. His men backed away, never taking their eyes off the knot of women, then disappeared through the archway.

"This isn't over," Dullard promised before following them.

A rifle barked in the distance. Kit raised his head from where he'd been helping Harry position the springboards in the massive tree so they could use the long crosscut saw. Axes stilled as Jesse and Drew waited, listening.

No other shot came.

"Not again," Harry moaned, but he grabbed his ax, and they all went running.

James and Simon were there ahead of them, as were Rina, Catherine, Callie, and Katie Jo. But Kit didn't spot Ciara until Rina and Catherine stepped aside.

She was sitting on the porch, arms cradling Grace, who had her thumb in her mouth, eyes huge.

His heart stuttered.

He dropped the ax and ran to kneel in front of them. "What happened? Are you all right?"

Her face was pale, but her chin was up and determined. "They came for Grace."

He helped her to her feet and kept one arm about her

waist in support as he turned to the others. "Who? Mrs. Virden? What happened?"

"Catherine, Callie, and I were picking huckleberries when we heard Grace scream," Rina explained. "I found three men on horseback surrounding her and Ciara. I took down the rifle and confronted them."

James tugged her closer. "Brave, mad woman that you are."

"It was your blast that called us in," Drew realized.

Rina nodded.

"We retreated to the loft," Catherine told her husband, moving to his side and laying a hand on his chest. "But they nearly took Grace anyway. The sight of Rina and the rifle and Callie and the revolver daunted them, and the sound of help coming set them to running."

"That and Catherine's reminder that they'd never be safe again if they harmed one of us," Callie put in. "But I don't think we've seen the last of them. Their leader warned they'd be back."

Kit felt the shudder go through Ciara. "It was that Mr. Dullard," she told him, gaze rising to his and filled with indignation. "He said he'd been watching us. He knew where you all were."

"No, no, no, no, no," Grace argued. She shook her little fist at Kit to emphasize the point.

Anger burned through him like a white-hot flame. "Where are they now?"

"We aren't certain," Catherine said. "The horses were gone by the time we ventured down." She looked to James.

"I was first to respond," he allowed, "but I didn't catch sight of them either."

"Just in case they headed south," Catherine said, "Nora took the forest path to check on Dottie and the children. Dottie was caring for them this morning, so we could pick."

His shoulders tightened as they all gazed down the road back to Seattle. If anything happened to any of the Wallin children because of the trouble he'd brought to their door…

Simon broke away at a run, and Kit sighted Dottie, Nora, and the children hurrying from behind the barn, where the forest path to James' and John's claims began. He wasn't the only one counting heads. Mothers and fathers hurried forward to gather their loved ones close.

"We're fine," Dottie said, Peter up in her arms. "Nora told us what happened, but we never saw those men, coming or going, and we were all out on the front lawn where we would have noticed anyone on the road."

"Could Dullard have a hideout in the area?" Simon asked, one arm protectively about his wife.

Ciara shook her head. "I thought he worked for Elodie Virden." Once more her gaze brushed his. "You had nearly decided to let her raise Grace. Why come steal her now?"

"I don't know," Kit answered. "But I'm not letting them get away with this."

"We'll track them," Drew said. He raised his chin and glanced around. "Where's John?"

"Riding for the mail," Dottie said. "I don't expect him back until evening."

Drew's face fell.

"It's all right." Kit heard his voice at a distance. "I can track them. John taught me how. We need to find them and let them know they can't get away with threatening those we love."

Ciara sucked in a breath. He smiled for her sake, arm tightening at her waist.

"Right," Drew said. "Kit will be our eyes. See if you can spot which way they went from the clearing."

The confidence in the words made Kit's shoulders relax as he nodded.

"Simon," Drew continued, turning to his next oldest brother, "fetch down your horses. Harry, go get the other of John's pair. James, we'll take Lance and Percy as well. Jesse can help you saddle them."

Frisco and Sutter shouldered their way forward from among the children. "We can come too," Frisco offered, eyes narrowed and frame stiff.

"Levi taught us to shoot," Sutter added. "Though I don't think he meant us to shoot people." He glanced at his sister, Callie, as if for support.

Before she could speak, Frisco rounded on him. "These aren't people. They're no good skunks."

"They are people."

Drew's deep voice was as loud as a thunderclap.

"People who have broken the law," he went on. "As such, they will be captured and turned over to the sheriff. Understood?" His dark blue gaze held each man's in turn. Kit nodded again and saw others doing the same.

Drew turned to the twins, whose heads were now hanging. "I appreciate the offer to come with us, but I have more important work for you. I need you to stay and protect our family."

Their heads popped up.

"Yes, sir," they chorused.

"I can go with the menfolk," Katie Jo spoke up. "I can shoot."

Harry frowned as if noticing her for the first time. "Who are you?"

"Katie Jo McAllister," she said, raising her head to meet his gaze. "I'm Miss Ciara's assistant."

"And I need you here with me," Ciara said, voice as determined as her chin. "I'm going to have dinner waiting for you all. I suggest, gentlemen, that you don't want to be late."

She pressed a kiss against Kit's cheek and marched into the house, Katie Jo behind her.

The group split up. Most of the women and children headed for the farm with Nora at the front like a band leader drilling for a parade. She carried off Grace as well. The men went for horses and equipment. For a moment, he felt useless, all the old complaints from Hannah and Rudy pummeling him anew.

But he wasn't useless.

Ciara was right. All the things he'd done, everything he'd learned, were tools in a chest, not toys to be cast aside when they no longer amused him. He could bring them out to help his family.

His family. Ciara. Grace.

He would let nothing harm them.

He began casting about the clearing, gaze on the ground and senses tuned. The dirt around the big cabin was a jumbled mess from the horses and the number of people who had trod it in the last hour. He fanned wider, until he was standing at the head of the tunnel of trees back to Seattle. Something about it struck him as wrong.

James came to join him, leading his prized horses. The steeldusts looked none too pleased to be wearing saddles. Lance kept tossing his black mane, and Percy picked his way carefully, as if expecting the tack to slide off otherwise.

"I can hold Lance while you mount," James offered.

Kit shook his head. "There's no dust."

"Well, I do my best to keep my tack in order," James allowed. "Though I haven't polished the brass in a bit." He grinned at the pun.

"No, there's no dust on the road," Kit said, turning. "I haven't felt a breeze today, and we haven't had rain for several days. If three men on horseback had gone pelting down that way a short time ago, the dust would still be lingering."

James peered into the shadows. "You're right."

Kit's gaze fell to the road. "And not a sign of a hoof

print. Tell the others. We may not be riding after all."

As James led his horses back toward the barn, Kit turned for the overgrown garden at the side of the house. He skirted the forest until he'd reached the southeast corner of the garden, nearest the lake. Sure enough, branches were snapped, about at the height of a horse's belly. Deeper in, he could see ferns crushed.

The others were heading in his direction. Simon reached him first.

"They're heading along the lake," Kit reported. "You were right. They must have a hideout in the area." He shook his head. "Was he working for Mrs. Virden after all, then?"

"Perhaps they both were," Simon said, following Kit's gaze into the forest. "The so-called aunt and her henchmen. Still, the grandmother must know you wouldn't allow Grace to be kidnapped."

"Mrs. Virden thinks very little of me," Kit said.

And he was about to prove her wrong.

From the depths of the wood, a loon called, low and mournful. A moment later, another answered.

A chill went through him. "Those aren't loons," Kit murmured to Simon. "They call mostly at twilight. They're watching us, waiting for us to head to Seattle so they can make another try to kidnap Grace."

Simon lay a hand on his shoulder. "Then we wait for the others, and we confront them."

Kit purposely turned away from the woods, as if the cry of the loon had meant nothing to him. "No, I think we should give them exactly what they want. Let's get the others."

CHAPTER TWENTY-THREE

"**S**TILL NO SIGN of them," Katie Jo reported from her place at the window in the main room of the cabin. "Not sure why all the menfolk decided to ride for Seattle, but I've never seen Wallin Landing so quiet."

Ciara had stirred the ham and bean soup enough to cause a froth. She forced herself to pull out the wooden spoon. She had to concentrate on something in her control, namely, dinner, or she'd go mad. A loaf of her molasses oat bread was sliced and ready, with butter and peach preserves to go with it. Gingerbread was baking in the oven, the scent drifting through the cabin. She clung to the smell of home.

Home. Until recently, that had meant Maddie, Aiden, and Michael. Now it meant Kit and Grace.

As it was, Catherine, Nora, Callie, Rina, and Dottie had taken all the children up to the farm on the top of the hill, where they planned to barricade themselves inside the big farmhouse. They had taken Grace with them. It had seemed the safer location, given that Dullard and his men had seen her more often at the big cabin. She and Katie Jo might have gone too, but Ciara had craved the comfort of her kitchen. She had commenced chopping and mixing, anything to keep her hands and mind busy.

Anything to stop thinking about what might happen.

About all she stood to lose.

Had he been injured? Had they captured those men? How would she and Kit keep Grace safe in the future if Mrs. Virden persisted in her threats?

Katie Jo's breath hissed so loud Ciara heard it over the bubble of the soup. Glancing out the archway, she saw that her friend had plastered herself against the wall on the other side of the window. Catching Ciara's eye, she tilted her head toward the glass.

Ciara went to the kitchen window and peered out. Dullard and his men were crossing the clearing, heading for the path up the hill.

"No!" She ran to the kitchen door, yanked it open, and barreled out onto the porch, reaching for the one thing that would call help to her side. Her hand met air.

Rina had taken the rifle.

Even as she opened her mouth to shout, to scream, anything to bring help running, Drew and Simon rode out from behind the schoolhouse.

Dullard and his men pulled up short.

James and Jesse rode out from behind the barn.

Dullard's men turned tail.

"Go back inside, Ciara," Kit called as he and Harry strode past. "We're almost done here."

She stood there, mouth agape, as the Wallin men, Harry, Jesse, and Kit surrounded the would-be kidnappers.

Something tugged at her arm, and she glanced over to find Katie Jo beside her.

"Come on," her friend urged. "You don't want to be out here when the shooting starts."

With a shudder, she allowed Katie Jo to lead her back inside.

But neither of them could stay away from the window. They peered out of the kitchen at the tangle of people, Ciara keeping an eye on the wild black curly hair of the man she loved.

Katie Jo sniffed, then glanced toward the stove. "Is something burning?"

Her soup!

She ran to the stove, yanked the pot off the burner.

"Tell me what's happening!" she begged as she checked for scalding.

"Mr. Drew and a bunch of them have the fellows tied. Your other two loggers are heading into the woods. Kit's a talking something fierce. Wish I knew what he was saying."

So did she.

Ciara was pulling the gingerbread out of the oven when Katie Jo stiffened. "Here they come!"

She dropped the pan on the warmer and raced out the kitchen door.

Kit met her on the porch and caught her to him. "It's all right," he murmured, holding her close. "Everything is going to be all right."

With his arms around her, she could almost believe that.

"What happened to the rest of them?" Katie Jo asked, joining them.

"Heading to Seattle," Kit supplied. "Taking Dullard and his men to jail."

"That's it?" Ciara demanded, pulling back. "Kit Weatherly, explain yourself this minute!"

"I will," he promised. "But first, there's something I have to do." He took her face in his hands and kissed her.

She closed her eyes, savoring the taste of him, her heart, her home.

"I love you, Ciara O'Rourke," he murmured as he drew back. "And I want to spend the rest of my life with you. I'm starting to see things your way."

She cocked her head. "My way?"

"That fellow you're so fond of might not be such a bad one after all," he allowed.

Her smile grew as she straightened. "Not a bad one at all. In fact, I'd say my frontier sweetheart would make the perfect groom."

He grinned. "Well, then, I guess we have an understanding."

"We do," she agreed, heart overflowing. "And I'm going to hold you to it."

It wasn't until two days later that they learned the whole story. Drew, Simon, James, and Harry had come home immediately after their trip to Seattle, so Ciara knew that the Dullard gang had been turned in to the sheriff. But none of the three villains had been willing to speak about why they'd wanted to kidnap Grace.

"Trying to keep their necks from the noose," Simon had said.

Ciara wasn't so sure. Could they be protecting Mrs. Virden? Or was Grace's grandmother so powerful they were afraid of her retaliation if they implicated her? She found herself watching the road to Seattle, waiting.

A gentleman rode in on Thursday. She was out on the porch churning when she spotted the fine bay all but prancing out of the trees. She lowered the paddle into the cream and straightened, mentally tallying the closest help. Grace was up on the ridge with Nora and Simon, but James was at the mercantile. Kit and the others were working fairly close. She glanced quickly at the rifle before the rider reined in by the porch and swept off his short-crowned hat to reveal light brown hair neatly trimmed.

"Good day, madam," he greeted in a warm tenor. "Could you confirm I've reached Wallin Landing?"

"That you have," Ciara said, head up. "What brings you to the settlement?"

He swung down from the horse, offering a brief glimpse

of tailored trousers under his leather duster. "I'm seeking Christopher Weatherly. I understand he resides here."

Oh no! She put her hands on her hips. "Kit's had enough trouble, so you better not be bringing more."

His brows went up, then he put on a pleasant smile. "No trouble, I promise. In fact, I hope he'll be highly pleased by what I have to say." He glanced around. "Would little Grace be nearby?"

That was it. No one was taking her family. She dropped her hands, marched to the porch support, and unslung the rifle. He started backing up even as she pointed at the ground and fired.

He held up his hands. "If you mean to warn me off, you've mistaken your man."

"And if you think I'll stand by while you threaten Kit and Grace, you've mistaken your woman," she said, cradling the gun across her chest.

His mouth quirked as he cautiously lowered his hands, as if he were fighting a smile. "You must be Ciara O'Rourke. Mrs. McCormick said you might be on your guard."

"Just because you use my friend's name doesn't mean I'll trust you," she warned him.

"Understandable," he said. "But she and Deputy McCormick promised to follow me out here. I expect them any moment."

He threw his hands back up as James swung around the porch. She caught a flash among the trees on the hill, Simon, on his way.

"Another one?" James demanded, shaking his head.

The stranger gave him a nod. "Dixon Hitchcock, attorney for the Virden estate, at your service, sir."

Could it be? Ciara took another look at the long leather duster, the fine horse, the tooled saddle. Either he was a lawyer with wealthy clients or one of the best outlaws in the area. She was willing to bet on the former.

She lowered the rifle, relief pulsing through her. "You should have introduced yourself the moment you rode up. We've been hoping you'd arrive for days. Kit has so many questions for you!"

They all had the opportunity to ask when Kit, Harry, Jesse, and Drew thundered out of the woods a short time later to discover that Beth and Hart had arrived as well. It took a few moments to gather the rest of the Wallin adults to the big cabin. They allowed most of the children to play in the yard, under the questionable supervision of Frisco and Sutter, though both Nora and Rina were stationed at the window to watch as well. Mica was napping upstairs in her old cradle. To be on the safe side, Kit had placed Grace in the tall chair next to him and Ciara, where they sat on the bench at the long table.

"So why are three men trying to kidnap Grace Virden?" Drew demanded, dark blue gaze moving from the attorney to Hart.

Hart spoke first where he stood by the hearth, Beth in her mother's rocking chair beside him. "We only have an inkling thanks to Mr. Hitchcock. Turns out the Dullard gang was wanted for armed robbery and horse theft around Olympia, Yelm, and Tacoma, though this was the first time they'd tried kidnapping."

"They had to know I didn't have enough money to make the effort worthwhile," Kit protested. "Did they hope to ransom her to Mrs. Virden instead?"

"But I thought they worked for Mrs. Virden," Ciara put in.

Mr. Hitchcock raised a hand. "If I may?"

Hart nodded.

He stood, moved into the center of the braided rug, and struck a pose, as if prepared to address a jury. "I have served Mr. Rudolph Virden for the last five years. It was my sad duty to carry out his final wishes and that of his late wife, Hannah Weatherly Virden. Among them was to see their only child delivered to her uncle, Christopher Weatherly."

Kit leaned forward. "Those were Rudy's wishes, not just Hannah's?"

"Indeed," Mr. Hitchcock assured him. "Mr. Virden made his will some time ago, and he confirmed its stipulations with his wife before his untimely demise. I was making the necessary arrangements when a maid in the house alerted me that strangers had been seen prowling about the premises. I notified the local authorities, but when we arrived at the house, we discovered that the valet had disappeared, and so had little Miss Virden."

"Bottles must have decided to safeguard Grace," Kit mused. "That's why he tried to bring her to me."

"So we surmise," Mr. Hitchcock agreed. "But the disappearance gave us a bad few days, I promise you. There was no reason to think she had come to you, and I didn't want to reach out until she was found."

Hart took up the tale. "We figure the prowlers were Dullard and his gang. News of Virden's death, and the size of his estate, were reported in the papers."

"Against my strict orders," the lawyer added. "But once the word was out, Dullard saw an opportunity too good to pass up."

"What about Miss Virden?" Harry asked. "The sister."

Dixon Hitchcock regarded him sadly. "Rudolph Virden was an only child. He has no sister."

Harry stiffened. "You mean she was a fraud?"

"A very talented actress," Beth said. "From a troupe currently touring Tacoma and Olympia. I've no doubt Mr. Dullard hired her for her winning ways."

Harry grunted, but he dropped his gaze.

"I've already alerted the sheriff in Pierce County to look further into the lady," Hart said.

Mr. Hitchock nodded. "And I at last can do my duty." He turned to Kit. "You wondered why Dullard wanted to kidnap Grace. You might be surprised by how much money you have available to you. The Virden estate is one of the richest in the territory, and Grace is the heir."

"An heiress," Rina said with a look to Catherine.

"A considerable heiress," Beth assured them.

Ciara shook her head. "Heaven help us when she reaches the age she can court."

"At least we're past the point where fathers were betrothing their daughters at birth," Catherine said.

"That's one of the reasons Mr. Mercer wanted us all to come to Seattle," Nora remembered, taking her gaze off the clearing for a moment. "So there would be grown women for the men to marry."

"We certainly did," James said with a smile to his wife.

"Then the matter is settled?" Drew asked, gaze on the lawyer.

She wished it were that easy. "It can't be," Ciara said, slipping her hand into Kit's. "What about Mrs. Virden? She threatened to take Grace away from us."

Mr. Hitchcock drew himself up and looked down his nose at her. "Mrs. Virden is outside her rights, and so I have informed her. I can assure you, she will be of no further trouble. In fact, you will shortly find her coming to plead for the opportunity to visit Grace. It is your choice how to answer her."

Everyone seemed to be waiting for their response.

Ciara met Kit's gaze. "I say we give her a chance. With one of us standing watch, of course."

"Agreed," he said. "It's time we were a family again."

Smiles blossomed all around.

Mr. Hitchcock nodded as if that were that. "I'll stay for a few days to explain everything to your satisfaction, Mr. Weatherly. As Grace's guardian, you'll have to be the one to manage things until she reaches her majority at twenty-one."

Ciara stared at Kit as he blinked in obvious surprise.

He had run all the way to Japan and back to escape a life of wealth, privilege, and expectation. Was this his sister's way of forcing him into it at last? How did a marriage to a frontier restaurant owner fit in the picture?

"Do you want to be a captain of industry, Kit?" she asked.

His laugh settled her heart. "Not me," he promised. "That's not where my strengths lie. But I think, with advice from my friends, I can choose good men and women to lead the company so Grace will be well represented. She can decide what she wants to be when she grows up."

"I'll endeavor to be of service to you both," Mr. Hitchcock assured him. "I recognize the responsibility that has been thrust upon you."

Kit slipped an arm about Ciara. "My only responsibility is to take care of my ladies, starting with my Irish rose."

His rose. His sweetheart. There was nothing she'd rather be.

Dixon Hitchcock bowed to them both. "Many congratulations." He returned to his seat as if he rested his case.

Beth clapped her hands. "Then we can plan your wedding?"

Kit met Ciara's gaze, and hope set her head to nodding. He grinned.

"Yes," Grace said. "Yes, yes, yes, yes, yes."

"I agree," Ciara said with a laugh. "We can start planning today. But we'll need to fit it around the restaurant. I'm hoping to open for business Monday through Saturday next month."

"Have you finally decided what to name it?" Beth asked.

She cast a quick glance at Kit, who nodded his support. That look, that smile, had become so dear.

She turned to the Wallin leader. "In a way. Drew, I'd

like to make you another proposal. If you help Kit raise a cabin nearby, Jesse can have the one you gave me until he proves up his claim. I understand Harry's cabin is nearly done. Then this cabin and restaurant can be the Wooden Rose Inn."

Kit beamed at her. "Perfect."

"Sounds good to me too," Drew said. "John, bring down the survey maps, and we'll locate a plot to Kit's liking."

"Our liking," Kit corrected him. "Ciara and I are a team, in everything."

"The way it should be," Levi said.

The way she had never known could be so wonderful.

Beth clapped again. "Oh, this is marvelous. Now all we have to do is get the new schoolmarm here."

Harry and Jesse perked up.

"She telegrammed to say she will arrive on the steamer from San Francisco in two weeks," Rina reported.

"I'll fetch her," Harry offered.

"I think it should be Jesse," Beth said.

Harry frowned. "Why?"

"Call it intuition," she said with a wink in his direction.

Harry huffed. "You promised me a mail-order bride. Ada Rankin even wrote the ad."

"And you didn't like any of the candidates who responded," Beth reminded him. "You never seem to reach the point of *I do*. Until you can, I'm not sure what else I can do for you."

As Harry's face reddened, she turned to Jesse. "Miss Dennison will likely have a number of trunks and bandboxes for this move. You're the strongest fellow out here, Jesse. Would you be willing to bring her in?"

"Sure," Jesse answered. "Like Harry says, always happy to oblige a lady."

"So am I," Kit said, and he kissed Ciara to the delight of everyone in the room.

"Dada," Grace said, waving a hand in their direction. "Mama."

Sweeter than any pie, warmer than any stew, rising higher than any bread. Ciara couldn't imagine being any happier. She had come to Wallin Landing to start a new life. She would stay as a new wife, mother, and business owner.

She had finally found where she belonged. Home.

Thank you for reading Ciara and Kit's story. We all need a place where we are loved for who we are.

If you missed any of the stories set in frontier Seattle, you can find the full list of Frontier Matches books on my website *www.reginascott.com*. Sign up for my newsletter to know when the next book is out or on sale. I offer exclusive stories to my subscribers. Don't miss out.

Looks like Harry and Jesse might be vying for the attentions of the new schoolmarm. Or will Katie Jo catch someone's eye? Turn the page for a sneak peek of the next Frontier Matches story, *Frontier Cinderella*.

SNEAK PEEK
Frontier Cinderella
Book 3 in the Frontier Matches Series

Seattle, Washington Territory, September 1876

IT SURE TOOK a lot of work to be a lady.

Katie Jo McAllister glanced around at the busy Seattle street. Plenty of menfolk were going about their business, dressed like her in loose wool trousers and collarless flannel shirts. But every one of them stopped to doff their hats and smile as the few ladies walked past, skirts swishing and swaying like aspens in the breeze.

She lifted a hand to the slouch hat mostly covering her hair. The other ladies' hair was curled around their foreheads and piled up to tumble down behind them in heavy braids and waves. That swung too as they walked. And every feller watched them go.

None of them watched her. Most probably didn't even notice she was female. But if prim and fussy dresses dripping with bric-a-brac and hair hanging every which way would get Uncle Cole to see her as a lady, and allow her and Zeke to get on with their lives, she was ready to give any amount of work a try.

"Here we are," Beth McCormick sang out. Now, she knew how to dress like a lady. Her dress was a pretty shade of pink, with flowers embroidered all over it, and it had extra skirts front and back draped in a darker pink, with gathers all along the hem. Under a hat trimmed in ribbon and flowers, her hair was the color of the gold Uncle Cole wished he could get the stream on their claim to spit out, and it fell behind her like a waterfall.

Beth had insisted that Katie Jo and their friend, Ciara O'Rourke, come in to Seattle from the settlement of Wallin Landing to purchase gewgaws for Ciara's wedding, which was less than a week away. One of the other ladies at Wallin Landing, Mrs. Nora Wallin, had made Katie Jo a dress for the occasion.

It was a pretty dress too. Katie Jo had picked out the blue gingham because it was the color of the sky on a summer's day, like her eyes. But standing in Nora's bedchamber with Ciara, gazing at herself in the standing mirror, Katie Jo had become aware of a distinct settling of her spirits.

"It doesn't look good on me," she had said.

Nora's kind face had sagged. "Perhaps more trim?"

Nora liked trim. Her dresses boasted embroidery, lace, fringe, and double and triple skirts, for all she lived in a house on a wilderness farm and cared for the little ones of the settlement when their mas and pas were busy.

Ciara had studied her critically. "What you need is a corset."

Katie Jo blushed now, remembering, as she glanced up at the sign over the door of the establishment two blocks above the waterfront. Mrs. Blanchard's Selection was written in curling letters washed over with gilt. Painted on the glass window were the words *For the discriminating lady of fashion and elegance.*

That wasn't her. But that didn't mean it couldn't be her. She just had to try. Anything to help her little brother.

She pulled open the door and held it wide to the tinkle of the shop's bell. "After you, ladies."

Smiling, Beth and Ciara stepped inside.

Katie Jo followed them. She'd been to the mercantile in Wallin Landing, and she'd come in to Seattle once or twice with her uncle for some piece of equipment, but none of the shops she'd ever visited looked like this one, all pink and white, like Beth's skirts and the taffy candies her brother begged her to bring him. Forms shaped like a lady's bodice were covered with corsets in white, cream, or black satin, the tops edged in lace and some with embroidery along the panels. One was even scarlet! She tried to imagine herself in it and failed.

"Welcome, ladies," called a tall woman with hair swept back like a raven's wing from her face. Her dress too was covered with lace and beading and trim. "May I ask your brother to wait outside? My clients prefer their privacy."

Katie Jo glanced behind her to see what feller had had the temerity to step into this lair of femininity, but she saw no one.

"This is our friend, Miss McAllister," Ciara said, steel in her voice, as Katie Jo faced front again. "She requires a new corset."

The lady's lashes fluttered, as if she'd been swarmed by gnats. "Of course. Something in a durable cotton?"

That sounded practical. Katie Jo nodded.

Beth shook her head. "Durable, certainly, but Miss McAllister is a lady of some refinement. Satin covered, lace along the top. Comfortably boned. Sturdy laces."

Katie Jo stared at her.

Mrs. Blanchard, or so she assumed the lady to be, nodded. "Certainly. This way, Miss McAllister, and we'll get you measured."

The thought of undressing in front of this lady was as horrible as getting stuck in the privy on a winter's morn. Katie Jo fumbled in the pocket of her trousers. "Mrs. Nora already took my measurements." She thrust the piece of paper at the dressmaker. "She thought it would be easier if I just gave them to you."

Mrs. Blanchard took the piece of paper with two fingers as if Katie Jo had somehow dirtied it, then studied it a moment. Her brows went up, and she gazed at Katie Jo so fixedly she wanted to turn and run out the door.

This is for Zeke. Uncle Cole is never going to let him go unless you can prove you are a lady grown.

Besides, she refused to let down her friends. She just smiled politely.

"Are these correct?" she asked, gaze now jumping from Ciara to Beth.

"Absolutely accurate," Ciara said. "Miss McAllister has an enviable figure."

"Which I'm certain you will know how to show to advantage," Beth added.

For the first time, Mrs. Blanchard's smile blossomed. "I most certainly can, and it will be my pleasure. I'll just gather some material, and we can come to an agreement on how she'd like it made."

Beth held up a finger. "Two, if you please. Long stays and short. Miss McAllister's maid has to take a day off on occasion."

Katie Jo nearly snorted. Maid. Who did Beth think she was kidding? Anyone looking at her would know she was more likely to be a maid than employ one.

"Do I really need two of the contraptions?" she whispered to her friends as Mrs. Blanchard hurried off.

"Yes," Ciara whispered back. "A lady can more easily deal with short stays when she's alone."

She wasn't really alone on the claim, but she understood. Zeke would have been mortified no end if she'd asked him to do up her stays for her. And Uncle Cole would have told her she was being a fool to wear them, if she'd dared to ask him for help.

Which she wouldn't have. She was just thankful he'd agreed to allow her to go into Wallin Landing for a whole week to help at Ciara's restaurant, The Wooden Rose Inn, and prepare for the wedding. She still couldn't quite believe Ciara had asked her to stand up with her, but she was going to do her best to make sure she did her friend proud.

Hence the need for a corset. She'd never owned one in her life. She'd been twelve when Ma had passed, and Uncle Cole had sold her mother's clothes to help make ends meet. As soon as Katie Jo had outgrown the dresses her mother had made for her, she'd been relegated to store-bought trousers and shirts, usually ones Uncle Cole no longer fancied.

"Whole lot easier," he had told her. "You don't have to fuss with seamstresses and the like, and they're less likely to wear out or get torn. Besides, you're not a lady yet."

Ten years later, he still didn't like to acknowledge she was a lady any more than he liked acknowledging that Zeke, now seventeen, was about old enough to be on his own too. Together, she and her brother did the bulk of the work to maintain the house and critters, while her uncle attempted to coax gold out of the creek. Uncle Cole had given up his own dreams to raise her and her brother. She understood the need to pay him back for his trouble. But it was time he let her and Zeke go.

She could only hope he'd be patient with her brother while she was gone. Zeke did his best to please, but it wasn't his fault he'd been born puny. Any little thing overset him. And Uncle Cole wasn't always good about standing in front of him, so Zeke could read his lips and understand what was expected of him.

The shop door tinkled again, and she glanced back in time to meet the gaze of Harry Yeager. Her heart plummeted to the soles of her sturdy boots, then shot up into her throat. Likely even he could hear it pounding as he sauntered closer.

Like her uncle, she might sometimes forget she was a gal, but when Harry was around, she was acutely aware she was female.

Maybe it was because he was such a male. That

confident swagger, that drawling voice. He had hair the color of her mother's mahogany chest she'd carried all the way across the Plains, and it waved around a strong-jawed face with a smile that could melt butter. When those dark brown eyes twinkled, she felt warm all over. He was taller than she was, which, she was coming to realize, was rare, and he was strong enough to swing a double-headed ax with precision. All in all, a gal could go all swoony in his presence.

It had been hard enough sitting beside him on the bench of the wagon as he'd driven her and Ciara in from the Landing this morning. Facing him here? Impossible!

She whipped around, tugged down on her hat, and prayed he wouldn't pay her any more mind than usual.

"Sorry to interrupt, ladies," he said from behind her. "I just wanted to let you know that the steamship is offloading passengers. It might take an hour before I have Miss Dennison and her things in the wagon."

"Thank you, Harry," Ciara said. "We should be ready by then."

Katie Jo heard the shop door tinkle a third time as he must have left.

She sighed.

She hadn't realized the sound was loud enough to hear, but Ciara put a hand on her shoulder. "You wait, Katie Jo. Harry's going to be singing a different tune when he sees you in your new dress. He'll forget all about Miss Dennison."

Katie Jo shook her head. "Thank you, but I realized straightaway that I'm not what Harry Yeager is looking for in a wife. That's not going to change with some new finery."

But something inside her pressed upward, as if reaching for the moon. Maybe it wasn't only Uncle Cole who she hoped would see her as a lady.

Harry Yeager whistled to himself as he strolled down the street toward the wharves. His wife could be coming in on that steamship. Beth McCormick might be the town matchmaker, and she'd picked out Jesse for the new schoolmarm, but Harry had something Jesse didn't.

A powerful will.

Harry considered it a blessing, even if some called it a failing.

"He's a headstrong lad," his third cousin had complained to the town constable when Harry had run away from the backbreaking work expected of him at only nine years old. "But never fear. We'll beat it out of him."

So far, no one and nothing ever had. Not the various distant relatives who had passed him around after his parents had died when he was eight. Not the ministers and schoolteachers who had tried to settle his spirit with kind words or harsh reprimands. Not the plowing, milking, and wood chopping he'd been required to do to earn his keep. Not the employers who generally saw him only as another strong back.

Not even the first friends he'd found, after joining Drew Wallin's logging crew.

"What would I have to do to convince you to let me bring home the new schoolmarm?" he'd asked his friend, Jesse Willets, last night as they'd sat at the table in the cabin they shared now that Ciara O'Rourke was turning their former home into the Wooden Rose Inn.

Jesse had eyed him. He was bigger than Harry and Kit Weatherly, the third member of the crew, nearly as big as the legendary Drew Wallin himself. He too hoped to find a wife in an area with eight and a half bachelors for every unmarried lady. "Mrs. McCormick asked me to collect her."

"I remember," Harry said. He put his elbow on the table and raised his fist. "Arm wrestle you for it."

Jesse couldn't resist a game. With his lopsided grin, he'd planted his elbow and clasped Harry's hand.

Oh, but Jesse was strong. Harry's muscles, honed by years of hard work, protested the pressure. His fist moved over and out as Jesse shoved harder.

No. This was his chance. Ever since his parents had died, he'd been looking for a family. He'd found one in the Wallin kin, but he wanted one all his own.

A wife, children. Home.

Jesse blinked and stared down at his arm, pinned to the table, with Harry's on top. "You won."

Harry released him, arm aching worse than if he'd felled a dozen trees in one day. "Looks like it. Thanks, Jesse. I promise not to propose until she's at least had a chance to meet you." He grinned. "But not much beyond that."

So here he stood. On the edge of the wharves, watching small boats bobbing in on the tide as they crossed the blue-gray waters of Elliott Bay from the San Francisco steamer. One step closer to having a family again.

He frowned, counting heads in the two closest boats. All men, if those hats were any indication. Then again, he knew of a female who wore a man's hat.

His mind conjured the image of Katie Jo McAllister in that lady's shop. For one moment, when their gazes had brushed, he'd thought he'd seen something like admiration in her look before she'd spun and put her back to him. He hadn't thought of Katie Jo McAllister as having those kinds of feelings, especially not toward him.

He had to appreciate her grit, though. He understood enough about what went on in such shops to know ladies were pinned and prodded every which way to fit into their dresses. He wouldn't have wanted to let some stranger measure him and possibly find him wanting. He was done with that part of his life.

"Mornin,' Harry." Mr. Bartholomew, the young assistant harbormaster, nodded from his booth at the top of the wharves as Harry drew up next to him. "You expecting something from San Francisco?"

Harry grinned. "Yes, sir. Miss Alice Dennison. The new Wallin Landing schoolteacher."

Bartholomew frowned down at the manifest he must have been given and scratched his clean-shaven chin. "Odd. I don't see a lady on the list."

Harry frowned as well. "Let me see."

Bartholomew handed over the paper, dark brows high and nose higher, as if he scented a story in the making. Harry ignored him to scan down the list. Not a miss, missus, or Dennison was in evidence.

"Must be some mistake," he said, shoving the paper at the assistant harbormaster. "She telegrammed to say she would be coming on this boat."

Bartholomew shrugged and tapped the pages on the edge of the booth to straighten them. "Happens all the time. Some ladies like San Francisco too much to continue to Seattle. Look at Miss Williamson. She only lasted a few weeks before hightailing it south."

Harry *had* looked at Melinda Williamson, sister to Ada, who had married Scout Rankin. She was beautiful, charming, and sweet-natured. But there had been something about her, a fragility, a fascination with her own needs to the exclusion of all else, that had kept him from pursuing her.

Beth said he was too picky, but a man had to have some standards in a bride. It shouldn't be too much to ask for one that was pretty as a picture, clever—but not so clever she'd think she was better than him—and strong, so she could help him prove up his claim. And if she could cook as well as Ciara O'Rourke, well, that would be a real blessing.

It wasn't as if he had nothing to offer in return. His

claim was one hundred and sixty acres abutting Lake Union, in an area that was sure to grow as Seattle expanded. His two-room cabin was about finished. All he had to do was lay down the plank flooring, dig a well, and put in a pump. And he had a good job, for good pay, in a settlement worthy of calling home.

A lady could do worse.

For some reason, Katie Jo came to mind again. Sometimes, when he could see up under that slouch hat, he would swear she was pretty. She was clever enough to take care of herself, and she didn't act as if she was better than him. She was plenty strong. She helped Ciara clear the tables and wash the dishes at the inn. She might even have learned a thing or two about cooking.

But Katie Jo McAllister had spent a lot of time with Beth and Ciara lately. She might have her own ideas about courting and marriage. He'd tried courting multiple times over the last two years, and every gal had chosen a different groom. It was enough to make a feller wary of opening his heart.

Which made a stranger like the new schoolmarm a safer bet than Miss Katie Jo McAllister.

Learn more at *www.reginascott.com/cinderella.html*

OTHER BOOKS BY REGINA SCOTT

Frontier Bachelors/Frontier Matches

The Bride Ship (Allegra and Clay)
Would-Be Wilderness Wife (Catherine and Drew)
Frontier Engagement (Rina and James)
Instant Frontier Family (Maddie and Michael)
A Convenient Christmas Wedding (Nora and Simon)
Mail-Order Marriage Promise (Dottie and John)
His Frontier Christmas Family (Callie and Levi)
Frontier Matchmaker Bride (Beth and Hart)
The Perfect Mail-Order Bride (Ada and Scout)

American Wonders Collection

A Distance Too Grand
Nothing Short of Wondrous
A View Most Glorious

Fortune's Brides Series

Never Doubt a Duke
Never Borrow a Baronet
Never Envy an Earl
Never Vie for a Viscount
Never Kneel to a Knight
Never Marry a Marquess
Always Kiss at Christmas
Never Pursue a Prince
Never Court a Count
Never Romance a Rogue
Never Love a Lord

Grace-by-the-Sea Series

The Matchmaker's Rogue

The Heiress's Convenient Husband
The Artist's Healer
The Governess's Earl
The Lady's Second-Chance Suitor
The Siren's Captain

Uncommon Courtships Series
The Unflappable Miss Fairchild
The Incomparable Miss Compton
The Irredeemable Miss Renfield
The Unwilling Miss Watkin
An Uncommon Christmas

Lady Emily Capers
Secrets and Sensibilities
Art and Artifice
Ballrooms and Blackmail
Eloquence and Espionage
Love and Larceny

Marvelous Munroes Series
My True Love Gave to Me
The Rogue Next Door
The Marquis' Kiss
A Match for Mother

Spy Matchmaker Series
The Husband Mission
The June Bride Conspiracy
The Heiress Objective

The Regent's Devices Trilogy (writing as R.E. Scott with Shelley Adina)
The Emperor's Aeronaut
The Prince's Pilot
The Lady's Triumph

ABOUT THE AUTHOR

REGINA SCOTT STARTED writing novels in the third grade. Thankfully for literature as we know it, she didn't sell her first novel until she learned a bit more about writing. Since her first book was published, her stories have traveled the globe, with translations in many languages including Dutch, German, Italian, and Portuguese. She now has more than sixty published works of warm, witty romance, and more than 1 million copies of her books are in reader hands.

While she adores the elegance of the Regency period in England and has penned many stories set then, she loves getting to write about history closer to her home in the Puget Sound area of Washington State, where she lives with her husband. She also loves diving into history headfirst. She has dressed as a Regency dandy, driven four-in-hand, learned to fence, and sailed on a tall ship, all in the name of research, of course. Learn more about her http://www.reginascott.com/